She lif...
teasing smile...

'Shall we gallop...

Author Note

You might already have met Alistair and Julia, in *One Night as a Courtesan*. They are a couple who kept interrupting other stories to remind me that while I had married them off I had not given them a proper happily-ever-after. They were quite insistent that after what looked like an excellent beginning things were not going well, and they needed me to give them a helping hand. So I did.

Along the way I also learned that kaleidoscopes were invented during the Regency era, and learned a new name for a swarm of butterflies.

I do hope you enjoy their story.

If you would like to know more about me and my books you can visit me at annlethbridge.com, where you can sign up for my newsletter, prizes offered with every issue, and find my links to your favourite social media.

SECRETS OF THE
MARRIAGE BED

Ann Lethbridge

Published in Great Britain 2016
by Mills & Boon, an imprint of HarperCollins*Publishers*
1 London Bridge Street, London, SE1 9GF

© 2016 Michèle Ann Young

ISBN: 978-0-263-92552-4

Our policy is to use papers that are natural, renewable and
recyclable products and made from wood grown in sustainable
forests. The logging and manufacturing processes conform to the
legal environmental regulations of the country of origin.

Printed and bound in Spain
by CPI, Barcelona

In her youth, award-winning author **Ann Lethbridge** re-imagined the Regency romances she read—and now she loves writing her own. Now living in Canada, Ann visits Britain every year, where family members understand—or so they say—her need to poke around every antiquity within a hundred miles. Learn more about Ann or contact her at annlethbridge.com. She loves hearing from readers.

Books by Ann Lethbridge

**Mills & Boon Historical Romance
and Mills & Boon Historical *Undone!* eBooks**

Rakes in Disgrace

*The Gamekeeper's Lady
More Than a Mistress
Deliciously Debauched by the Rake* (Undone!)
More Than a Lover

The Gilvrys of Dunross

*The Laird's Forbidden Lady
Her Highland Protector
Falling for the Highland Rogue
Return of the Prodigal Gilvry
One Night with the Highlander* (Undone!)

Linked by Character

*Wicked Rake, Defiant Mistress
One Night as a Courtesan* (Undone!)
Secrets of the Marriage Bed

*Haunted by the Earl's Touch
Captured Countess
The Duke's Daring Debutante*

*The Rake's Inherited Courtesan
Lady Rosabella's Ruse
The Rake's Intimate Encounter* (Undone!)

Visit the Author Profile page
at millsandboon.co.uk for more titles.

This book is dedicated to my sister-in-law, Ro,
who entertains me and my dear husband in grand style
whenever we visit her in Wales and never minds
if I have my nose in a book or my head in a story.

Chapter One

This picture of domestic bliss should have sent Alistair, Duke of Dunstan, haring off for a brandy at his club. Instead, standing in the shadows outside his wife's withdrawing room, watching her delicately ply her needle, he wanted…more. A painful twisting in his chest for something he could not name, along with the far more easily controlled inconvenience of lust. When he really should not want anything at all.

A bitter smile pulled at his lips. The only woman he'd wanted this badly in years he couldn't have because she was his wife.

What the devil had he been thinking when he'd offered marriage? A question he'd asked himself more than once these past two weeks. He didn't need a wife. Hadn't wanted one. Why be tied to one woman when any number of them, from princess to pauper, were ready to fall into his bed? Marriage was his worst idea ever.

And he'd had more than his share of bad ideas.

If she ever learned the truth, she likely would turn away in disgust.

Of course, he hadn't been thinking the night he'd met her. At least not with the brain atop his shoulders. Drunk on the aftermath of exquisite passion, the legend of the Dunstan rubies had put words in his mouth he would never have uttered had his mind been in full working order. Pride hadn't permitted a retraction.

A Dunstan never went back on his word. That was something he should have recalled before he'd opened his mouth, having sworn years ago to put old mistakes right. Mistakes that made marriage out of the question. And yet here he was… married.

He lingered in the dark, out of sight, when he should have walked away.

Her head bent towards the light of the candle, her gaze fixed on her needle, Julia might have been posing for a portrait. From this vantage point, he had a perfect view of her profile. A small straight nose, a high intelligent forehead, a seductively elegant neck rising from a gown of the finest pale blue silk. A gown that covered a body every curve and swell of which he knew intimately.

He would not think about that. An odd longing clutched at his heart. What would it be like, just for once, to bask in a woman's affection?

Affection. His lip curled at the word. He had never known it and didn't want it. Men who craved affection were weaklings, led around by the nose, or some other part of their anatomy. He only had to look at his father with Isobel to know better. After Alistair's own mother's death, his father had been a pawn to Isobel's queen. Alistair had had a few happy years with his half-brother, but eventually, to please Isobel, his father sent Alistair away to school for being sullen and difficult with his new mama, while keeping Isobel's precious son close to home.

At first, in hopes of being allowed to come home, he'd been the perfect student. As time went on, and he realised it wasn't working, he'd instinctively taken the opposite tack, getting into every sort of scrape available to a wealthy young man away at university. Until finally, the bagwig had sent him down.

He'd been so glad to get home he'd even tried to be nice to his stepmama. It hadn't done him a bit of good.

Within a month Alistair had found himself

with a boring elderly scholar as bear leader and a ticket to France. His father had seen the Treaty of Amiens as the perfect opportunity to send Alistair on his Grand Tour.

Too bad the peace had ended less than six months later, leaving Alistair stranded in Italy and trying to avoid being arrested by Napoleon's soldiers.

By the time he'd made it home, his father was dead and Alistair's youthful missteps had caught up to him with a vengeance he would never have foreseen.

Now, to top it all off, like some soft-hearted fool, he'd married Julia. He should have given her the money she'd needed and sent her on her way instead of entering into a hollow shell of a marriage. Had he been any sort of honourable man, he would never have bid on her and bedded her in the first place.

He'd known at first glance she was not usual bordello fare. Known it deep in a part of him he'd thought long dead. A part that was a mere shadow of the decency and honour he'd once taken for granted. A part he'd been ignoring for years, while denying himself nothing except a family. The one thing he certainly neither deserved nor wanted.

Somehow that little corner of his brain, inexplicably overcome by the sight of her lovely body draped with blood-red rubies, had caused words to spill from his lips. *Marry me.* They rang in his ears even now.

Lunacy.

Devil take it. He couldn't even use over-indulgence as an excuse for replacing the *carte blanche* he'd first intended with an honourable offer. He'd been nowhere near cup shot.

The only reason he could attribute to that particular piece of madness was his desire to put his stepmother in her proper place for all time. To force her into the role of Dowager instead of allowing her to swan about as the reigning Duchess.

At least marriage had given him the satisfaction of imagining Isobel's rage and fear at the thought that her darling son Luke would be supplanted as heir by a child of Alistair's marriage.

Revenge, though, was not as sweet as he'd expected. Julia was too nice, too good, to have been dragged into a cold marriage of convenience. At least, she appeared so, up until now, but as Alistair knew to his cost women were not to be trusted. He'd learnt that the hard way.

In the meantime, it pleased him to torment his stepmother, despite that there would be no resulting children from his marriage. Not when he already had a son.

He let go a breath of impatience. He should not be lingering here.

Julia lifted her head from her work, glancing towards the door. 'Your Grace?'

He ground his teeth at the sound of his title on her lips. She'd taken to using it since the day after their wedding ball when the *ton* had turned up to meet his new bride. No doubt every female of that august group had blistered Julia's ears with stories of his depraved and dissolute past. That, compounded by his coldness towards her, must have brought home to her what a bad bargain she'd struck.

When he made no response, she looked down at the work on her lap with a shake of her head, clearly thinking she'd been mistaken.

This was his opportunity to beat the retreat and head off to his club.

What was he, then? A coward to be outfaced by a woman? His wife no less?

He strode into the room.

She looked up with a hesitant smile. Despite the shadows in her eyes, beauty shone in that smile. A welcome full of hope and promise. Her lips were lovely. Full and soft. Kissable. Sinful temptation, like the rest of her slender body with its graceful curves and its power to make him lose reason. Her skin was as soft as silk, he recalled, her limbs long and elegant, yet softly formed. He bit back a curse.

'Good evening, Your Grace.' A calm cool voice with a throaty, inviting quality that, like the rest of her, called to him on a visceral level. He could not hear her voice without recalling the passion of their night together. He half turned so she would not guess at the interest she aroused and propped an elbow on the back of the chair facing her across the hearth.

'Good evening, my lady.' He deliberately curled his lip, dropping his gaze to the scrap of cloth covered in coloured shapes and patterns in her lap. 'What a picture of domesticity you are, my dear. It always astonishes me, the kind of things you ladies like to do with your hands.' When they could be making so much better use of them.

Hades, could he not get his mind off fornication in her presence?

She must have heard the edge in his voice for she put the work aside. 'I'm sorry. Does it annoy you?' Cool civility edged each inflection. With each passing day, she became chillier, a little more reserved, exactly as he'd planned.

So why this irrational sense of disappointment? He'd always revelled in his bachelor life. His freedom to come and go as he pleased. Family obligations kept to a minimum. An unpleasant duty, to be avoided whenever possible. In his experience, when relations weren't dunning one for money, they were stabbing one in the back. He ought to know, he'd done his share of knife work. His stepmother was still bleeding from the loss of her status.

Her gaze swept his person. 'You are going out, I see. I wish you an enjoyable evening.' She reached for her needlework.

His jaw clenched, even though she hadn't asked a question. She'd quickly realised that he refused to be interrogated. About anything. Yet irrationally, he found her lack of interest cutting. 'I am going to my club. I have arranged to meet friends.' Why was he explaining when he had no reason to think she cared?

Her shoulders relaxed. A little.

She no doubt imagined him with an *inamorata*.

Blast. He'd forgotten to give Lavinia her *congé*. Yet another detail that seemed to have slipped his mind recently. He'd have Lewis, his secretary, take care of it first thing in the morning. Given that he hadn't visited his mistress since before his wedding, she must already understand they were finished. He'd been bored by her weeks ago. Likely another reason he'd bid for Julia at the bordello.

'I will let the staff know you will not be here for dinner,' she said quietly.

Always quiet. Always controlled. It rubbed him the wrong way. Made him want to incite the passion he knew resided beneath the calm surface. But it was an urge he would never indulge again, given his promise. Distance was his watchword. Security hers. They were all he had to offer. All he wanted.

'I informed Jackson.' His valet.

A shadow passed across her face. Her lips tightened a fraction.

He ignored this faint show of annoyance. 'What will you do while I am off having a jolly time?'

She glanced down at the needlework and back up to meet his gaze, her chin lifting a fraction. Defiance. She was a spirited woman, his wife. His body responded with a pulse of heat.

'Perhaps I will select a book,' she said. 'There are several in the library I have not yet read.'

Hundreds more like. If he had wanted to be a good husband, he would be escorting her to balls and such. Introducing her to the people of his set.

Yet he hadn't been good since his teens. Wickedness for which he now paid the price.

The very thought of failing in his husbandly duty made him want to lash out. Not at her. But at something. Life, perhaps. The cruelty of the Fates. After all, it was not her fault they were married. The fault lay entirely with him. To mitigate the damage, the best he could do was keep her at a distance.

Because when he came close, when he inhaled her delicious scent of jasmine, touched the silk of her skin, basked in the warmth of her welcoming smile, she was far too tempting.

'I bid you good evening.' He bowed and left.

Julia frowned at the sprig of lilac she was embroidering on a handkerchief. Why had Dunstan married her if he held her in such contempt? If their one night together had not been so deliciously sensual, so different from her experiences with her first husband, she might never have agreed to his proposal.

Indeed, having suffered eight years of her husband's brutality when he realised she was never going to give him the heir he so desperately wanted, she'd thought never to marry again. If not for her desperate straits, she would never have accepted Dunstan's offer the way a drowning man clutched at a bit of flotsam.

He certainly had not avowed undying love or anything close. She'd perfectly understood theirs was a marriage of convenience, a kindness on his part, but surely there could be more to this marriage than chilly reserve?

Judging by his lovemaking that first night, he had found her as physically attractive as she did him. His skill in the bedroom had proved his reputation of legendary lover to be unassailably true. Not that *she'd* had much experience from which to judge, but she recalled every intimate detail of their one night together and it had been lovely.

She squirmed on the sofa cushions at the memory. A skitter of pleasure tightened her insides.

Since their wedding less than two weeks ago, she had done her best to be the kind of wife she assumed he wanted. A duchess, no less! Her stomach pitched as it always did at the terrifying thought. Apparently, however, he was not pleased with her efforts.

Her heart sank. To be embroiled in yet another unpleasant marriage loomed like a waiting nightmare. She shuddered at memories of her first husband's vile temper each month or so, when he realised she was not about to produce a son. The constant criticisms. Her physical revulsion. The blows raining down on her when she made a mistake. She pushed the recollections aside.

The Duke was nowhere near that bad. But since their wedding day, most of his remarks had been biting to the point of rudeness. Could this marriage be heading in the same direction as her first? Something had to be done. She shot to her feet and hurried out into the hall to where Alistair was being helped into his coat by a footman.

'Your Grace?' Her voice echoed around the grand space of polished oak panelling and marble flooring. The ducal town house was more like a palace than a home. A cold place, full of stiff formality.

His shoulders tensed as he turned to face her. In this light, the slightly cruel cast of his thin lips gave his golden good looks an aura of decadence. A devil disguised as an angel.

Yet every time she saw him, his cold beauty made her heart skip a beat.

One blond eyebrow arched in question, his grey eyes silvery in the light of the huge chandelier above the staircase.

Her blood heated as the realisation struck her anew. This glorious apparition was her husband.

The footman retreated to his place beside the door.

Servants were everywhere and that was part of the reason she had such difficulty approaching him about anything. The lack of privacy drove her to distraction. She was terrified of making a fool of herself in front of his people. Likely they already scorned her for her ignorance with regard to running such a grand household. Thank the heavens they did not know exactly where he had found her or they might refuse to serve her at all.

'I wonder if I might have a word with you, Your Grace?' She barely managed the words, in the light of his obvious impatience.

'If you must?' As always his voice sounded icily polite. And bored.

'In private?' she whispered, with a quick glance at the footman.

With a huff of breath, he gestured for the man to take his redingote and followed her back into the drawing room. He closed the door.

She twisted her hands together, her courage deserting her in the face of his wintery gaze. A golden David as cold as the marble from which the statue had been carved.

His expression changed to one of concern as she hesitated. 'What has happened?'

She took a quick breath. 'If I have offended in some way, I wish you would tell me.' Oh, she sounded so weak, so tentative, but her first husband had found her very existence offensive. Ultimately she'd been afraid to address him, unless he spoke first, but at least then, she had known why he found her lacking.

Alistair's eyes widened for a second, then a bored expression fell over his face like a shield. 'You mistake, madam. I am not in the least offended.'

She gritted her teeth at his indifference. 'Can we not at least be friends?'

He recoiled. 'You are my wife.'

One could not be friends with a wife? And why did he look so grim? She grasped the back of the nearest chair to stop herself from beating her fists on that wide impervious chest in frustration. How *did* one ask why a husband never came to one's bed without looking like some sort of strumpet?

But was that not what she was? After all, he'd bid for her at a bordello while she'd stood on a pedestal practically naked. Her stomach roiled at the recollection. Clearly, there really was no way to keep one's dignity after such a display. Likely every man he knew had also seen her that night, though as far as she was aware, none had recognised her, since she had taken the precaution of wearing a mask. And little else. She repressed a shudder of shame.

Still, he had known all this before they'd wed.

Anger trickled up from her belly. Her chest ached with a slow burn. 'Why do you never come to my chamber?' There, she had said it. Announced the desires that haunted her nights.

His expression shuttered, but not before she saw a flash of what she thought might be anger. 'I am in no rush to saddle myself with a parcel of brats.'

Inwardly, she flinched. Should she tell him there was likely no hope of her ever having children, or did she continue to hide behind what little was left of her dignity? And an even smaller shred of hope.

And besides, what would it hurt to try? It wasn't as if he could beget an heir with anyone else.

Perhaps he was now regretting his chivalry. Regretting it so much he disdained to have a child of hers inherit his title? Much as that thought hurt, it also rang true. The Duke was a proud man. Proud of his name and his title. She met his gaze and lifted her chin, unwilling to show how much the possibility hurt.

When she made no reply his mouth hardened to a cruel line. 'Was there anything else you required of me?'

Crushed by his coldness, his deliberate scorn, she looked down and shook her head. 'Nothing.'

'Then if you will pardon me, I am late.' He hesitated for a second, then turned and left.

Pardon him? If she could have picked him up, she would have thrown him out of a window to be rid of him. She also wanted to cry. Her knuckles whitened, her grip painfully tight on the chair back.

Finally, she let out a long breath. She needed to think with her head, instead of feeling with her heart. She wasn't a fool. *Something* had sparked between them that first night. A very heated something. That was the reason she had dared marry him in the first place. The hope that the attraction they *both* felt could lead to more.

She was not going to give up that hope. Not without a fight. She'd had one dreadful marriage, she would not have another. She would not permit this man to destroy what was left of her spirit.

She wanted a proper husband and, should a miracle occur, a proper family. It wasn't so much to ask.

Either they found a way to resolve what was coming between them, or... Well, she must, that was all. There had to be something she could do to rekindle the spark.

The next morning, Alistair stopped short in the doorway of the breakfast room. Never had he seen his wife up and about this early in the morning, nor had he seen her looking more delectable. Dressed in a riding habit of royal blue with black frogging closing the front, she perused the sideboard. The high ruffled shirt rising from the collar framed her beautiful face. A mischievous smile played about her lips and sparkled in her eyes as she glanced his way.

'Good morning, Your Grace.' She added a scoop of scrambled eggs to her plate.

Devil take it, he hated conversation before he'd had his first cup of tea. Why couldn't she take a tray in her room like any other self-respecting noblewoman? Although come to think of it, none of the women he'd been around in the morning were at all self-respecting, or he would not have been there.

'Good morning.' At least that was what he intended to say. It came out sounding more like a grunt.

She took her place at the table adjacent to his normal seat. He marched across to the sideboard, loaded up his usual poached eggs and steak and set his plate down. He glanced at the newspaper which had been carefully ironed, folded and set beside his fork so he could glance at the headlines.

He gritted his teeth. Not today. One did not

read at the table when one had female company. Even he remembered that from his youthful lessons in manners. His nursemaid, Digger, would be proud of him.

Maybe.

'Tea?' she asked.

He preferred to pour his own. 'Thank you.'

She fixed two cups, added cream and sugar to one and passed it across. He took a sip. Perfect. Exactly how he liked it. How had she known? His temper improved leaps and bounds with each mouthful.

'I see you plan on riding out?' Hah! A whole sentence and perfectly polite.

'I do. Your stable master, Mr Litton, introduced me to Bella earlier in the week and since it is such a fine morning, I thought to put her through her paces.'

He hadn't known she liked to ride. He should have asked. 'Hmmph.'

'My riding out does not meet with your approval?'

Blast the woman, did she have to ask him questions? He took another sip of tea. For some stupid reason the morning seemed altogether brighter than it had when he arose from his bed.

'I will ride with you. I always ride first thing in the morning.' As she probably knew quite well. 'There is no reason why we should ride out separately.' No reason at all, except his confrères might think he had run mad. For years he'd mocked any man so smitten as to ride with ladies at so early an hour. Too dull by half. Yet he had a duty, did he not? To make sure she could handle Bella, as well as see to her safety? A mere groom would not take nearly enough care.

She raised a brow and looked at him speculatively over the rim of her teacup before taking a sip. She gave a little grimace of distaste.

'Something wrong with the tea?'

'Oolong is not a favourite with me.'

'Tell the kitchen.'

'I will.' She put her cup down and glanced down at his untouched food. 'I will be ready in say…half an hour.' With him or without him being implied. On that note, she daintily consumed the remaining food on her plate and left the room.

After skimming the political headlines, checking on the arrival of a ship in which he had an interest while he demolished his breakfast, he headed out to the stables. Litton had both horses saddled and was saddling his own. Of Her Grace there was as yet no sign. He was a couple of minutes early and he hoped she would not keep him waiting too long.

He gave Bella's tack a thorough inspection, before turning his attention to his own horse. Not that he expected his staff to do anything but an excellent job. 'Her Grace will not be needing you today, Litton.'

The man's eyebrows shot up. 'Bella's not been out under a lady's saddle for months, Your Grace. She'll need a close eye.'

A warning if ever Alistair heard one. It seemed Litton had decided to add his wife to the list of people he cared about. Up to now the list had only had one name on it. His own.

'I'll take care,' Alistair said.

Litton's glance flickered over Alistair's shoulder, warning him that their topic of conversation had arrived.

Alistair turned to greet her. Her hat was a version of the one he wore, a black beaver, the crown not quite so tall, and adorned with a scrap of net and a peacock-feather cockade. Very stylish. Hopefully it wasn't only for show and she rode just as well as she looked.

Julia had patted her mount's neck, checked the girth and adjusted the stirrup with a confident hand before signalling her readiness to mount.

He bent, lacing his fingers together. She adjusted her habit, raising it a fraction, presenting him with a view of a beautifully cut riding boot and a smidgeon of pretty calf. His breath caught in his throat as he recalled the last time he'd had his hands on that calf. How silken her skin had been. How responsive her body to his touch. Once more his body hardened and he bit back a curse at the discomfort. She stepped into his palms and he boosted her into the saddle.

Bella, who up to that moment had been a perfect lady, shifted uneasily.

Alistair's heart gave a thump. He reached for the bridle, then snatched his hand back as Julia expertly brought the animal under control. She patted Bella's neck. 'Easy, girl. You know me. We have had several conversations these past few days.' The mare settled under her soothing hand and quiet words.

That. He wanted that, her hands on him, soothing, stroking, gentling and perhaps even— He cut the thought off.

Self-disgust at this rare lack of restraint rose in his throat. He forced it down where it belonged— with the shame of his past. He reached for Thor's reins, while she continued to pat Bella's neck.

He quelled his body's unruly response with effort and forced his mind to the task at hand. It seemed his wife was an accomplished horse-woman. What else about her did he not know?

And why would he care?

He swung up on to his horse and they moved off. Outside in the square, Alistair brought Thor up alongside Bella. 'We'll go by way of Park Lane. It should be reasonably quiet at this time of the morning. Stay close.'

'Lay on, MacDuff.'

He'd like to lay on her. The thought crept into his mind unbidden.

Damnation. More adolescent nonsense he could do without. More visions of temptation. He shifted in the saddle.

Chapter Two

While her husband might not have been thrilled at having her along on his morning ride, at least he had accepted her presence with a modicum of graciousness. She'd half expected him to refuse to allow her to go at all. Her first husband had refused her anything that might give her pleasure. In his eyes, she hadn't deserved it.

The day was perfect for riding. A slight breeze, a few puffy clouds and not too much heat. With years having passed since she'd been on horseback, she intended to make the most of every moment.

'What do you think of Bella?' the Duke asked and, to her surprise, he seemed genuinely interested in her answer.

'Lovely mouth. Beautifully responsive. A perfect lady.'

He muttered something under his breath that

sounded suspiciously like *I meant the horse.*
Surely not? She glanced over at him and his expression remained a blank slate. Unless that really was a fleeting twinkle warming his eyes.
Was it possible?

'I beg your pardon, I did not quite hear what you said.'

His lips twisted. 'I'm glad. She's not been getting out much recently.'

Was he glad she hadn't heard what he said? Or glad that she liked her mount? Not wanting to risk spoiling the accord between them, she decided to let the matter drop.

His horse, Thor, was a huge black gelding with four white feet. A big horse for a big man, whereas Bella was definitely a lady's mount. For which lady? She tried to ignore the pang to her heart at the thought of the kind of ladies who must have ridden this horse with him in the past, for there was no mistaking that the animal seemed used to riding alongside Thor.

'Are Bella and Thor always kept in town, or do they go with you to the country?'

'It depends where I go.'

Hardly forthcoming. She knew he had several country houses scattered around England and visited them once each year in strict rotation, according the housekeeper. Julia had questioned the woman closely the morning after her wedding. At the time, she'd supposed he would want his wife to entertain his friends and arrange his household. It had quickly come to her attention that he did not welcome her meddling in his bachelor arrangements.

Apart from their wedding ball, attended by every member of the *ton*, not once had he entertained in any formal way and his only forays from the house were to his man of business, his club and his morning ride. The last, the only activity where a wife *might* be welcome.

They passed through the gate into the park and the noise from the streets faded until one might imagine they were deep in the heart of the countryside. Julia took a deep breath. 'What a beautiful morning to be sure.'

He frowned and looked around at the trees and the glitter of the Serpentine as if he had never seen it before. 'Hmmph.'

'I agree,' she said.

He raised a brow questioningly, his eyes narrowing in suspicion.

'I agree with your sentiment. While it is a good day, the weather being unusually bright and fine, it is too bad there is nowhere to give the horses a really good run.' Oh, dear, the widening of his eyes said she had let her tendency for sarcasm run away with her. Something she had learned never to do with her previous husband. A couple of good hard slaps had cured the habit. Apparently, she had started to forget his lessons.

Having planned this morning as a way for her to get to know him better, to try to rekindle some of the liking he had shown her, even if he no longer felt passion, she had probably ruined it all by speaking out of turn.

Men did not appreciate being teased about their foibles, Dunstan's being a marked lack of conversation. At least it was where she was concerned. Perhaps he was a veritable gabble-monger amongst his friends. She pretended nothing was amiss and fixed her gaze straight ahead down the length of Rotten Row.

Bella tossed her head as if asking for permission to do more than a sedate walk. In the distance a group of riders were cantering.

She clenched her jaw to stop herself from asking if they too could pick up their pace.

'Let us see how she is at the trot, shall we?' Alistair said.

When she glanced at him she was sure she saw a slight twitch at the corner of his mouth, as if he was trying not to smile. Perhaps he had not been annoyed by her teasing after all.

Quite likely fearsome dukes weren't accustomed to teasing. It might do him good.

The horses moved easily into the trot and she was aware of her husband watching her with a critical eye. A comforting thought. This was the first time she had ridden Bella. She was glad he wanted to assure himself that she knew what she was doing.

He moved into an easy canter. Bella responded to the request to do likewise and they rode side by side. At the end of the Row, they drew to a halt. He glanced over at her. There was something in his expression she couldn't quite fathom.

'You have a good seat.'

A compliment? Her spirits lifted. She arched a brow. 'You already knew that.' The naughty innuendo tripped off her tongue before she could catch it.

His eyes widened. And, as sudden as a bolt of lightning, a crack of laughter broke free from him. Delight lit up those grey eyes, turning them a sparkling silver. 'Race you back.'

Her heart somersaulted in her chest at the sight of the tempting curve to his lips. She remembered the feel of kissing those lips. Then they had wed and he'd thrown up his barricade. For some mad reason she had the urge to kiss him again. Right now. Very shocking. While it certainly wouldn't do for a married couple to be showing any signs of affection in public, she was absolutely ready to take up his challenge of a race. 'Why not?' She turned Bella around.

'Go!' she said. Bella responded without hesitation. She let the little mare have her head, aware all the time of the thunder of the larger horse behind them, catching up, and then they were neck and neck.

Julia risked a glance at her husband. There was grim determination on his face, but also a smile of pure pleasure she had only seen once before, in a small candlelit room in the brothel.

As if he sensed her gaze, he looked over, grinned and pulled ahead, the long-legged gelding stretching into a gallop, only to slow a few moments later.

She came up beside him. 'Thank you.'

He raised a brow in question.

'For not pretending and letting me win. It wouldn't have been fair to Thor.'

Indeed, Thor was pawing and prancing, so very proud of himself. Alistair grinned at her. 'I haven't raced like that since—' he shook his head '—I can't remember when.'

'Nor me.'

He glanced around them. 'We should—' A frown crashed down. 'Damn.'

She followed the direction of his gaze to where two gentlemen were riding swiftly towards them.

'Someone you know?' she asked, holding Bella steady.

'Perhaps.'

A calm, coldly spoken word. The wall was back up. Likely he was annoyed that people had witnessed their display of high spirits. Not that they had done anything too outrageous. Or perhaps it was the thought of introducing his wife to his friends.

Chilly fingers crawled down her spine. Might they have been at the brothel when she had shamelessly allowed herself to be auctioned?

She lifted her chin and pinned a teasing smile to her lips. 'Shall we gallop *vente à terre* in the other direction?'

Once more a corner of his mouth twitched with the hint of a smile. 'Now that really would be rude.'

Hope bubbled in her veins. Was the distance between them closing, this barrier meant for others and not for her? 'Do we care? Being of the ducal sort?'

His eyes flashed amusement. 'Behave, madam.'

Thrills chased through her stomach. He'd used that deep seductive growl the night they'd made love. Her insides softened, liquefied. Longing filled her. For him. For his touch. For the way he had made her feel. 'I will behave if you will,' she quipped. He had intended to arouse, she was sure of it. The man did nothing without purpose.

Yet as the men drew close, his expression cooled.

'Duke,' spoke a handsome fellow on a big grey who looked familiar.

'Beauworth,' her husband replied, helping Julia to make the connection. 'You know my wife.'

Beauworth bowed, which was difficult to do with any elegance when astride a horse, although he made it look easy. 'Good day, Your Grace.'

Julia inclined her head and smiled. 'How do you do. We met at our ball.'

'Kind of you to remember,' the Marquess said.

Alistair had been icily cold that evening. She'd been terrified of doing something to put him to shame and had memorised the name of each person she'd met.

The younger man, clearly leaning towards dandyism with fair hair and plump apple cheeks, doffed his high-crowned hat. This was a man she had not met before, she was sure, yet he regarded her with a puzzled frown.

'My cousin, Your Grace,' the Duke said, his voice full of *ennui*. 'Percy Hepple. He was not at our ball.'

None of his family had been at their ball.

The plump fellow, his shirt collar impossibly high and his coat straining at the seams, bent awkwardly in the middle. 'Good day, Coz.' He frowned. 'Though may I say you look vaguely familiar? Must have seen you at somewhere around town.'

Julia's blood turned to ice. Her only other public appearance had been on stage at Mrs B.'s auction. Fortunately, the fellow seemed to lose interest in her and almost at once turned back to Alistair.

'Now I am in town again, Your Grace, I'll look for you at your club. I've a mind to challenge you to a game of piquet and recover some of my losses.'

Her stomach sank. More reason for her husband to leave home and hearth every night. She kept a smile pinned to her lips and hoped her dismay did not show.

'I doubt you can afford the stakes at my table,' the Duke said, his voice arctic. Was he always so unfriendly?

An awkward silence fell, during which Beauworth gave each of them a distinctly piercing stare.

'It is a beautiful day for a ride—' she said.

'I must be getting along—' Hepple said at the same moment.

'Yes,' Beauworth said. 'Run along, Hepple. Thank you for your company.'

Another awkward bow and Hepple rode off.

'Do you go to Sackfield Hall any time soon?' Beauworth asked, his gaze still on Hepple, his mouth curled in distaste.

'I had planned to go in a couple of weeks,' her husband said.

Julia swallowed a gasp. He had said nothing of this to her. Her glance shot to Alistair and he gave a slight shrug that told her nothing.

The Marquess smiled rather like a cat that had spotted a dish of cream. 'You will bring your wife to visit us, Duke, or my Marchioness will want to know why.'

Julia waited, breath held, half expecting Alistair to say she would not be going with him.

'Naturally,' he said. 'I will send a note when we are in residence.'

The Marquess nodded and turned to Julia. 'We are no more than five miles from you as the crow flies and normally, we would ask permission to call on you, Your Grace, but with young children underfoot...you will forgive us for not venturing forth.'

'Congratulations on your growing family,'

Julia said, a slight pang in her heart, envy for the Marchioness she had not yet met. It was unlikely she would ever conceive when she hadn't after eight gruelling years of marriage. She ignored the feeling and crushed the tiny tendril of hope that a younger, more virile husband might succeed where an old man had not. The fact that her husband never came to her bed didn't help, but the doctors had been adamant she was unsuited to conception.

The recollection of their harsh words made her chest squeeze, but she kept her composure. 'I shall look forward to making your wife's acquaintance.'

'She will be thrilled to have someone nearby close to her own age. Up to now she has been surrounded by dowagers and ageing matrons. Now if you will excuse me, I have business requiring my attention before I head home.' He gave her another elegant bow, nodded to Alistair and rode off.

Julia knew better than to carp at her husband for not telling her his plans to remove to the country. She knew now, after all.

'About our removal to Sackfield Hall,' she said. 'Do you have a specific date in mind?'

'Lewis will give you the details.'

Lewis, his amanuensis. Apparently it was

his secretary's job to inform her of His Grace's wishes. She bit back a sharp retort. This morning had afforded a ray of hope for improvement in their relationship. It would be foolish to ruin it with words spoken in irritation. This fragile beginning needed careful nurturing. And time. 'Very well, I will speak to Mr Lewis upon our return.' She managed to say the words without gritting her teeth and felt proud of her forbearance.

As they turned their horses towards the gate, an unpleasant thought crept into her mind. Perhaps he had not intended that she would go with him and had been driven into a corner by Beauworth's assumption.

A chill invaded her stomach. Had he planned to take someone else? A mistress, for example? 'Was it your intention that I remain in town while you visited your estate in Hampshire?'

She regretted the words the moment she spoke them, but it was too late to call them back.

'Did you want to remain in town?'

The tone of his voice said he didn't care one way or the other. Dash it all. 'A visit to the country would be pleasant at this time of year.'

He didn't react.

They headed home, the silence between them becoming impenetrable. Every time she thought of something to say, she discarded it as being too bold, too weak sounding or just plain ridiculous. While the Duke had not shown himself to be the sort of man to strike his wife for impertinence, she did not want to make him angry.

Bah. Such cowardice. She did not know who she wanted to kick harder, herself or him.

They arrived back at the stables without having said one word.

Julia went in search of her husband's secretary. As Duchess, she must have some duties to perform in regards to their removal from town. She also wished to know exactly where Sackfield Hall was located.

'Ah, Grindle,' she said, when the butler appeared in answer to her ring. 'Where will I find Mr Lewis?'

'In his lordship's estate office, Your Grace.'

Another room in this monster of a town house she had never heard of. 'And where will I find the office?'

'Would you like me to take you there, Your Grace?' He frowned. 'His Grace is not at home at the moment.'

She knew that. He had set out on some errand or other; she'd seen him pass the drawing-room window. 'Lead the way, please.'

Grindle bowed and set off.

Sometimes being a duchess had its advantages. People did not question your requests, never mind your orders, though she had noticed a faint wrinkle of concern in Grindle's brow as he turned away. Apparently, His Grace not having left instructions to the contrary, he had decided there could not be any harm in showing her into the omnipotent presence of His Grace's amanuensis.

Stop it, Julia. Sarcasm was unbecoming, even in the recesses of her own mind.

Mr Lewis was an important person in this household. It was to him Alistair referred when asked if he wished to attend this ball or that rout. And it was he who always sent Julia a note of regret, His Grace always, *always* having made some prior and far more important commitment.

It hadn't taken Julia long to stop asking and to simply decline every invitation she received. Now she would meet Mr Lewis in person.

The estate office was located at the back of the house. The room was bright and inviting—cosy, despite the large desk on one side of the room facing a bank of French windows overlooking a small walled garden. The glazed double doors were open and a fresh breeze redolent with the scent of roses wafted in.

A young man rose from a smaller desk off to one side. His expression was that of astonishment.

'Her Grace wished to see you, Mr Lewis.' The butler swiftly withdrew.

The fair-haired, blue-eyed young man bowed. He was not a tall man, but he was handsome and as he straightened, he gave her a smile of such sweetness she warmed to him instantly.

'Mr Lewis, I regret that His Grace has not had an opportunity to introduce us and I apologise for interrupting your work, but I understand you are to inform me about our move to the country in the next week or so.' She decided attack was the best mode of defence.

Lewis came around from behind the desk. 'I am?' He gave a little cough. 'I mean, yes, Your Grace, I am.'

Julia kept her face blank in light of the revelation that her husband had either neglected to inform his secretary in this regard, or had not intended that she be informed at all.

Her stomach dipped. She wandered over to the grand polished oak writing table where an ornate writing set of silver and cut glass occupied pride of place. A red leather-covered box with gold trim sat on one corner. The leather was beautifully tooled and engraved. Spanish, she thought. A work of art. A gift?

Julia dropped her gaze. She had no wish to pry, yet there was a little pang in her heart. The box was obviously something one would give to a woman. Surely Mr Lewis would not have looked quite so distraught if the gift had been one intended for her. There was no reason for Alistair to be giving her gifts. The bridal gift had been deposited on the night table beside her bed on the morning of her marriage, a set of sparkling diamonds, and her birthday was not until August.

'What a lovely view,' she said, turning towards the window.

'It is, isn't it?' Mr Lewis said. 'This was the room His Grace's mother used as a private parlour.'

And His Grace spent many hours here during the day, before he went out in the evening in search of entertainment. She had met him during one of those quests, had she not?

'I had no idea the garden existed,' she said pondering this hint of sentimentality in His Grace's soul. Even if it was directed at his mother. Another lady whom he had never once mentioned.

'His Grace says the light in here is the best in the house for doing paperwork,' Mr Lewis continued.

Clearly looking for sentiment in her husband was wishful thinking.

'About our move to the country,' she said, metaphorically grasping the nettle. 'Where is it exactly we are going?' She smiled and sat on the sofa near the open French door. 'Ring for tea, would you, and you can inform me of the plans.'

Mr Lewis's shy smile returned in full force.

Walking into his office and finding his wife taking tea with his secretary ought to have added to the misery of Alistair's day. In fact, the sight of her sitting on the sofa listening intently to Lewis lifted his spirits to the point of ridiculousness.

She looked up at his entry into the room with a smile so welcoming it plucked at a painful chord deep within him. An alien need to belong.

'I'm glad to find you having such a rollicking good time with my Duchess, Lewis,' he said and wanted to kick himself for the instant wariness on both their faces. He had no reason to feel jealous. None at all.

His wife, goddamn it, *his* wife, lifted her chin. 'Mr Lewis was regaling me with stories of organising your processions around the countryside. Will you join us for tea? I took the liberty of ordering an extra cup should you return in time.'

She'd thought of him? When was the last time anyone at all had thought about him in his absence and so kindly as to hope for his arrival? Surprised, he took a seat beside her on the sofa.

She set a cup of tea in front of him, then offered him the plate of shortbread. As he lifted the delicacy to his mouth he inhaled a faint scent of orange. A taste confirmed he was not wrong. The shortbread not only smelled lovely, it was delicious. He sipped at his tea and found it prepared exactly to his liking.

'Her Grace wanted to discuss the move to Sackfield next week,' Lewis said. 'I have given her the date of our departure and an outline of the usual travel arrangements.'

'Mr Lewis has been extremely helpful,' Julia said, but while her voice was light and even, he sensed an underlying unhappiness. Did she not like the countryside? For him, it was always a blessed relief, though his business affairs remained as demanding as they were while he was in Town. Putting the Duchy in order after his prolonged absence had been trying indeed, though his half-brother, Luke, had done his best with it, under the circumstances. Keeping it that way required equal effort.

'You will like Sackfield Hall, Julia.' He hoped she would. It was the only place in all of the estates owned by the Duchy he felt any affection for. He put down his cup. 'However, Lewis and

I have a great deal of business to conduct before our departure.' He glanced over at his desk.

The man jumped to his feet.

'Indeed, Your Grace. The documents arrived from the lawyer's office this morning.'

His will. He'd added a codicil to ensure Julia received his personal fortune in the event of his death. Everything else would go to the Dunstan heir.

Julia rose, graceful, elegant, and clearly unhappily aware of her dismissal. 'I will ask Grindle to collect the tray, if you have finished?'

Alistair, having risen with her, glanced down at the biscuit in his hand. He hadn't even realised he had taken another. 'I have. My compliments to the chef. The shortbread is delicious.'

'I will let him know.' A small smile curved her luscious lips and he wondered if the orange had been her idea. The idea that his compliment had pleased her gave him a feeling of warmth in the pit of his stomach.

When nothing about her should warm any part of him.

He sat down at the desk, finished off the letter of dismissal and handed it to Lewis. 'Send it round with a footman, would you, please. Lavinia will be well satisfied.' He'd been more than ready to let Lavinia go for some time. Even if he had not, he would have done so. While he did not tolerate jealousy in a mistress, his wife deserved what little respect he could give her. He certainly wasn't going to flaunt other women in her face.

'Yes, Your Grace.'

'Now, let us take a look at the documents from the solicitor.' He wanted to be sure they had followed his instructions to the letter. There must be not the slightest opening for Luke or his mother to contest the new provisions he had made for his wife and there had been too many accidents in his life to leave her welfare to chance.

Chapter Three

Alistair's staff needed no guidance from Julia. All questions were directed to Mr Lewis on the Duke's orders. Julia hadn't packed so much as a handkerchief. She unclenched her hands. There was no sense in complaining. If she wanted to make herself indispensable to her husband, she would have to work a great deal harder to find her niche in his well-ordered life.

'The carriage is at the door, Your Grace,' her dresser, Robins, announced.

In truth, she reminded Julia of a robin. Her movements were quick and deft and her nose, while small, came to a sharp point. She was exceedingly officious and exacting when it came to Julia's wardrobe. She clearly felt her skills as dresser to a duchess were very much on display and she had a reputation to uphold.

Julia sat down at her dressing table so the poor

woman did not have to stand on tiptoe to perch her hat on the elaborate coiffure that had taken what felt like hours to accomplish. Why a duchess could not manage the simplest of tasks for herself, Julia wasn't sure, but any rebellion in this regard, like putting on one's dressing gown without aid, or the removal of a shawl, sent Robins into a twitter.

The dresser tied the cherry-coloured ribbon under Julia's left ear, tweaked at the curls framing her face and stepped back. Julia rose and held out her hands to be encased in York tan gloves.

Robins ran a critical gaze from her head to her heels.

'Will I do?' Julia could not help asking.

'Your Grace does me great credit.' Robins's smile seemed oddly forced, her eyes remaining dull.

Julia repressed the urge to question this extravagant expression of approbation from the toplofty dresser when her expression belied her words. 'Thank you.'

'You are welcome, Your Grace.' The woman frowned mightily and Julia quailed. 'I notice that you ate little from your breakfast tray.'

Julia glanced at the remains of her breakfast on the night stand, the toast and preserves. The pot of chocolate. 'I am not hungry.'

The woman twisted her fingers, a sign of obvious distress. 'You will need something to sustain you on the journey, Your Grace.'

The kitchen had made the chocolate a little sweeter than she liked. Almost sickly. Or perhaps the niggardliness exhibited by her previous husband when it came to sugar—well, everything really—had ruined her taste for sweet things. She didn't want to make a fuss and cause a stir in the kitchen. Not for so small a thing. French chefs were renowned for their temperamental ways.

'I will likely travel better if I do not eat too much.'

'A piece of toast, Your Grace, and a sip of chocolate. We don't want you fainting along the way.'

Heaven forefend.

To please the woman, who while autocratic was clearly trying to be helpful, Julia nibbled on a point of toast with orange marmalade. A sip of chocolate had her repressing a shudder. A knock came at the door, giving her an excuse to set the cup aside while Robins bustled to the door.

It was a footman coming for the last of Julia's bandboxes. 'Be careful, Samuel,' Robins scolded as he hefted a hatbox under his arm. 'Those are easily crushed.' She turned back to Julia. 'Your Grace, please be so good as to await my arrival at the inn before you attempt to remove your outer raiment. The hat, if removed improperly, is likely to disturb what I must say is the perfect arrangement of your hair.'

Julia sighed inwardly. Robins despaired of her long straight hair and insisted that no proper duchess could set foot out of her room without the appropriate length of time spent with curling papers and pomade. Apparently a duchess required more curls than any lesser mortal.

As the sister of an impoverished earl, for Julia, curling and primping had been abandoned in favour of marriage to a very old, very rich and very unpleasant man.

Naturally, a duchess could tell her dresser to desist fussing and ignore the resultant sulks. But that would be unkind, when the woman was trying so hard on her behalf. Instead, Julia suffered silently. 'Thank you. I will keep your warning in mind.' The last thing she wanted was another hour in front in the mirror.

Being perfectly turned out might seem less of a task if one's Duke took an interest in one's appearance instead of seeming to wish her to Jericho. Despite her best efforts, she had never again managed to ambush him at the breakfast table and thereby force him to escort her on his morning ride. A new plan of attack was required. Hopefully, such strategies as ambuscade and flanking would work better in the country. Surely there, they would be required to ride out to visit neighbours and tenants.

Indeed, they already had one invitation from Lord Beauworth. The thought cheered her. As did the prospect of riding in the carriage with Alistair for the next few hours. The opportunities for a wife to connect with her husband in such close quarters were endless.

In a far more cheerful frame of mind, she walked out of the town house. Only to have her hopes dashed.

The travelling carriage, pure luxury on wheels in shiny black and silver, certainly awaited, but clearly her husband intended to avoid her company yet again. A groom was holding Thor saddled and ready for Alistair to mount.

Said Duke was inspecting the second coach loaded with their luggage and giving last-minute directions to Mr Lewis. Once again she was startled to note how tall her husband looked beside other men. How commandingly powerful and masculine. Her insides fluttered pleasurably, while sadness crept into her throat and formed a hard lump. What a waste. The lovely man who could have been cosily ensconced with her in the privacy of a well-sprung carriage preferred to exhaust himself hacking across a good chunk of England.

If that wasn't a travesty, she didn't know of one. Only if she could discover why he had taken her in dislike could she find a solution.

As she approached the elegant equipage in which she was to ride, a footman sprang forward to open the door and let down the steps.

'Thank you.'

His Grace turned at the sound of her voice. 'Finally,' he said, in the tone of the aggravated male of the species.

A clock within the house struck ten.

She raised a brow. 'You did say ten o'clock.'

'Hmmph.'

'Apology accepted.' She climbed into the carriage and, once her skirts were settled, looked through the door and into his startled expression. 'Are we leaving or are we not?'

'Yes,' her husband said. 'We are.' He stared at her, a glint of something in his eyes.

Julia wanted to kick herself for the odd sense of humour that always caused her trouble. She wanted to please her husband, not put him in a temper.

It was the thought of the journey that was making her lose her calm. She hated the idea of being shut up alone all day, much as she had been shut up alone in her last marriage.

* * *

Alistair wanted to kiss his wife's saucy mouth. She was likely the only person in his life who dared take him to task about anything. He was learning that she was a delight and a wonder. Not something he had ever expected in his life. Or wanted.

His good spirits plummeted. A wonder deserved a far better marriage than he was able to provide. Perhaps they could be friends as she had requested. A daunting prospect around an impudent sumptuous mouth that offered so much temptation for kissing, particularly when kisses would naturally lead to other far more dangerous activities.

Thought of said activities caused a stir behind his falls, confirming the impossibility of friendship.

It was far better to maintain a civil distance. He'd been thinking about leaving her at Sackfield when he went off to visit his other estates. It was easier to put the erotic memories of their one night together out of his head when she was far away. Unfortunately, that meant leaving her open to importuning visits from family members who were nothing but a trial.

As a rule, he looked forward to the ride out to Hampshire. The feeling of homecoming was a subtle draw, but this time a strange feeling of dread filled his heart. He closed the carriage door, swung himself up on to Thor and gave the signal for the off.

Naturally they made much slower time on the road than when he travelled alone. The cavalcade didn't arrive at the Bull and Bear until some eight hours and five changes of carriage horses later. Had he been alone, he would have pushed on to Sackfield Hall, but at the last toll gate he'd notice his wife's pale complexion and her answer to a passing remark had been unusually terse.

A stab of guilt tightened his gut. He had not thought to ask if she travelled well or ill. A husband should know that sort of thing about his wife. He leaped down and handed the reins off to a groom.

Setting her hand in his for only the briefest moment, she stepped down and gazed about her. 'Is this where we spend the night? Ah yes, the Bull and Bear.' Relief coloured her tone, despite her calm expression.

He offered his arm.

Though she took it, there was a reluctance in the action. Was she angry with him? Or... 'Are you unwell?'

'I am perfectly fine, thank you.' The strain

around her eyes said otherwise, but he didn't care to argue in front of the servants. It was bad enough that they would have noticed their estrangement in the marriage bed.

Inside the inn, the landlord, a chubby jolly fellow he'd known for years, Harry Bartlett, escorted them up the winding stairs to their chambers. Lewis had written ahead and their rooms were ready.

The moment she stepped inside the chamber, she released her grip on his arm. 'Would you have Robins sent up the moment she arrives, please?'

He bowed. 'Certainly.' He hesitated, inexplicably loath to leave her looking so fragile. He'd suffered travel sickness as a child. He recalled how he'd dreaded every promised journey. Dreaded the embarrassment of casting up his accounts to the pity of all concerned, along with the disgust.

Was that why she had not told him? 'Are you often ill when you travel?'

A crease formed between her brows at the sharpness of his tone. 'Not generally.' She sank into the nearest chair. 'I must admit, though, I have been feeling queasy since early this morning.'

If anything her face looked paler than before. She really was not well, poor thing. The urge to take her in his arms and offer comfort had him stepping closer. She froze, eyes wide.

He brought himself up short, shocked by his irrational need to ease what ailed her when he'd always avoided being drawn in by female megrims. Even so, and despite her obvious lack of trust, he could not bring himself to remain unmoved by her obvious discomfort.

'Is there anything I can get for you in the meantime?' he asked, surprised at the tenderness in his voice. He forced himself to sound calmly practical. 'Peppermint tea, perhaps?'

Surprise replaced the anxiety in her gaze. She gave him a brave smile. 'Peppermint tea would be very welcome. Thank you.'

It wasn't the smile or the bravery that shook him. He'd seen her courage first hand that night they'd met. The way she'd braved the leering stares and catcalls of the men waiting to bid for her. No, it was her surprise that came as an unpleasant shock. Her expectation that he would care nothing for her welfare. The idea was a bitter taste in his mouth, but he could not deny he deserved such condemnation.

Nor did he want anything else, since keeping his distance was already difficult enough.

She drew off her gloves and glanced about their shared sitting room. 'Would you care to join me?'

Temptation held him silent for a second, as he battled with the urge to say yes. Simply to assure himself she recovered, of course. Nothing else. But she might see it as something else.

A clever woman would certainly see his need to protect her as weakness and more than once he had seen his wife's cleverness at work. Forcing him into taking her riding in Hyde Park had been a masterful move. One that had, for a time, pierced a hole in his defences. That day he'd let emotion rule rational thought.

'No tea for me. I must oversee the stabling of the horses.'

The smiled died from her eyes. She leaned her head back against the chair cushions and closed her eyes briefly. Wearily. 'As you wish.'

He gritted his teeth. Nothing was as he wished. His wishes were not at issue, here. He certainly hadn't wished her to keep silent about feeling ill. Though nor had he encouraged her confidences. Far from it.

Dash it all, if he was fit for nothing else as a husband, at least he could ensure her safety.

He bowed. 'I will have your tea sent up right away and look forward to seeing you at dinner.'

Puzzlement filled her expression.

Because he *looked forward* to sitting down with her to eat? Did it sound so far-fetched? Before he said anything else that might make her rethink her opinion of the distance between them, he withdrew.

The moment her husband left the room, Julia closed her eyes, hoping to ease her dizziness.

Every pin of the elaborate coiffure seemed to have its point stuck in her scalp, along with the hatpin Robins had used to affix the bonnet. She didn't care what the woman said, it was coming off. Her fingers searched amid the feathers and flowers on her hat.

'Your Grace!'

Julia winced at Robins's sharp tone. The woman had slipped into the room without making a sound. And while she was always perfectly polite and indeed sometimes unbending enough to be almost kind, Julia sometimes had the feeling the woman was not quite comfortable in the ducal household. Still, Mr Lewis had been delighted that he had been able to secure the services of such a superior creature. Julia hadn't had the heart to refuse her, or the courage, if the truth was told.

She got up and went to sit at the dressing table. 'I have a bad headache,' she said quietly. 'The hat is making it worse.'

Robins's lips pursed. 'You see, Your Grace.

I was right. You did need to eat more. Now the journey has made you feel ill.'

The self-congratulatory tone was almost more than Julia could bear. She clamped her jaw shut before she said something she would later regret.

To her great relief Robins divested her of her bonnet with deft efficiency. Unfortunately, the throbbing behind her temples did not diminish.

A scratch at the door had her swinging around. A maid of about fifteen, with rosy cheeks and wheat-blonde hair, entered with a tray.

Robins frowned. 'I did not order a tray.'

Julia swallowed another surge of nausea. 'His Grace did. Peppermint tea.' She managed a weak smile. 'Please put it on the night stand, if you would.'

The girl bobbed a curtsy. 'Will there be anything else, Your Grace?' she said carefully, her country accent soft.

'I will let you know if Her Grace requires ought else,' Robins pronounced, glaring so hard that the young woman turned tail and fled.

Did Robins fear to be thought lacking, because someone else had seen to her welfare? Servants could be jealous, though they usually kept it amongst themselves. It was best to ignore it. She rose from the dressing table. 'I think I will lie down for a while.' And sip at the tea. It might help settle her digestion.

Robins rushed to plump the pillows. 'Your Grace, please, be careful. Your hair—'

'Stop!' Julia closed her eyes at her sudden loss of patience. 'I beg your pardon, Robins, but I really do feel unwell. Please, pull the curtains against the light and I will close my eyes for an hour or so.'

Robins did as asked, stiffly inclined her head and left.

The woman was becoming insufferably possessive. Yet suffer Julia must, for when she had hinted to Mr Lewis that she might like someone a little less toplofty, he had been most concerned she had found his judgement at fault.

And besides, Alistair had made it clear he did not want her changing anything in his household. Or hanging on his sleeve. She could always try to assert herself, as she had at the beginning of her first marriage. The pain and humiliation of having her husband take a birch switch to her palms to remind her to keep her hands out of his affairs had been a bitter lesson.

She did not think Alistair would beat her, he was too much the gentleman, but his coldness was in some ways worse. She never knew quite where she stood with him. Did she offend, or merely bore him? Doubtless it was the general regret of marrying a woman so far beneath him.

Her blood ran cold. Did he, too, fear someone might recognise her from the night of the auction?

She crawled up on to the bed and leaned back against the cushions Robins had arranged so that her hair would not touch either the pillows or the headboard. She poured herself a cup of tea and inhaled the soothing fragrance of mint. A sip told her it had been perfectly prepared.

Slowly her head seemed less inclined to spin. Her eyelids felt weighted. Sleep beckoned.

Something deliciously cool pressed against her forehead. 'Julia.' A male voice. 'Julia, wake up.' A demand.

She forced her eyelids open. A face wavered in and out of focus. 'Alistair?'

He muttered something under his breath that sounded a little like a prayer. Or not. He looked irritated rather than prayerful. She glanced around. Why was it so dark? And where—? Oh, yes, the inn. Robins had closed the curtains.

She stretched. For long seconds her husband gazed at her chest, his hard thin mouth softening sensually. There was no mistaking his interest in that unguarded moment. Was this then the way through his armour?

His gaze rose to her face, full of concern. She offered a smile of apology. 'I must have fallen asleep.'

'So it seems,' he said. His voice sounded rougher than usual. 'How do you feel?'

She pushed herself upright. Everything stayed where it should. She felt refreshed and her headache was gone. 'Much better, I must say. The tea helped enormously.'

'I'm glad.' For once he sounded relieved, rather than bored.

'I do beg your pardon. It was not my intention to sleep so long. I wonder that Robins did not wake me.'

'You aren't late. Yet.' He grimaced. 'I told Robins to let you sleep a while longer, but when I didn't hear any movement, I thought I should look in on you.'

An unlooked-for courtesy. One that made her heart stutter.

He rose from his seat on the edge of the bed. He had exchanged his riding coat and boots for evening dress, whereas she still wore her carriage gown.

'I must change.' She began undoing the buttons. He watched her hands with a peculiar intensity. Her face warmed. 'Will you ring the bell for Robins, please?' Oh, now why had that popped out of her mouth? Wasn't being alone with him exactly what she had wanted?

She pinned what she hoped was a seductive smile on her lips. 'That is unless you don't mind doing the honours?'

Surprise warred with another expression she could not read.

She held her breath. What would he choose?

'I will ring for your dresser.' He strode to the bell.

Chapter Four

Julia watched her husband leave with a sense of frustration. And sadness. Whatever passion he had felt for her that night at the brothel had gone as if it never existed. That was a disappointment she did not want to examine too closely, because it hurt too much.

Her stomach rumbled. Oh, goodness, she really was hungry. Whatever had ailed her earlier was clearly over and done.

Robins strode in and gave a heavy sigh. 'Your Grace, your hair! We must start again.'

Julia wanted to cut the whole lot off. She forced a pleasant smile. 'No, Robins. You will find a way to repair the damage. After all, we are in the country and dining *en famille*. I am sure His Grace will not care if my hair is a little less formal.' He might, however, care if she kept him waiting for his dinner.

Robins made an odd little noise.

Julia frowned. 'Did you sniff at me, Robins?'

The woman started. 'Naturally not, Your Grace,' she said and her mouth softened and, yes, almost smiled. Perhaps there was a human being behind the façade of dresser after all.

'Very well,' Julia said. 'Do your best to salvage what you can, but for heaven's sake do not fuss for too long. I do not want to keep His Grace waiting.' A man hungry for his dinner was likely to lose his temper. And that was not something she wanted to witness.

As instructed, Robins had swiftly made her look respectable and with half the usual number of pins, and she was on her way to dinner in less than half an hour.

A swarm of butterflies flapped around in her belly. Did butterflies swarm? Perhaps they flocked. Or buttered. Grinning at her foolishness, she entered the dining room set aside for their private use.

Alistair, rose. He arched a brow. 'What has you smiling so mischievously?'

Oh, dear. What would he think of thoughts brought on by a bad case of nerves? 'I was trying to recall what one would call a group of butterflies? A flock? A swarm?'

His eyes widened. She winced inwardly. Now he would think her perfectly stupid.

'I would call it a flutter, I think,' he said perfectly gravely and yet there was a twinkle in those intense grey eyes.

Her heart warmed to see it. 'The best I could come up with was a butter. I like flutter much better.' She laughed at how wonderfully foolish the words sounded coming out of her mouth.

'A butter of flutterbys.' He grinned. 'I mean butterflies, though they certainly do flutter by, I suppose.'

They exploded with laughter.

The transformation was almost magical. In that moment, he seemed younger, almost boyish. And sweet. An odd little pang pulled at her heart.

'May I offer you a sherry before dinner?' he asked, the laughter still in his voice, giving it a warmth she had never heard before.

'No, thank you.'

He sent her an enquiring glance. 'You do not object if I pour one for myself?'

'Not at all.'

After pouring himself a drink, he seated her on the sofa and sat at the other end, half turned towards her. He raised his glass in a toast. 'To my lovely and exceedingly speedy wife.'

She inclined her head in acknowledgement of

the compliment. It seemed that her illness today had brought out the compassionate side of her husband.

'Butterflies remind me of stained-glass windows,' Alistair said musingly after sipping from his glass.

'They do, don't they?'

'If I remember correctly, they are called a swarm.'

'How dull for such…an explosion of colour. One only has to think of the peacock butterfly, or the red admiral, to see it does not fit.'

'Mmm. More like the view through a kaleidoscope, don't you think?'

She blinked. 'I have never seen one, but I have heard of them, of course.'

'Old Brewster, the inventor, gave me a demonstration. They are remarkable. Fascinating, in fact. Turned out to be a profitable investment, too.' He smiled at her. 'A kaleidoscope of butterflies.' He nodded. 'That is it. A perfect description.'

My word, her husband actually seemed to have a little romance in his soul. What a revelation. 'I should like to see if your analogy is correct.'

He sipped thoughtfully on his sherry. 'Perhaps one day you will.'

Silence fell, but it contained no awkwardness.

She leaned back against the cushions. 'How long will it take to reach Sackfield from here?'

'Three hours if the weather remains fair. Can you bear it?'

'I hope so. Though I find it tedious in the extreme to be imprisoned all the livelong day.'

An expression flickered across his face. She wished she could read him. She had no idea why he had reacted to what she had said, when he so rarely reacted to anything at all, or why was he being so charming now, when for days he'd been positively brusque in their dealings.

Could he be missing the company of his mistress? Another little stab of jealousy under her ribs took her aback.

She forced a smile. 'Perhaps I will invite Robins to travel with me tomorrow as a diversion.'

He tilted his head, his eyes dancing with amusement, his lips curving in a wry smile. 'You would prefer your dresser's company to mine?'

Mouth agape, she stared at him. Now he wanted to ride with her? Because she'd been ill? Most gentlemen would run a mile. Perversity was this man's middle name. 'But—' She swallowed her protest along with her frustration—something she knew all too well how to do in the face of a husband's odd ways—and smiled instead. 'I would delight in your company, Your Grace, if that is your wish.' She'd be thrilled. It had been her initial plan, after all. 'Though I do not wish to discommode you.'

If he came unwillingly, with ill humour, it would not suit her purposes at all, though teasing the man out of a bad mood might have rewards. Another man, perhaps. With Alistair she wasn't sure how he would react. She wasn't sure of anything with regard to her husband.

'Thor will appreciate the rest.'

Of course, his horse. Well, that certainly put her in her place. She quelled the dart of pain and smiled brightly. 'Then I will look forward to your company. We could read poetry to each other for entertainment.'

His expression of horror, quickly masked, made her want to laugh. It also made her feel a little guilty, but really, didn't he deserve a little torment?

But perhaps he'd noticed her amusement, for he was now eyeing her speculatively, the way a fox might eye a henhouse. 'I hope you will allow me to select something we will both enjoy.'

A quick recovery. Judging from the teasing light in his eyes he had something wicked in mind. 'What do you suggest?'

'Why don't I surprise you?'

Everything that had come out of his mouth

this evening had been a surprise. A pleasant one. The man could be utterly charming when he wished. 'Very well.' Though she sensed a trap, she thought it would be interesting to see what he had planned. Certainly she would far prefer his company to that of Robins. She could only hope he would not return to his usual taciturn self in the morning, because it was distraction she needed, if she was to survive more hours trapped inside a box on wheels.

Though hopefully she would not be ill again.

The door opened to reveal Grindle. 'Dinner is served, Your Grace.' He bowed them into the dining room.

'Did you travel with your chef as well as with your butler?' she asked, seeing the array of dishes awaiting them on the table.

Alistair raised a brow. 'I have standards to maintain and a finicky appetite. Given my consequence, what else would I do?'

Her jaw dropped. She'd been jesting. 'Really? Is that not doing it a bit too brown?'

He laughed and his face changed from coldly handsome to gorgeous and alive. Her heart tumbled, not at his handsomeness but at how approachable he seemed in that moment. An odd sense welled in her chest, a feeling of tenderness. A sense that behind the chilly demeanour resided a man who cared more than he liked to reveal. If she could find a way to reach that man… The idea caused her heart to still.

Hand on the small of her back, he guided her to her seat and held her chair. 'I bring Grindle because he has family nearby and of course my valet and your dresser and a couple of footmen, but not my chef. The cook at Sackfield would not approve.' He helped her to sit, leaning close enough for her to feel his warm breath on her cheek. 'You know, your face shows your every thought, your surprise, your puzzlement.'

Glad she had her back to him so he could not read her most recent thoughts, she fought for composure as he moved to the adjacent seat. 'I am glad you find me entertaining.' And…there it was, sarcasm, her defence against hurt.

He moved around to his chair. 'You have a saucy mouth.'

She froze, terrified that she had ruined the evening. 'I beg your pardon. I did not mean to be rude.' Or shrewish.

He frowned.

She held her breath. Would he send her from the room in disgrace as her husband had done on more than one occasion? She clenched her hands on her lap. Or would he find more subtle means of punishment?

He gestured to the table. 'I hope you do not mind the informality. There are only the two of us dining and we can be more comfortable serving ourselves.'

Confused by the sudden change of subject, she nodded her assent.

Alistair couldn't remember when he had enjoyed a dinner more. He'd thought he'd become immune to the need for companionship. Then Julia had come along and was giving life to feelings he'd frozen out of existence.

A tide of longing rushed along his veins and stole his breath. Longings that belonged to a time when he'd been young and naive. Before he'd understood how badly a man could be led astray by his primitive urges. Before he learned first-hand how easily women pretended they cared for a man to suit their own ends. Never again would he be taken in. Especially not by the woman who was now his wife.

Bleakness filled him. The idyllic boy he'd once been didn't want to be always alone.

Alone was better than giving in to a weakness that could be used against him. He'd had enough of being used to last a lifetime.

Civility, common courtesy between them, had to be enough to see them through this marriage.

He picked up his wine glass. 'To our summer idyll and butterflies.'

Her smile lit up her face, filled the dark-panelled room with brightness. 'A whole kaleidoscope full of butterflies.'

Against his wishes, a chuckle rose up in his throat, the sound rusty to his ears. Life, the future, would be so much simpler if he liked her a whole lot less.

They each sipped their wine.

He carved the meat, she served the vegetables. He was surprised to see how much she ate, given her illness not so very long ago.

'The food is excellent,' she said as if guessing at his thoughts.

'Yes. Bartlett's wife has a reputation hereabouts.'

'Needs must, given Your Grace's finicky appetite.'

She was teasing again. When was the last time anyone had cared enough to tease him? And why did that matter?

'I'm glad your appetite is recovered,' he said.

'Me, too. I am feeling perfectly well now. I can't think what made me feel so dizzy.'

'Something you ate, perhaps.'

She frowned as if his words had struck a chord. 'Possibly. I do not recall ever suffering illness when travelling by coach, but I have never been on such a long journey.'

He rang the bell at his elbow. Grindle appeared instantly, along with the footmen to clear away the dishes.

The butler returned shortly afterwards with a decanter of port. 'Tea is served in the sitting room, Your Grace.'

She inclined her graceful neck. 'Thank you.'

Alistair rose to assist with her chair. He glanced down at her vulnerable nape and wanted to sweep aside the fine hairs that had escaped the confines of her coiffure and brush his lips over the delicate skin…

She sucked in a quick breath as if she had guessed at his fleeting thoughts. Thoughts he must not entertain if she could so easily guess at their direction.

'I'll take my port in the sitting room,' he said, surprised by the impulsiveness of the decision, his lack of forethought. 'That is if Her Grace is amenable.'

She glanced over her shoulder, her eyes warm. 'Very amenable, Your Grace.'

His blood heated at the implied promise.

Right at this moment, he realised, he was at a crossroads. He could give in to his desires and abandon the last shred of his honour by making her his wife in truth, or they could limp along in friendship, avoiding all temptation.

The choice was simple. Much as he wanted her, his duty, to the dukedom and to his heir, must come first. Otherwise he really was nothing more than a slave to lust.

He escorted her into the sitting room and, having accepted a glass of port from the butler, settled beside her on the sofa, one arm along the back to rest behind her head, his legs stretched out before him. 'That will be all, thank you, Grindle.'

The butler bowed and left.

Watching the graceful movements of his wife's hands in the ritual of pouring tea was as sensual as feeling them glide over his skin. An erotic sensation he remembered only too well.

Lush full lips pursed slightly as she tasted the concoction. He recalled how those lips had felt against his own. Soft. Full. Warm. The knowledge that he must not taste them again was pure sensual torture.

Deservedly so.

He sipped at his port, letting the tawny liquid slide over his tongue and down his throat, wrestling his unruly body under control, fighting to put his own needs aside and serve merely as a friend. Even so, he could not prevent a surge of heat at the way her hand shook as she placed her cup in the saucer.

She, too, sensed the tension in the air, the awareness, heavy, like perfume. She sipped at her tea and after a moment or two straightened her shoulders, as if coming to a decision. 'If we are to set off early again, I should likely retire very soon,' she said softly.

The breathiness along with the slightest break in her throaty voice would have been all the encouragement he needed, if she was not his wife.

'I agree,' he said coolly. 'After your illness you need your rest.'

A quick glance from beneath lowered lashes was the only signal she gave that she had heard the chill in his voice.

He helped her to her feet and they strolled arm in arm up the stairs. At the door to her chamber, he turned her to face him, cradled her face in his fingertips and bent his head to brush his lips lightly against hers. The feel of her lips so pliant, so welcoming, almost overcame reason.

He reached around her and opened her chamber door. 'Goodnight, Your Grace.'

The expression of puzzlement on her face, the hurt in her eyes, made him wince. As did her words. 'Would you care to join me in a nightcap?'

They'd enjoyed a nightcap at the brothel. It had

been one of the most erotic experiences of his life. He quelled his body's clamour for more of the same. Those clamours were one of the reasons he'd forgotten his duty and offered her marriage.

The thought of a similar encounter almost changed his mind. Beyond her, inside the room, her dresser hovered, trying to look busy. It would be easy enough to turf the woman out and have his way with his wife.

Temptation beat hard in his blood. Again. He would not allow it to control his decisions.

'You have been ill,' he said with a smile he hoped would temper his refusal. 'We have a long journey on the morrow. You need your rest.'

Her expression eased. Somewhat. Though regret figured largely in her eyes. Along with physical weariness. It was true what he had said earlier; her expressions made her an open book. Or at least, so it seemed. He also was enduring a certain amount of physical regret.

She passed him by and turned in the doorway. 'Thank you for a pleasant dinner. I—I will see you in the morning.'

'Indeed. An early start will ensure a timely arrival.' He took her hand and pressed it to his lips. 'I am looking forward to showing you around Sackfield.'

He was, he realised with surprise. He had

never brought any of his women there, but he
would enjoy showing his home to Julia.

He bowed and closed the door firmly, before
he changed his mind about leaving.

The next day proved fine and clear. Dressed
and seated at the dressing table, Julia munched on
a piece of dry toast while Robins worked on her
hair. Her stomach felt much better this morning,
but she had asked Robins to bring up a breakfast tray after hearing that His Grace had already
breakfasted and had gone out to the stables.

Would he keep his promise to join her in the
carriage? She hugged the warmth that thought
engendered deep inside. While she might have
preferred to ride a horse with him rather than
spend another day cooped up, undertaking such
a long journey on horseback would be foolish in
the extreme.

Robins worked another pin into her hair. She
forced herself not to wince. Or complain. One had
to suffer if one wished to be fashionable.

'What about your chocolate, Your Grace?'
Robins enquired around a hairpin held in her
lips. 'It will be cold if you do not drink it soon.'

Julia bit back her impatience. The woman was
being kind. 'I should have asked for tea. I think
it might sit better on my stomach.'

Robins frowned. '*Would* you like me to ring for tea, Your Grace?'

The door opened and Alistair stepped in. He was not avoiding her then, as a little niggling doubt had suggested. Not regretting the new accord that had reigned the previous evening, despite his rejection of her less-than-veiled offer to join her in bed. Afterwards, she had worried he might have thought her too bold for a respectable duchess.

And he'd had the right of it. She had been exhausted, despite her earlier nap. She'd slept so soundly, Robins had been required to shake her awake. Most unusual.

'Are you ready?' he asked. Dressed in his outer raiment and holding his gloves in one hand, he looked handsome and noble and thoroughly kissable. She swallowed her surprise at the unruly thought.

Stemming the waywardness, Julia glanced at Robins. 'Almost.'

'The coach will be at the door in ten minutes.'

Robins huffed out a breath, but even she did not dare gainsay the Duke.

'Ten minutes it is,' Julia said, smiling, feeling as if she had won a minor skirmish and could be ready for anything.

'Good.' He glanced at the triangle of toast in

her hand and over at the tray on the nightstand. 'You haven't eaten much.'

Robins shot her an I-told-you-so look.

'I will finish the rest when my hair is done.' What she really wanted to know was if he truly intended to travel with her today, but she didn't want to risk seeming overanxious.

'Good.' He nodded his approbation.

The moment he left, Robins brought the tray from the bedside table to the dressing table. 'Please, Your Grace, finish your breakfast. It will not take me a minute to help you with your bonnet and pelisse, but who knows when you may have a chance to eat next?' She sounded almost desperate.

Ashamed of her unkindness when the woman was trying to help, Julia downed the chocolate and finished the rest of her toast, slathered with butter.

Robins immediately sprang into action with bonnet, pelisse, gloves, and finally held out a shawl.

'Do I really need a shawl?' Julia questioned. 'It is June, after all.'

'There is a cool wind today, Your Grace. If you find you do not require it in the carriage, you may of course put it to one side, but shawls are *de rigueur* at the moment, you know.'

Julia swallowed a sigh. 'Very well. It seems I am ready. I will see you at Sackfield Hall.' Even if Alistair changed his mind about joining her, it seemed she had decided not to invite Robins's company for the rest of the journey.

The woman dipped a curtsy as she passed out of the door. 'I will come to you as soon as they have fetched in your trunk, Your Grace.'

On her way downstairs, a surge of dizziness took Julia by surprise. Oh, dear, it seemed Robins had been right about her needing sustenance. Hopefully it would pass in a moment or two, now she had eaten.

The carriage was waiting outside the front door, Thor was tied to the back. Her heart gave a little hop of joy. All at once the prospect of the journey became a whole lot more pleasant.

She glanced around for Alistair. He was in deep conversation with Mr Lewis, beside the coach carrying the luggage and the servants. Mr Lewis glanced her way, a frown on his face, then nodded at something Alistair said to him.

Were they talking about her? Why?

One of the footmen opened the door and let down the steps. 'Thank you, Matthew,' she said as he handed her in. 'Mrs Robins is waiting with my trunk.'

'I'll go up right away, Your Grace.' He touched

his forelock and strode around the corner, where the servants' stairs were located. Such a nice young man. Intelligent, too. He knew exactly what to do.

So Alistair really was going to travel with her in the coach. Desire fluttered low in her belly at the thought of several hours in her husband's company. She settled herself in one corner and folded her hands in her lap, trying to look as if her heart wasn't ready to leap from her chest and to keep her smile on the inside. A man as reserved as her husband would not appreciate a wife behaving like a besotted schoolgirl.

While she waited, her trunk arrived carried easily on Matthew's shoulder accompanied by a stream of instructions from Mrs Robins as if she suspected the young man of either preparing to toss his burden to the ground, or to open it and rifle through its contents.

Julia grinned to herself as she realised Matthew had developed a case of bad hearing and was marching along as if she was no more than an irritating fly.

The coach dipped on it springs as Alistair entered. He removed his hat, set it on the seat in front of her and sat down at her side. 'What on earth made you hire such a fussy woman?' he asked once the footman had closed the door. 'If I was Matthew, she'd be throttled by now.'

Julia pressed her lips together. She had no wish to get Mr. Lewis into trouble with his employer. 'I will have a word with her when we reach Sackfield.'

He made a non-committal sound. 'I hope we can make good time today.'

The coach jerked and moved off, its wheels grinding on the cobbles. Her husband put an arm across her front, steadying her, and then they swung out on to the toll road where the ride smoothed out. He stretched his longs legs out as far as he was able and stared out at the passing countryside.

Should she speak? Would he prefer silence? She glanced sideways at him, to discover him doing the same thing. She laughed.

He grinned.

And the awkwardness dissipated.

'Since I gather you did not bring the promised book, please tell me about Sackfield,' she said, broaching a topic that had been at the back of her mind for several days. She had hesitated to ask Mr Lewis in case he wondered why she hadn't sought the information from her husband. 'What should I expect? A castle? Something huge with hundreds of servants?'

'Quite the opposite,' he said. 'It is small compared to the other properties held by the Duchy.

A manor house. It came to the family in recognition of our loyalty to the Stuarts. Though I rather think my ancestors walked a fine line between pragmatics and ideology.'

Her own family had been staunch Protestants in Cromwell's era, but it was not until later that they had been raised up to nobility for services to the crown. 'Your family's gain was another's loss, I presume?'

'In some respects. My ancestor was a political being. He married the daughter of the ousted baron to his eldest son, thus eliminating future friction.'

Another arranged marriage. 'I wonder how they felt about it. The couple, I mean.'

He turned his face to look at her, his grey eyes speculative. 'You sound sorry for them.'

Did she? Did he see it as a criticism of their circumstances? Certainly out of the two of them, her lot had improved dramatically, while his... She still wasn't at all sure why he had offered marriage. Out of pity, she assumed, since their marriage was clearly pro forma. She certainly wasn't going to spoil what seemed to be a growing rapprochement in their relationship by reminding him of his coldness. She might have made some mistakes in her life, but she was not a complete fool.

'Simply curious.'

'You are interested in history?'

'In the history of your family, certainly, for it is now my family, too.'

'So it is.' There was a note of wonder in his voice, as if he hadn't yet adjusted to the idea of a wife. 'Sackfield is likely one of the places where you will learn a great deal about us, for it is the oldest of the Dunstan holdings.'

'I am looking forward to seeing it.' She leaned back against the squabs and watched the countryside drift by. She yawned.

'Tired?' She heard a frown in his voice and turned her head. He was watching her intently.

'Your carriage is wonderfully sprung. The rocking...' She lost the thread of her thought. 'Soothing.' She yawned again. What on earth was wrong with her? She never slept during the day.

'What crops do you grow at Sackfield?' Always ask a man about what concerns him most. With her first husband it had been his bargaining at the wool exchange. He had lectured her for hours on end about his dealings. And about her shortcomings.

'Wheat,' he said. 'Barley. We rotate...' His deep voice was sensual no matter what he was talking about...

'You will end up on the floor if you are not

careful,' a voice muttered in her ear. A strong arm went around her shoulders. 'Lean on me, if you must sleep.'

He did not sound pleased. Well, he wouldn't. She was supposed to be keeping him company. She tried to force her eyelids open. But the harder she tried to stay awake, the heavier her eyelids felt. Along with a strange feeling that something was not quite right…

She felt something hard beneath her cheek. Her body rocking oddly. Oh, dear heaven, that was a heartbeat. She jerked away. Her heart racing. Her gaze trying to focus on the face of…

Alistair. Frowning. Deeply.

Not Algernon. Of course not. He had died. And he would never have permitted her to sleep on his shoulder. He'd have poked her awake with a bony finger. Or slapped her.

She pressed a hand to her rapidly beating heart. 'I beg your pardon. I must have dozed off.'

He was eyeing her warily. 'You did.'

She slowed her breathing, tried to still the panic she had felt on awakening. 'I am sure I do not know what came over me.' She swallowed hard. 'Have I slept long?'

'Two hours, or so.'

So long. How could that be? She groaned. 'I apologise for being such poor company.'

'And here I was thinking it was my treatise on crops and yields and mangel-wurzel that had you snoring.'

'Snoring?' Horror filled her. She squeezed her eyes shut. 'Oh, I do beg your pardon.'

He frowned. 'Julia, I am jesting.'

'It is hard to tell when your expression is so stern.' She winced at the words she had meant to keep to herself.

He half turned to face her. 'You are my wife, Julia. Am I not entitled to undertake a little teasing?'

She stared at him wide-eyed, aware of the small curl at one corner of his mouth signifying amusement, but the shadows in his grey eyes showed concern. 'You must forgive me, I was not quite awake,' she said, miserably aware she was apologising yet again.

'Someone hurt you.'

She stared at him blankly.

'You flinch, Julia. When your speech is unguarded. You startle when I move too quickly. When you awoke a moment ago, you seemed nigh on terrified.'

There was an accusation in his tone, yet it did not seem directed at her.

'Who, Julia?'

It was the first time he'd used her first name

for an age. She shook her head, the memories of her husband's cruelties too raw, too filled with unhappiness because of her own failures as a wife. She shook her head. 'It is all in the past.'

He reached out slowly, the way one might reach out to a skittish horse, and took her gloved hand. His steady gaze rested on her face. 'I will make you a promise. Never will I raise a hand to you or physically cause you harm.' He spoke as if he was taking a vow. 'Do you believe this?'

His gaze was so intent upon her face, she felt as if every thought, every memory was bared to him. Yet she did not want him to know how cowed she had been by her husband. Or how she'd failed him.

Naturally, Alistair was irritated by signs she did not trust him. It likely impinged on his honour as a gentleman. And truly he had never given her cause to think he might raise his hand to her, even if his words at times sliced at her feelings.

She nodded her agreement and promised herself she would do better.

He brought her fingers to his mouth and kissed her knuckles.

Her stomach tumbled over and her inner muscles tightened. The hot restless feeling low in her abdomen increased tenfold. She swallowed a gasp of shock.

The twinkle in his gaze said he knew exactly the reaction he had provoked. He kept her hand in his, resting on his thigh. Her heart gave an odd little thump. She tried to ignore the heat of his hand permeating through her cotton gloves and the strength of his muscled thigh against the back of her hand.

He glanced out of the window. 'Not long now.'

She leaned forward to look out of the window. Her head spun. Her stomach rebelled. She slapped a hand over her mouth. 'Oh, no,' she whispered through her fingers.

His expression hardened, but he didn't waste a second. He hammered on the roof. 'Pull over.'

He held her around the shoulders as the carriage came to a halt.

Her stomach heaved.

She lurched for the door.

'Steady. Let me help you.' He held her while he opened the door with the other hand.

She wasn't going to make it. 'Please.' She swallowed.

And then he was swinging her down to the ground and holding her by the shoulders as she emptied the contents of her stomach.

Oh, how she wished she had not drunk that chocolate. He guided her a little way away and she hung limply on his arm, bent over, fearing to raise her head in case the dizziness should begin again.

Patient and strong, he stood beside her until at last she felt she dared stand upright. A blur of vision, a feeling of spinning. She held still a moment longer.

'All right now?' he asked in a voice rather devoid of warmth. A clean handkerchief, neatly folded, appeared before her face.

Shuddering with distaste, she wiped her lips. 'Better.' How horrible a way to end what had been mostly a lovely morning. 'I beg your pardon. I cannot understand what is going on.' She pushed away from him and leaned against the coach.

When he came closer, she waved him off. 'I will be better in a moment.' She hoped. Her head was still floating above her shoulders. Her stomach roiled at the thought of any movement.

'Perhaps if you sat in the carriage—'

'It must be the carriage that does this to me.'

'Likely so.' He sounded almost bored.

Feeling steadier, she risked a glance at his face. His eyes were hard, his lips thin.

His face softened as he looked at her, became concerned. He dived inside the carriage and returned with a flask. 'Perhaps some brandy will help?'

Despite his obvious distaste, he clearly was

trying to be kind, but instinctively, she knew brandy was the last thing she needed. 'No, thank you.'

He blew out a breath and glanced around. 'I wish I had thought to bring along a flask of water.'

She closed her eyes and opened them again. No senses swimming. She walked a step or two. No heaving stomach.

'How much longer before we reach our destination, do you think?'

He frowned. 'An hour at most.'

'Then we should continue. I think I shall manage.'

An odd look passed across his expression. She could not tell quite what it meant. She didn't know him well enough. It could be anger. After all, he was not the sort of man who would relish taking care of anyone else. Or it might have been sympathy.

'As you wish,' he said. He took her elbow, supporting her again. As if she was some sort of fragile invalid.

He helped her back into the carriage without a word. When she was settled in one corner, he took the other, stretching out his long legs, and when the carriage started, he stared grimly out of his window, their earlier accord nowhere in evidence.

This was not how she had wanted to spend the day with him. She had wanted to show him she was not such a bad choice for a wife.

Moisture welled behind her eyes. Now she was weepy. This was not like her. She blinked them back. 'I really am sorry,' she whispered.

He turned his head to look at her, his eyes as cold as a grey winter sea. 'What can't be cured...'

Must be endured, she finished in her mind. She'd ruined everything. She shivered.

He reached across the carriage, picked up her shawl and wrapped it around her, his gentleness surprising. He narrowed his eyes. 'Let us get rid of this...' he pulled at the ribbons of her bonnet '...and make you more comfortable.'

Startled, she could only stare at him as he skilfully divested her of the hatpin and then lifted the bonnet clear of her hair. She let go a sigh of relief. 'Thank you.'

'Rest. We'll be there soon.'

She nodded and clutched at the shawl, knowing she must look a fright, with her hair in disarray, her gown rumpled. She leaned her head back against the squabs and closed her eyes.

The carriage jolted and turned.

Julia opened her eyes. Oh, no. She must have fallen asleep. Again? This was so unlike her. And once more she was leaning against her husband's broad chest and he had one arm around her shoulders, keeping her steady. She struggled to sit up and he released her instantly.

A glance out of the window revealed a beautiful house of yellow sandstone. Not a huge house, but still one of impressive proportions. The house of a gentleman of means, with neatly trimmed ivy climbing the walls and a columned portico where… She swung around to face Alistair, the movement too rapid. Her vision blurred for a second.

'The servants—'

'Expect to meet my duchess,' he said calmly.

She put a hand to her hair, glanced down at her creased gown and the limp shawl. She wanted to disappear under the seat. 'I couldn't possibly.'

If anything his expression became more remote.

He was going to insist. She dived for her bonnet.

'Leave it.' His tone brooked no argument.

How could he expect her to meet those people looking as if she had been pulled through a hedge backwards? Of course the servants would be waiting to greet their new mistress. They had gone through all that at the town house and it was perfectly normal, and if she had been feeling more herself she might have thought of it. 'But—'

'You can meet them later.'

But they were all standing there... In a line.

The carriage halted at the front door. A footman hurried forward to open the door and let down the steps.

'Wait here,' Alistair said and jumped down.

She hunched forward, not feeling ill so much as feeling hopelessly inadequate. It seemed no matter how she tried, she was destined to be useless as a wife.

A moment later her husband returned.

She forced herself to her feet, but before she could step down, he gathered her in his arms. Once out of the carriage she could see all the servants were gone. She braced herself for him to set her on her feet. Instead, he carried her a few short steps across the drive, up the steps and into the house.

Across the threshold, like a bride. Something he had not done on their wedding day. He continued up a beautiful marble staircase that seemed to float in the great hall and up another flight and into a chamber all cream and gold and beautiful. It was a sitting room, she realised.

He set her down on a *chaise longue* and ran a hand through his hair as he looked about him. He strode across the room and rang the bell. He frowned. 'Would you like tea? Something else?'

'Tea would be wonderful.' She was never drinking chocolate ever again. She shuddered.

A knock came at the door. He went to it, opening it only a fraction, and she heard the murmur of voices before he closed it again. 'Tea will arrive shortly.' He put her bonnet and pelisse on the chair. 'I have told them to send Robins to you the moment she arrives.'

'Thank you. You don't need to stay. I am sure you have other things…'

His gaze narrowed a fraction and he bowed. 'Try to rest. Take some sustenance from the tray and if you are well enough I will see you at dinner.'

More orders. Sensible ones given the way the room seemed to pitch and yaw around her. He'd been very patient. And kind. She inclined her head. 'Your Grace?'

Already at the door, he stopped and turned back with a look of enquiry on his face.

'Thank you.'

He bowed elegantly and walked out, obviously displeased.

She sighed. And she had hoped this visit to the country might be a new start.

The next morning, Alistair sat in his study, staring at his empty desk. All his paperwork was in the third carriage, a lumbering affair carrying the last of their trunks which had not yet arrived. Burying himself in the work had always served to take his mind off problems of a personal nature. A suitable distraction. But never had he felt quite so anxious as he did now. About his wife.

Well, she was his duty, too.

Cook had reported that the Duchess had eaten nothing of the meal taken up to her on a tray last night, while he had dined in solitary splendour in the dining room. She'd drunk only peppermint tea for breakfast, sending everything else back untouched.

Why had she again not told him she felt ill in the carriage? He'd been so occupied talking about the place he held close to his heart, he'd failed to notice her growing pallor. The damned bonnet hadn't helped. It had hidden her face while she slept. And the look of terror on her face when she awoke had taken him aback.

Had she thought he might be angry at her illness? For a moment she'd actually cringed. Anger gripped his gut tight. Her previous husband had a great deal to answer for. Too bad the man was already dead.

He closed his eyes against the memory of how fragile and vulnerable she'd looked leaning against his shoulder for those last few miles.

He'd failed her, badly. He struck the table with the side of his clenched fist.

Shocked at the pain, he shook his hand out and stared at it. What the hell was the matter with him? He'd done everything in his power not to care about this woman who was his wife, but it seemed the more he knew her the more he wished things were different.

Enough! Things were as they were. He would not be weakened by this strange protective need. Or the foolish desire to make her happy.

Even Lewis had thought he was being ridiculous for sending him back to London. That he had actually allowed himself to succumb to such nonsense was the source of his anger. Nothing else. He'd let down his guard. He could not afford weakness where a woman was concerned. It stopped now. Today.

Still seething, he got up and strode to the window, looking out on the formal gardens at the back of the house. Everything was as it should be. Hedges trimmed. Roses blooming. Walkways swept. Edges neat. Usually the sight from this window brought him peace. All his memories of this place were good ones.

This house, filled with his earliest memories before Isobel had come into his father's life, normally felt like home. Not today. The ruination he had made of his life, the mistakes he had made, hung over him like a pall. He inhaled a deep breath. Duty. It was now his watchword if he was to make amends.

He turned at a scratch on the door. 'Lunch is served in the breakfast room, Your Grace.'

'And Her Grace?'

'Robins reports that she will not come down, Your Grace.'

An urge to see her for himself had him moving towards the door. He halted. 'Did a tray go up to my wife?' My wife. Not the Duchess. Not Her Grace, but *my wife*. He had to stop this sense of possession. She was not his in any way that mattered. And she never could be.

'At any moment, Your Grace. Tea is all she requested.'

'I will join her.'

If Grindle was surprised, he didn't show it. 'I will make sure the kitchen knows, Your Grace.'

'Make the tea peppermint. And send sandwiches. For me. Chicken broth for Her Grace.'

Grindle's eyebrow twitched, but he managed to maintain his bland expression before he bowed. 'I will let Cook know.'

Alistair blinked. What the devil had happened to his resolution to maintain a sensible distance from his duchess? Nonsense. He was only doing his husbandly duty.

The thought echoed back to a time when he'd thought he was worthy of a dukedom and a wife and family. A time he did not care to think about.

Chapter Five

Julia closed her eyes and lay back against the *chaise* in the sitting room adjoining her bedroom. Surely she should feel better by now. If only Robins would stop bustling about in the other room, she might actually be able to rest.

There was something about the way she felt that reminded her of being ill as a child.

If her courses had started, she might have ascribed her general weakness to that occurrence. They were always frightfully painful and terribly irregular. And they were due in a week or so, though they were often late. A sign, the doctors had said, of an inability to have children. But these sensations were quite different. The nausea. The dizziness.

Could she have contracted some sort of illness? Should she ask for a doctor?

A door opened and the rattle of cups alerted her to the arrival of the tea tray.

'Is that the girl with the tea, Your Grace?' Robins called from the other room. 'Shall I pour?'

Julia forced her eyes open as Robins scurried in from the bedroom. The woman stopped short, her mouth agape.

'I will pour for Her Grace.'

Alistair?

Julia went to swing her legs down and sit up.

'Stay where you are, madam,' he said. He glowered at Robins. 'Have you finished unpacking?'

'No, Your Grace.'

'Come back later.'

With a gasp, the woman curtsied and disappeared from whence she came, no doubt leaving by way of the dressing room off Julia's bedchamber.

Alistair frowned. 'Did she sniff at me?'

Julia couldn't help chuckling even if it did sound a little weak. 'I think she may have. Do not feel special, she sniffs at me, too.'

'Good Lord. How very odd. Perhaps you should get someone new.'

And hurt Mr Lewis's feelings? 'She hasn't done anything that requires such drastic measures. And she is really very kind though her manner can be a little presumptuous.'

'You are braver than I. The woman leaves me quaking in my boots.' He brought the small table holding the tea tray and set it beside her. He pulled up a chair. 'I had them make peppermint tea. I hope that is all right? It seemed to help yesterday.'

'It did. Thank you.' How kind. And after such a horrid display of illness yesterday. Tears welled. She blinked them back, shocked by the sudden surge of emotion. This was not like her at all. Perhaps her courses really would be early for a change.

In truth, only the last part of the journey had been awful. The earlier part had been nice, even if she had fallen asleep. She recalled his promise to never cause her harm with a feeling of tenderness. The man had a kind streak. Of course, she had already known that or he would not have offered marriage. But his coming to see how she was faring was an unexpected thoughtfulness.

Perhaps he was missing his mistress. She ignored the pang in her chest. If he was, perhaps she could find a way to replace her in his affections. A trickle of heat ran through her veins at the naughty thought. Heaven help her, she really was becoming wanton. If so, it was all his fault, him and his fallen angel looks and the heat flaring in his eyes. She lowered her gaze in case he saw the direction of her thoughts. The man saw too much.

Alistair handed her a cup and saucer and she took a sip. He watched her intently. Oh, dear, did he think she was going to be ill again and was preparing to leap clear? Or worse yet, make a dash to fetch the chamber pot?

'I am feeling a good deal better, today,' she said as much for herself as for him. 'It is strange how I am ill one moment and then an hour later I feel fine.' She hesitated. 'I felt a great deal worse yesterday than the day before.'

He straightened. 'Worse?' His frown deepened.

Oh, she had not meant to cause him further worry. 'Perhaps. I am not sure.'

'You have been refusing your food, madam. It is no wonder you are weak. Once you have drunk your tea you are going to eat something.'

'I am not sure I could.' Or that she should.

'I insist. The kitchen is bringing up broth for you and sandwiches for me, and we will see how you do.' His expression became grim. 'If you are not better by morning, I am sending for the doctor.'

Relief filled her. She had wondered how she might raise that very issue. Doctors were expensive and she was not sure he would appreciate spending the coin. But then he was nothing like her first husband, begrudging every penny. She had to remember that. She lifted her brows at him over her cup. 'You are very dictatorial, husband.'

'Someone needs to take you in hand,' he said, his voice strangely gruff as if he found the words uncomfortable. 'It might as well be me.'

And if not him, who else would? The loneliness she had tried to ignore since leaving her home eight years ago threatened to overwhelm her. If she had not been barren, she would have had a child by now. Children. In that event, she would not have had to worry about loneliness.

A knock on the door heralded the appearance of another tray. While one footman whisked the tea tray away, the second replaced it with the other, bearing a plate of sandwiches and little cakes and a steaming bowl of clear soup. They left as soundlessly as they had arrived.

Julia put a hand on her stomach. 'To tell the truth, I do feel a little peckish.'

'But you did not send down for food.'

'I did not think of it until now.' Oh, dear, she was sounding defensive. Argumentative. 'I thank you for your thoughtfulness.'

His grey eyes warmed, as if her thanks pleased him. 'Good.' He removed the plate of sandwiches, balanced the tray with the soup on her lap and handed her the spoon. 'Now eat.'

A smile tugged at her lips. Clearly her husband, while his bedside manner left much to be desired, was trying his best to be sympathetic in the practical way of a man solving problems. 'Thank you, Your Grace,' she said meekly.

A twinkle appeared in his eyes. Was there really amusement there? 'I see what you are about, madam. Do not think I will be fooled by your cozening ways.' He picked up a sandwich and took a bite.

He had lovely white teeth and his face, though very masculine, was also quite beautiful when that little smile curved his lips. It made him look devastatingly handsome. Her insides fluttered as she recalled their one night of lovemaking. He had smiled then, too.

Apparently, given the direction of her thoughts, she was indeed feeling better. She sipped at her broth. Delicious. Seasoned to perfection. She finished it in short order. 'My compliments to your chef.'

'Cook. And she was quite perturbed at your lack of appetite.'

Or was it he who was perturbed? The idea that he cared was a warm sensation around her heart.

He inspected the three remaining sandwiches

on the plate resting on the arm of his chair, held there by one large, but elegant hand. 'Do you think you could manage one of these? There is ham, roast beef, or breast of chicken.' He gave her the most bashfully boyish smile she had ever seen.

He looked so young, almost hopeful.

It seemed he had saved her one of each kind so she would have a choice, rather than leaving what he least preferred. 'Chicken, please.'

Looking thoroughly pleased, he passed it over and watched while she ate, as if to make sure she did not tuck it into the chair cushion when he wasn't looking, like a recalcitrant child.

Protective.

If he had children, that is how he would be with them, too. Longing stole into her heart to be swiftly followed by the ache of regret. The expectation she might give him children was practically nil. When he realised this was the case, would he also hate her, the way her first husband had? What of his promises then? His disappointment?

The warm glow dissipated. She finished the sandwich.

'Another,' he asked.

'No, thank you.' Thinking of children had stolen the rest of her appetite.

He regarded her intently. 'I will not have you fading away to nothing.'

'No, Your Grace.'

'Humph.' He paused, looking at her almost expectantly. When she didn't respond, a crease appeared in his forehead. 'I told Grindle you would greet the staff when you feel better. I was going to suggest you take to your bed for the rest of the afternoon, but then I wondered if you wouldn't prefer to take a walk. Get some fresh air. Put some colour in your cheeks.'

Instantly, her spirits lifted. 'I would love to go for a walk.'

His face brightened. 'Excellent. Let us send for that dresser of yours.'

'I think I can manage to wrap myself in a shawl and put on a bonnet,' she said, not liking the idea of Robins's fussing.

'I am sure you can. With my help.'

They walked down the hill to the stables set away from the house. This was closer to what Julia had expected would be her lot in life as a girl. A handsome husband whose large gloved hand held hers against the crook of his elbow. A home in the country, similar to the one she had lived in growing up—before Father died and her brother took over the estate and her life.

Not that she'd ever imagined reaching as high as a duke. Her family had lost much of their land and influence after generations of lackadaisical earls who had preferred the spending of wealth to accumulation. And yet her breeding was as good and as old as his, so it wasn't a complete *mésalliance*, even if they had met in unusual and potentially scandalous circumstances.

The stables were a long low red-brick affair reached by way of a path across the lawns, or by way of a turn off the drive further down the hill. They passed through a red-brick arch and into a quadrangle laid with cobblestones in diagonal patterns that sloped into a runnel. In the centre was a large stone horse trough fed from a wrought-iron pump. The stables, red brick with a thatched roof, had sufficient room for a great many animals.

'My goodness, how many horses do you keep here?'

'The east end—' he pointed '—holds various equipages. The rest are stalls. At the moment we have ten animals, most of whom are out to pasture. Several of the mares are in foal. Would you like to meet those in residence?'

'I would love to.'

He strolled on. 'When my father was alive, he kept a great many more horses, mostly for hunting. Now we have become more discerning and turned our attention to the racecourse.'

He guided her inside and along a corridor along a wall set with large windows at regular intervals and three sets of double doors, one at each end and one in the middle. On the other side was a row of stalls and loose boxes with windows under the eaves. The whole thing had a bright airy feel, though of course it was thick with the usual aromas of manure, horse and hay. A couple of the residents poked their heads over the top of the half-doors to see who had come to visit.

'Your horses must count themselves fortunate to live in such modern accommodations,' she said, recalling the details of her girlhood home for the first time in a long time. The stable where her father and now her brother kept his horses had no windows at all at ground level, the ceilings were low and the stalls on each side of the central aisle were dark and dingy. One needed a lamp to see much at all, even in the middle of a sunny day.

'A happy horse is a healthy horse. Isn't that right, Thor?' His horse whiffled a greeting and nudged his owner with his nose. Alistair dug in the pocket of his jacket and produced a carrot.

Leaving the horse munching happily, they strolled down a row of mostly empty stalls.

'Ah, here is the lady I was looking for.' Julia,

standing next to him, once again realised how tall he was as he leaned one arm on the top of the stall door on a level with her chin. Inside the larger loose box was a beautiful grey and her leggy coal-black foal.

'Oh, how lovely.'

The mare wandered over to greet them. Alistair blew softly in her nose and she shook her head and pawed at the ground. 'I know, Princess,' he said. 'You want to be let out.'

'Princess? Is that her name?'

'Her name and her nature,' a voice with a faint Scottish burr said. The owner of the voice walked down the aisle towards them. He was a handsome man of about thirty, with sandy-coloured hair and bright blue eyes. He wore a homespun jacket and trousers of an indeterminate brown and a startlingly blue kerchief at his throat. 'Welcome home, Your Grace.'

'Jaimie, you rogue. Let me introduce you to my wife. Duchess, this is James McPherson, head lad here at Sackfield.'

'Your Grace.' Jaimie bowed with a little twirl of his wrist. 'Welcome to my domain.'

There was something oddly familiar about the man, though Julia knew she had never met him before. Perhaps it was the intensity of his piercing blue gaze. 'Thank you, Mr McPherson.'

'Call him Jaimie,' Alistair said. 'Everyone else does, from the land steward to the scullery maid. Jaimie charms them all.'

Clearly her husband liked this man. His expression was less chilly than usual. Julia smiled. 'It is a pleasure to meet you, Jaimie.'

Jaimie grinned back, then turned his gaze on Alistair. 'So... Here you are for another summer visit.'

'How is everything?'

The stable master began a report full of horses' names and various ailments and other needs. While the two men communed, Julia wandered further along the row of stalls. The stables were a wonder of cleanliness and care. Jaimie McPherson clearly knew his business.

'Bella!' she exclaimed as the little mare hung her head over her stall door.

'Found her, did you?' Alistair said, coming up beside her.

McPherson must have left, for all of a sudden there was no sign of him.

'When did she arrive?'

'I sent her down a few days ago. I assumed you would want to ride during your stay here.' He frowned. 'Perhaps being unwell you would prefer going about by carriage.'

'Oh, no. I am sure this will not continue. I

would love to ride out with…on Bella.' She had
been about to say *with you*, but after their one ride
he had not asked her to go with him again. She
had no wish to put him on the spot, either force
him to go with her when he did not want to, or
have him tell her she was not welcome.

He rubbed Bella's nose. 'Good. Why don't
we hack out tomorrow morning, if you are suf-
ficiently recovered by then? I have to look in on
all my tenants over the next few weeks and it will
be a good way for you to get to know the countryside and the people hereabouts.'

It seemed her fears were groundless. A light-
ness entered her chest. 'I would love to. We also
have to pay a call on the Marquess, once we are
settled.'

'I will send a note over and enquire when it
might be convenient to call.'

She smiled up at him and he actually smiled
back. A rather fleeting affair, but still a smile.
Who was this charming man? And what had he
done with her dark and dangerous dissolute duke?

The next morning, Alistair, at the sideboard,
filled his plate with fluffy scrambled eggs and
several rashers of bacon, his ears alert for the
sound of his wife, who had promised to join him
at breakfast. He had suggested she retire right

after dinner and had been wishing ever since that she had objected to leaving him by himself.

He shook his head at the irritating thought and the resultant restless night. Theirs was a marriage of convenience. Even had she not been unwell, he would not have joined her in bed. No matter what. Of that he was certain. Practically certain.

He turned the moment she walked in.

The dreadful pallor of her skin of the previous day had been replaced by a healthy glow. She was dressed in the habit she had worn in Hyde Park. Ready to ride out. Gladness washed through him. Because she looked well, nothing else. Oddly the feeling was far stronger than circumstances warranted, likely brought on by how attractive she looked. And that was not a good thing.

'Good morning, Your Grace,' he said, taking his plate to his usual place at the head of the table. 'It looks like a good day for hacking out.'

She smiled at him and his stomach lurched. He must be hungry. For food. He'd been up at first light. And not only because he hadn't slept well. In Lewis's absence, he'd been forced to attend to all of his correspondence rather than only the important items. After that he'd met with Jaimie and given him his orders for the day, or at least agreed on a plan of action. Giving Jaimie orders was like trying to instruct the tide when to turn.

He forked up a mouthful of eggs.

'I am looking forward to seeing more of Sackfield,' she said, browsing the platters of food.

'I can recommend the eggs and the bacon if your digestion is up to it. Both come from the home farm.'

'Thank you.'

Covertly, he watched her take a small amount of each and then add several strawberries and a slice of toast. It didn't look like enough to keep a bird alive. No wonder she was so slender. He pondered encouraging her to take more, but did not want that wary look back in her eyes.

A look he'd put there with his deliberate coldness.

She sent him a curious glance. A pretty pink washed across her face. A blush. Hell, he was staring at her like a besotted schoolboy.

Or a newlywed husband.

He forced his attention to his newspaper, an article on horticulture, a comparison of the benefits of pig manure versus cow manure. Something that would cool any man's ardour.

Or should. It did not blunt his awareness of Julia at his right hand, close enough for him to touch. His fingers twitched as if they might reach out and stroke her hand of their own volition. Abandoning the pretence of reading, he folded the newspaper and gestured to the teapot. 'May I pour you a cup of tea?'

'Thank you.'

He did so and watched as she added a generous dollop of cream and a mere sprinkle of sugar. She sipped it and sighed.

He raised a brow. 'Is something the matter?'

'Oh. No.' She gave him a hesitant glance. 'Why do you ask?'

'You sighed.'

She blinked. 'Did I? Oh, I suppose it was a sigh of gratitude. Robins insists I take chocolate in the morning and I really do not like it.'

'Then tell her no.'

She pursed her lips, but her eyes sparkled with amusement. 'I did mention it. She is determined I shall be all that is fashionable. Apparently, only dowds and dowagers take tea upon awakening. I fear I am a sad disappointment.'

She certainly was nothing of the sort. 'She sounds more like a governess than a dresser.'

'A very attentive governess.'

'It is your decision, of course.'

'Yes. It is.' She shot him a conspiratorial smile. 'This morning I tipped it out of the window into the flower beds while she was off fetching my bonnet.'

Confidences were a wonderful start to the day. 'Hardly a satisfactory solution.'

Her smile faltered and he felt as if he'd kicked a puppy. 'You are sure you feel well enough to ride this morning?'

'I do.' A puzzled frown creased her forehead. 'I cannot think what came over me on the journey.'

Intending comfort, he took her hand in his, small and fine boned and so very breakable. 'Travel sickness. It can affect the best of us at times.'

To his pleasure, she did not pull away. He brought her hand to his lips before reluctantly releasing her fingers. She was his wife, not his lover. 'We will not overdo things today. I have only one call I must make.'

She gazed at him, her amber eyes strangely soft. 'Did you remember to send a note round to Beauworth? We should not be remiss in answering his invitation.'

'As promised. I will let you know his response.' He glanced at her barely touched plate with a sense of unease. Was she not well and simply afraid to tell him? 'Jaimie said he thought it might rain later.'

She pushed the eggs on her plate around with her fork. 'Do Jaimie's predictions usually prove true?'

'About half the time.'

A small smile played about her lips. 'Good to know.'

Something painful tugged at his chest. Why, because he'd made her smile? Such nonsense. He picked up his cup and sipped at his tea. 'Eat.'

For a moment he thought she might take issue with his request, or rather his order. Apparently his wife was another one who did not respond well to orders and nor did he usually find himself dishing them out to the females of the species. He preferred to get his way by more subtle means, but seeing her pick at her food when she had eaten so very little these past two days was concerning in the extreme. He offered her a mollifying smile as she glanced at him from beneath lowered brows.

To his relief, she resumed eating and, while he pretended to read his newspaper, she finished everything on her plate.

He rose to help her with her chair, enjoying the scent of jasmine as she stood. 'Are you ready?'

'But for my hat and riding gloves.'

He walked her out to the hall. 'I will meet you outside.'

He paused in the hall to watch her mount the stairs, the sway of her hips in the full riding gown a delight to behold. He caught Grindle eyeing him with an indulgent expression and frowned. 'Something wrong, Grindle?'

The man flushed. 'No, Your Grace.'

Puzzled by his embarrassment, Alistair strode out the front door where Jaimie was waiting with Bella and Thor.

As he'd requested on the spur of the moment, a blanket had been tied on behind Thor's cantle. Another impulse brought on by his wife's company. He pressed his lips together to stop himself from requesting its removal. He was, after all, on his honeymoon in a sense.

Jaimie touched his cap and looked expectantly towards the front door.

Alistair narrowed his eyes. Apparently his duchess was fast becoming a favourite with the staff. As she had in London. He quelled a sudden welling of pride. Such emotions would be his undoing.

'How is Bella this morning?' he asked Jaimie.

'In fine fettle. Well rested after her journey, but not in the fidgets.'

'Good. Her Grace is an excellent horsewoman, but the terrain is unfamiliar.'

'Bella will stay close to Thor.'

True.

When Julia joined them, she smiled at the stable master. 'Good morning, Jaimie.'

The man gave her a shameless grin. 'Your Grace.'

Alistair boosted her up on to Bella, handed her the reins and swung up on to Thor.

'Where are we going?' Julia asked as they trotted down the drive.

'First to the home farm as we've some new arrivals, and then I thought I would show you one of the local villages and some of the park.'

Chapter Six

The home farm was a mile from the main house, outside the park and along a narrow lane. A middle-aged man with a ruddy face and greying-brown curly hair met them at the gate opening on to the lane.

'Your Grace,' Alistair said, 'this is John Bestmore. He and his wife are in charge of the home farm.'

Mr Bestmore bowed and opened the gate. 'Welcome to Manor Farm, Your Grace.'

Julia inclined her head. 'Thank you.'

They passed through. The Duke dismounted. 'All going well, John?'

'Yes, Your Grace.' They walked up the drive leading to a brick farmhouse and several out-buildings at the top of a hill.

'As I reported last month, the lambing went very well. The wheat should give us a fair crop

if the weather holds fine and Queenie has out-
done herself.'

'How many, John?' Alistair asked.

'Twelve, Your Grace, all healthy.'

'Twelve what?' Julia asked, thinking it would
likely be puppies or kittens.

'Piglets, Your Grace,' Bestmore said. 'Our
Queenie is a prizewinner, she is. Best litters at
the local fair three years running. Would you like
to see them?'

Alistair raised a quizzical brow. 'Smelly
things, pigs.'

But even as he offered her the choice, she could
see very well he intended to visit the lady in question.

'I would love to see them.'

Alistair mounted up. 'We keep the sty a little distance from the farmhouse,' he said as the
horses followed Bestmore up a fork in the lane,
'at Mrs Bestmore's request.'

The sty proved to be a brick-built three-sided
affair with a tiled roof and a large enclosure. And
while there was a certain earthy pungency about
it, it wasn't too unpleasant. Alistair helped her
down and they looked over a gate leading into
the covered portion of the sty. An enormous sow
lay on her side on a stone floor spread with straw
with her infants nestled against her, some suck-

ling, others fast asleep. Queenie, a reddish-brown animal with black spots, opened an eye, grunted and closed it again.

'Oh, they are so sweet,' Julia said. 'I love their little flat snouts and curly tails.' They also made her feel a little sad. A reminder that she would never have a baby of her own. She swallowed down the lump in her throat. Wishing for what could not be was foolish.

'They look fine, John,' Alistair said, his attention focused on the scene before him. 'Thank Mrs Bestmore. I know Queenie falls under her special care when it comes to table scraps and so forth.'

'That I will, Your Grace. She would have been here to greet Her Grace, but she went to visit our daughter for a few days.'

'Her Grace is sorry to have missed her. I'll have Lewis set up a time for you and me to go over the accounts when he is back.' He looked at Julia. 'Do you wish to continue on to the village? I told Grindle we would pick up the post since we were out. We can circle around and see a bit more of the park that way.'

A question about her health without making her feel like a nuisance. A kindness. Here in the country, he seemed different from his cynical man-about-town persona. He cared about this estate and his people. And today it seemed as if he was including her in their ranks. 'I'm game. We did not pass through a village yesterday.'

'No. Boxted lies further along the post road than we needed to go.' He helped her up on to Bella and, after a couple of quiet words with Mr Bestmore, mounted up.

They headed back past the farmhouse to the lane and a bare fifteen minutes later they entered a village with a triangular green bordered on one of its sides by a wide paved road. An inn bearing the sign of the Wheatsheaf dominated the other businesses around the green's perimeter. A smithy, a baker and a haberdasher, Julia saw.

Alistair left her with Thor and entered the latter establishment. He returned a few moments later with a bundle of letters which he tucked into his saddlebag.

Her husband glanced at her as if assessing how she was holding up. 'I hope I am right, that you are feeling quite well?'

'I have never felt better.' The queasiness that had beset her for the past two days had quite disappeared. It must have been something she ate. And yet there remained the odd sense of familiarity in her illness. Something she could not quite put her finger on.

'Excellent,' Alistair said. 'I would like to show

you our orchards. Our fruit trees are among the best in the county.'

They took the post road for a short distance and then turned up another lane that wound between well-kept hedges. 'Is it your land on both sides?' she asked.

'No. Beauworth is over there.' He waved a hand.

'So your estates adjoin.'

'Here they do. For a short distance only. Further that way we run up against common land.'

She smiled at him. 'So, we are to visit an orchard.'

'I thought we might,' he muttered.

'I should like that.'

'We have to pass it, anyway.'

Why was he sounding so defensive? Or as if he was attempting to convince himself of the wisdom of showing her a bunch of trees?

A short way along the lane, the fields gave way to the distinctive shape of fruit trees. He dismounted and opened a gate in the hedge. He walked the horses through and closed it again. Trees stretched in neat rows as far as the eye could see. It would be a grand place for children to play. Trees to climb and hide amongst. She decided not to mention those particular thoughts.

'This must be a sight to behold when the blossoms are out.'

His expression softened. 'It is. It smells glorious.'

'What do you do with all the apples?' She grinned at him. 'You couldn't possibly eat them all.'

'We make some of the finest cider in the country.' His voice held pride. 'Sackfield has no trouble getting and keeping labourers once they have tasted our home brew.'

'That is bribery, sir.'

He quirked a brow. 'Simply good management.'

She laughed. 'These trees are not the same as those back there. The bark looks different as does the shape and the apples are not as far along.'

'You are right. Those we saw first were Nonpareil. Here we have Golden Harveys and down that way Lemon Pippins for cooking. There are also pears and peaches against the wall at the south end.'

The horses wandered along the gap between the hedge and the first tree in each row. Alistair drew Thor to a halt and leaped down. 'There is something I want to show you.' The note in his voice was different. Darker, sensual. It touched her like a stroke across her shoulders. A little thrill ran down her spine.

Unhesitating, she put her hands on his shoulders when he came around to her side of Bella.

Grey eyes met her gaze, molten with silver. Heat rippled through her at the feel of his large hands on her waist. The slow sensual slide down his body, with his gaze locked her hers, left her knees weak. When he finally set her on her feet, he held her steady for a moment or two, giving her time to catch her weight.

He knew exactly what he was doing. Flirting. The dissolute Duke had made an appearance here in the country. And wickedly, her body came alive under his hands. Desire. Along with a smidgeon of anxiety. He hadn't approached her in this way since the moment they wed.

The thought hurt. She brushed the pain aside. He had saved her from a terrible situation with their marriage. She had no right to ask for more.

'All right?' he asked, his voice a low rumble.

'Yes.' Her voice sounded husky, breathless.

A wicked grin curled his sensual lips.

She swallowed.

He stepped away, tying the horses to a low branch on the nearest tree and unbuckling the rolled blanket from behind his saddle she had noticed, but not really thought much about. Clasping her hand firmly, he led her deeper into the orchard, ducking beneath low branches here and there, until they arrived at a huge tree with a gnarled trunk and low twisty branches.

'This is the oldest tree in the orchard,' he said. 'We think it is more than a hundred and fifty years old.'

'Positively ancient, then.'

He gazed upwards into the leafy canopy. 'There is a great view to be had from up there.'

Her mouth gaped open. 'Are you suggesting I climb it?'

'It isn't difficult. I'm told my mother did it.' Again there was that odd note in his voice. Nothing of the chill to which she had become accustomed. And he was sharing something with her that seemed to have special meaning.

If she wanted to come to a better understanding, she needed to take such opportunities when they arose or they might not come again. Though she wasn't exactly dressed for clambering about in trees. 'As long as you promise to catch me should I fall.'

'I won't let you fall.'

The intensity in his expression spoke of protectiveness and possession. Her insides gave a little pulse of pleasure. She swallowed a gasp of surprise and hooked up the train of her riding habit to allow for more freedom of movement. 'I think I might need a ladder to make the first branch.' After that, he was right, the branches were at easy distances and so thick, the climb wouldn't test a toddler.

'Come. I will give you a boost.'

No sooner said then he had her about the waist and lifted her to sit on the lowest branch. Placing the rolled blanket on the branch, he hauled himself up effortlessly and stood up. Holding on to the next branch up, he helped her to her feet. After that, with a bit of careful attention to her skirts and his steadying hand, she was soon a good few feet off the ground. Nestled in a fork at eye level was a structure. A narrow platform she hadn't noticed from below.

'A tree house?'

'Of course not,' he said. 'Anyone can see it is a fort. Or a pirate galleon. Or a castle.'

She laughed. 'But not a house.'

'Not for this generation.' An expression crossed his face. Was it sadness?

'You and your brother played here.'

'We did. And our father before us.' His wicked smile made another appearance. 'I was conceived in this tree, according to my father.'

Startled, she wobbled, her foot slipping. His grip on her arm tightened for a brief moment. She had no fear of falling, but his instinctive action to keep her safe made her want to lean against his strength.

'Then it must certainly be sturdy enough for two. How do we get up there?'

He grinned. 'Let me go first. I'll pull you up.'

Standing close to the trunk, she held on, while he nimbly went down for the blanket, whose purpose she now recognised, and then pulled himself up. He tested the three wooden planks by bouncing up and down. 'It seems solid enough.' He reached down.

She took his hand, following his directions of where to put her feet, and was soon seated safely on the blanket, her back against the tree trunk and her feet dangling. At this point in the tree, several branches had been trimmed back. Not only was the tree the oldest in the orchard, it also stood at a high point and gave a vista of some considerable distance. From here, she looked over the treetops to Sackfield Hall nestled in the centre of its park. 'What an amazing view.'

'I know.' He sat beside her, watching her face as she took in the view of rolling meadows and elegant stands of trees.

'Are there deer in the park?'

'No.' He leaned back on his hands. 'The Duchy has another estate for game.'

'How many estates do you hold altogether?'

'Six. Not counting the houses: one in London, one in Edinburgh and one in Manchester. I rent them all out, except the Richmond one.'

'Your housekeeper at Richmond said you visit each of the estates once a year.'

'Though I receive regular reports from my estate managers, I like to see things with my own eyes from time to time.'

'It is a great deal of work, being a duke.' He certainly spent a great deal of time in his office. She had wondered how he had any time left over to gain his wicked reputation.

He gazed at her thoughtfully. 'I find it fulfilling. Things were a bit of a shambles when I inherited. Fortunately, I have a good staff who help with much of the work.'

She would like to offer her help, too, but he had kept her at such a distance, she wasn't sure it would be welcome. 'Talking of staff, when will Mr Lewis return? You seem to be drowning in paperwork.'

His smiled widened. 'I expect him tomorrow.'

Silence fell, but for the twitter of birds and the rustle of leaves in a light breeze. A comfortable quiet. A bumble bee buzzed by, investigated them and decided they were not worth his trouble.

She breathed deep, inhaling the scent of new mown grass. 'I love the countryside.'

'Me, too. I am not so fond of this bonnet, however. Perhaps we can dispense with it for the moment. It hides your pretty face and the feather keeps tickling my nose.'

Pretty. He though her pretty. Her body warmed, but she managed to avoid giggling. 'Feathers do that,' she agreed, hoping she sounded calm. 'There is enough shade for me to take it off.'

'Let me.'

He untied the strings beneath her chin, unerringly found the hatpin and eased the hat off her head. He kissed her cheek and tossed the hat to the ground.

'Your Grace!' she said. She leaned over and saw it had landed on the grass. 'That is no way to treat such an expensive hat.'

He ran his knuckles along her jaw. The light caress made her shiver. 'You will call me Alistair when we are alone, will you not? "Your Grace" is far too formal when we are private.'

Finally, a chink in his armour. She could not help but feel glad, if a little cautious. 'If you will call me Julia.'

His expression softened. 'I will.'

His eyelashes lowered and she watched his hand draw a circle on her shoulder, reminding her of the first time they met when he had drawn words all over her body with a finger dipped in red wine. Her insides gave a pleasurable little pulse. Was he remembering that, too?

'I am a lucky man,' he said softly. 'It is not often one finds such an exotic bird in an ordinary English orchard.

She wasn't used to this. She didn't know what to say, but the ground did seem a long way below. 'This bird cannot fly.'

'I will not let you fall. Trust me. '

She did trust him. Somewhat. But it was hard to relax when the seat beneath one moved with every little breeze.

Then he leaned close and kissed her, a light brush of his lips, that was comforting. Reassuring. Delicious. Gradually, the kiss turned into something far more heated.

His lips roamed her face, ending up beneath her ear. One hand grazed her breast. Heat blossomed between her thighs. She gasped.

Her throat suddenly dry, her insides clenching, she swallowed. 'I do not think this is such a good idea.'

He straightened his legs and drew her into his lap, turning her face with fingers on her jaw and kissing her deeply, his tongue stroking hers until her heart was thumping wildly and she could scarcely breathe. He lifted his head and gazed into her face. 'Is that what you really think, sweetheart?'

Thinking was beyond her. 'Alistair,' she said, and sighed.

His lips descended once more, wooing, teasing, tormenting.

Returning his kiss, loving the silky slide of her tongue against his, she clutched at his shoulders, pressing her aching breasts against the satisfyingly hard wall of his chest. Though she had only ever known him carnally once, she had missed this. Missed the feel of him.

She sighed.

He shifted. The hard ridge of his arousal pressed against her hip. He desired her.

She stroked his shoulders, his back, then combed her fingers through his silky hair and felt as if she was flying.

But a niggling doubt wouldn't be ignored. Why on earth was he kissing her after all these days of cold reserve and why in a tree?

When he set out this morning, he'd simply wanted to show Julia his home. As well as gain a little of her trust. He had given the old tree fort a passing thought with the vague idea that she might be intrigued by his boyhood pursuits. Though he'd half expected the planks to be rotten. Or torn down.

He had not expected to be tempted into kissing. This delicious slide of tongue against tongue, her breathing warm against his cheek, her breasts soft against his chest. His body hardened.

He broke their kiss and let go a breath, slowly letting his desire ebb until it was no more than a minor disturbance, a faint beat in his blood he could ignore. A hard-won skill he had never expected to need so drastically.

'Easy,' he said.

Her breath hitched and she uttered a little sound of distress she tried to hide. He wanted to curse at that sound. Instead, he let out a long sigh. 'Any more kisses like that and we'll be testing our wings.'

She stilled. Tensed. 'Falling, you mean.'

Falling into bliss. He cursed the wayward thought when his shaft gave a little jerk of approval.

'You are quite safe.'

She snuggled her cheek against his chest. 'I know.'

'Nor will I risk life and limb for the dubious pleasure of outdoor intimacy.'

'Dubious?' she questioned, her expression hidden, but not the doubt in her voice.

'Uncomfortable.'

'And high.'

'That, too.'

Back in control, mostly, he ducked his head and brushed his lips across hers. She deepened the kiss and he savoured the plush feel of her tender flesh, the feel of her fingers at his nape, the small sounds in the back of her throat as a simple kiss once more brought them both the brink.

Not for years had he had so much trouble maintaining control of his base urges. Perhaps if he stopped remembering her wearing nothing but the Dunstan rubies...

The rubies and her sighs and moans and her delectable body.

And...once more he was harder than granite.

He lifted her so she sat between his legs with her back to him and her *derrière* a few decent inches from his falls. 'Do you hear the lark?'

She listened, her body alert, her head cocked to one side, the milky skin below her ear so very available to his lips, his tongue, his teeth. He resisted temptation. They were married. There was no need for sore knees and splinters in naughty places. No need for anything in a marriage that would never be consummated.

'I hear it.' She leaned back to look up into the deepest blue of the sky. 'I do not see it.'

'Nor me.'

A white butterfly fluttered past.

'Not much of a kaleidoscope, that one,' he murmured in her ear.

She gave a light gasp before a breathless utterance. 'No.'

He held her loosely and still he felt her heart-beat against his chest. 'Tell me more about your first husband.' He held his breath as her back stiffened. He cursed himself for spoiling what up to now had been a perfectly companionable interlude, if a little fraught with another kind of tension.

She rested her head against his shoulder, gazing out across the tree tops. For a moment or two he thought she would not answer.

Her voice was soft when she spoke. 'He paid my brother a great deal of money for the privilege of my hand. Very quickly he decided he'd got a bad bargain, as he never stopped reminding me.'

And that was the least of it, no doubt. Rage rose in his chest.

'I am sorry,' he said, hoping his anger wasn't apparent in his voice.

'If you don't mind, I'd prefer never to speak of him again.'

'Forgive me for asking, then.' He kissed her temple, her cheek, the hollow of her neck. 'Please.'

He sensed her smile rather than saw it. 'Forgiven.'

Her generosity of spirit almost made him feel ill. He did not deserve her forgiveness. Or her kisses. He should never have married her.

'We should go,' he said, knowing if he did not

leave now, his control might give way to carnal desires. 'The horses will think we've abandoned them.' Carefully he got to his feet. 'Give me your hand and I'll help you down.'

She stood up and bestowed a glowing smile upon him that was a tiny bit mischievous, too. 'Thank you for bringing me here. I know this place is special to you.'

He'd been glad to share it. Surprisingly glad, since he rarely ever shared anything with anyone any more.

Perhaps he'd made the right choice to bring her here. She'd trusted him enough to let him kiss her in a tree.

Some instinct he couldn't name urged him to do the same. To trust her, despite knowing full well what sort of reaction she'd have to his past and what he'd done. Since he despised himself for what had happened, he could hardly expect her to feel differently. Not that he cared what she thought of him. What he could not do was give her the power to cause his son harm.

Julia gained the ground and not for a moment did she feel unsafe. For the first time in a very long time.

'I assume we are headed straight home?' she said when they rode into the lane.

His gaze was fixed ahead. Two riders were approaching from the other direction. A man with a boy on a dun-coloured pony. Alistair cursed softly as the pair slowed from a trot to a walk.

Julia had the feeling that if there had been any way for Alistair to avoid them, like a break in the hedge, he would have gladly taken it. The other man seemed equally uncomfortable. She half expected him to turn his horse and gallop off. Manners apparently overcame instinct because they came to a halt facing each other in the middle of the lane. 'Duke,' the other fellow said in gentlemanly, if stiff tones.

His face a frozen mask, Alistair moved forward, angling his horse between her and the newcomers. 'Julia, allow me to present my half-brother, Lord Luke Crawford.' His tone held so much ice she would not have been surprised to see a frosty puff of air issuing from his lips. 'Luke, meet my wife.'

His half-brother, and the heir he had mentioned. The son of Alistair's hated stepmother. They certainly looked nothing alike. Lord Luke was as dark as Alistair was fair, built on leaner lines, his dark eyes set deep, his cheekbones standing out to the point of gauntness. If she had thought her husband stern, this man was positively austere. Joyless.

Lord Luke certainly looked no happier than her husband at this chance encounter. He was another family member who had not been invited to their celebratory ball. 'Estranged' was the word Alistair had used.

Nevertheless, Lord Luke offered her a fleeting smile that held a charm all of its own. 'It is good to meet you at last, Your Grace.'

'May I say likewise.' She held out her hand and he leaned across Thor's neck to touch her fingers. Barely.

He gestured the lad forward. He was a blond boy of about eight or nine. 'May I introduce my oldest son, Jeffrey? Unfortunately his brother could not come with us today.'

The boy cast them both a shy smile. 'Good day, Your Graces.' He bowed, clearly carefully schooled in his manners.

Alistair was staring at the boy as if he'd like to eat him for dinner. A muscle flickered in his jaw. 'Jeffrey, how do you fare?' He glanced at his brother and back to the boy. 'He's grown a great deal since I saw him last.'

He sounded strangely bitter.

'Papa says I am going to be as tall as he is,' Jeffrey said.

If anything Alistair's face became grimmer. 'You will outgrow that pony soon.'

He was right. The stirrups were well past the pony's belly.

'He'll do for now,' Lord Luke said stiffly. 'Jeffrey is perfectly satisfied with Rascal.'

It was a warning not to interfere as best Julia could tell from Alistair's glare.

The silence stretched between them.

Lord Luke ran a swift glance over Julia and a brief flash of amusement entered his dark eyes. 'Showing your bride the orchard, were you, Your Grace?'

Alistair glared. 'What of it?'

Lord Luke's eyes were a little too knowing as he stared back at his brother, before turning to Julia. 'It was a favourite haunt of ours as boys. Many a mischief has taken place in that orchard. Did my brother happen to show you the view, Your Grace?

In the tree, he meant. Julia felt her face heat, as if she'd been doing something more wicked than simply kissing. Yet oddly enough she had the feeling Lord Luke was not being unkind, but rather enjoying being part of the joke.

Alistair, on the other hand, looked disgruntled at his brother's teasing. Clearly, he was not particularly fond of his sibling. She assumed Luke was his only sibling. Did he have others lurking in unopened cupboards? That question she would save for later.

'A fort, Papa?' Jeffrey said, clearly having taken in only that part of the conversation. He sounded intrigued and hopeful all at once.

His father glanced at him, his gaze slightly guilty. 'I doubt there is much left of it after all this time.'

The boy's face fell as he realised he was not going to be invited to see it.

'What are you doing in these parts, Luke?' Alistair asked. 'I understood you were in Yorkshire.'

Lord Luke hesitated, then squared his shoulders. 'My employer died. The new owner of the estate did not need my services. Beauworth took me on.'

Alistair's expression darkened. 'Did he now?'

His brother glared back. 'Alistair, it is none of your business where—'

'You are right, it is none of my business,' Alistair said with indifference, yet he was not looking at his brother, he had once more turned his hungry gaze on his nephew. 'Since you are in the district, perhaps you would like to bring Jeffrey to visit the stables. I've a couple of steady beasts looking for a home.'

His half-brother shot him a look of impatience

when his son once again pinned him with a look full of small boy hope.

Feeling uncomfortable, Julia cast around for a way to ease the tension.

Perhaps this, at last, was something she could do for her husband. Heal the breach in the family. Or at least establish some sort of cordial relationship, so Alistair wouldn't be quite so isolated. 'We would be delighted if you and your wife would come for tea one afternoon. You could bring the boys and visit the stables?'

Jeffrey's face blanched. His gaze flew to his father's face, which had turned to stone. 'I am a widower, Your Grace.'

And Alistair hadn't seen fit to warn her. She wanted to shout at him. Or gallop over the nearest rise. 'I beg your pardon. I did not know.' She straightened her spine. 'The offer of tea remains.'

A wry smile twisted Lord Luke's lips as he looked at his brother.

Alistair bowed. 'Please let my secretary know when your duties at Beauworth will permit it and he will check our engagements.'

Julia wanted to lash out at him for his stiff unwelcoming formality. All she could do was smile.

Lord Luke moved his horse closer to his brother and lowered his voice, clearly wishing to speak privately.

Julia smiled at Jeffrey and moved out of earshot. 'You picked a good morning to go riding with your papa.'

The boy patted his pony's neck. 'The lads needed an outing and Papa needed to look at one of the drainage ditches.' He sounded as if a tree fort might have been a much more enjoyable prospect. Yet Julia admired the father for taking his boy with him. Boys needed their father's guidance.

Her own brother had certainly received none.

'I appreciate the forewarning,' Alistair said when his brother finished muttering. It was a rudeness she decided to ignore. A glance of understanding passed between the brothers, yet it held little warmth. Julia understood perfectly. She and her brothers had been out of charity with each other for years.

Lord Luke touched his whip to his hat. 'Good day, Your Graces. Duty calls. Come along, Jeffrey.' He clapped heels to his horse's sides and took off at a steady trot.

The boy bowed and trotted after him.

Alistair watched them go, then turned Thor towards Sackfield.

Julia waited until they had turned into a lane that ran at right angles before speaking. 'Is he your only sibling?'

'He is.'

'You do not like him?'

'My brother has every cause to dislike me.'

The bleakness in his expression forbade further questions. What was it that his brother had imparted that made Alistair look more like a threatening storm than usual?

It was not her place to pry, despite the better understanding they seemed to have reached over these past two days and the kiss they had shared. Instead she tipped her face to look up at the sky. 'I think this is one of those times when Jaimie will be proved wrong about the weather.'

From the corner of her eye, she saw him shoot her a piercing glance, but some of his tension seemed to evaporate. 'It appears so.'

Chapter Seven

After dinner, Alistair indicated he would join his wife for tea in the drawing room. Hedged about with servants since returning from their ride, he'd had no further opportunity for private conversation with her about the matter his half-brother had raised. A matter he had decided, after considerable thought, could not be ignored.

While she went through the ritual of pouring tea, he sipped at his port. To his surprise, he enjoyed the simple pleasure of watching his wife's graceful movements.

After their time in the orchard, he was beginning to wonder how long he could deny himself pleasure with his wife. And whether it was really necessary. As a punishment for past sins, he could tell himself it was fitting, though nothing would make up for those. But his abstinence was also punishing her, if the shadows in her eyes were anything to go by. A subtle punishment, that was true, nothing to cause her to flinch, but unkind. Ungentlemanly.

His intention had in no way been meant to make her unhappy.

Nor to ruin her health with worry. Though he could not be sure that was the cause of her recent bout of illness, she certainly seemed happier when he was not keeping her at a distance. She looked healthy enough now. Ravishing, in fact.

As long as he restrained his ardour, and he had no doubt he could…

Once she had her teacup in hand and was gazing at him over the rim, he raised his glass. 'To my lovely and extraordinarily forbearing wife.'

She blinked uncertainly.

No doubt because she wasn't certain of him. An indication of his bad behaviour.

'You are no doubt wondering what warning Luke imparted.'

She smiled faintly. 'Curiosity killed the cat.' She sniffed at her tea, then took a delicate sip.

Was that the sort of thing her first husband had said to her? 'I apologise for not telling you sooner.'

'My greater concern was that I had stepped where even angels should not tread.'

A gentle criticism indeed, when he deserved

a thorough dragging over the coals for not warning her. He let guilt rake its claws across his conscience. 'I am sorry for that, too. Luke's wife died years ago, after the birth of their second child. It did not occur to me to mention it.'

In truth, he hated recalling Elise, and how she had lured him into her bed, let alone speaking her name. How horrified he had been on his return from Italy to learn she'd borne his son after marrying his brother. No wonder Luke hated him. Their father had done neither of them any favours by spiriting Alistair out of the country and leaving Elise with no choice but to accept his brother's hand.

'I do hope he will bring his boys for tea one afternoon.' Another delicately phrased admonishment.

'When the honeymoon is over, perhaps.' Luke had categorically refused to have anything to do with Alistair after his miraculous return from the Continent's shores. No doubt Alistair's reappearance had blighted all his hopes of inheriting the dukedom. Harsh words had been spoken when Alistair had discovered the terrible state of the duchy's coffers. Now his brother was no doubt also resenting Julia's appearance on the scene at least as much as, if not more than, Isobel, given that an heir would cut out both him and Jeffrey.

Alistair had no intention of relieving his brother's mind on that score. Why should he? He would do his damnedest to outlive his half-brother and ensure the title went to the true heir. None of which he could tell Julia.

'His mother has arrived in the neighbourhood.'

'That is what you were whispering about?'

He took a long pull at his drink. 'While Luke knows I would sooner never set eyes on her again, he advises that we get the introductions over and done.'

A frown creased her brow. 'You think she won't approve of me?'

Alistair stilled at the anxiety in her eyes. 'I care nothing for what she thinks, but that is not the source of her unhappiness. She hates being merely the *Dowager* Duchess. It does not suit her pride.' Nor did the potential displacement of her son as Alistair's heir.

'Should we invite her for tea along with your brother and his children?'

He grimaced. 'I prefer to contend with them separately, if I must contend with them at all. Dealing with dear Stepmama is wearing enough without adding her darling son and grandchildren to the mix.' Although Alistair admitted he would like to see more of Jeffrey. Get to know the boy. Hear about his hopes and dreams. Luke had refused to bring the boy anywhere near him, out of petty revenge no doubt, since he knew Alistair could never acknowledge the boy as his own without causing a scandal.

He didn't care for himself, but Jeffrey did not deserve to carry such a burden.

A pause ensued, while Julia sipped her tea thoughtfully. She put down her cup. 'I enjoyed our ride today. I am looking forward to more such expeditions.'

It was a change of topic, when he had thought she might take him to task for his lack of familial feeling. A rush of warmth filled him, for her kindness and for her support in his decision.

'You have not noticed any ill effects from our outing?'

'None at all. In fact, I feel very much better, if a little tired. I think I will retire.'

He rose to his feet, took her hand and helped her to rise. 'I will escort you. If you will allow?'

She must have heard something in his voice for her eyes widened and her breath caught. 'I would be delighted.'

He brought her fingers to her lips, grateful for her honesty. The night they had met, she had been flirtatious, but also honest. He'd forgotten it was one of the things about her he had found so attractive.

When they reached her chamber, he dismissed her dresser, who for a moment looked as if she might dispute his right of entry, until he glowered. The woman sniffed and disappeared.

Julia stifled a giggle and he frowned at her.

She laughed outright. 'She will never forgive you, you know.'

He raised a brow. 'I am supposed to care?'

She turned her back and glanced over her shoulder with a smile. 'In her absence, perhaps you might help with my fastenings.'

'The pleasure will be all mine.'

Her little gasp sent great deal of pleasurable anticipation heading south.

As seduction went, the smile on his wife's face was surprisingly innocent. Yet undeniably welcoming. A look of such courage, it captivated a man used to the jaded ladies of the *demi-monde*.

Her brief glance touched every inch of his skin. Resided in every beat of his blood and had done so since their earlier kiss in the apple tree. Heat trickled along his veins.

Turning away, she dipped her chin, presenting her vulnerable nape. A delicate spot he ached to taste with his lips and tongue. A whisper brush of the pad of his thumb and tiny hairs rose along her hairline. A shiver, she scarcely repressed. She was so responsive, his wife.

Resisting the temptation to touch his mouth to the place where his thumb had grazed, he gently, carefully, unfastened the buttons of her gown, exulting in the occasional brush of his knuckles against the creamy skin of her back and the resultant hitch of her breath.

What man wouldn't want to unwrap such a delicious parcel? Desire, perhaps even need, roared through his veins. Hot. Demanding.

For years, lust had been little more than a physical nuisance. A function of being male, requiring an outlet from time to time. Or not. It had always been his own decision. Until Julia. From the first, he'd found control elusive.

Everything about her aroused his base urges: her voice, her smile, even her scent. He inhaled deeply. Jasmine and a deeper note he had never quite isolated. Clove? Delicious. Enticing. Uniquely her.

He pressed his lips to the curve of her neck above her collarbone.

She curved her spine, like a cat seeking more stroking. He half expected her to purr. A tiny vulnerability that hit him like a blow to the heart. A strange longing deep inside him battered his carefully constructed walls. Seeking the light. Her light.

He could never let her see how much this husbandly act meant to him. Never know how she pulled at his deepest desires. While he did not deserve such bounty, perhaps they could enjoy each other on the physical plane.

The gown slid down her hips to the floor. Lips parted, eyes slumberous, she laid it on the end of the bed.

He swallowed a growl of frustration at the sight of her stays. The dresser had threaded them in some complex arrangement that caused a man anxious to see his wife to wish for a pocket knife. He started at the bow at the bottom.

She inhaled a deep breath when he'd worked halfway up her back. 'That feels better.'

He frowned at the relief in her voice. 'Why lace so tightly if it is uncomfortable?'

'To improve the drape of the jacket.'

'Are you some sort of mannequin that you must conform to the shape of your clothes?'

She threw a glance over her shoulder. A teasing smile curved her lips. 'That, Your Grace, is fashion. It is a hard little god who must be obeyed or one suffers the consequences.'

Teasing he could handle. He welcomed the distraction of conversation. He tackled the last few holes. 'Consequences such as letters to the editor of *The Times*, perhaps?'

The Times would no doubt prefer the story of a

duke come back from the dead. The true story—a sorry tale of hiding behind a woman's skirts while the gendarmes searched from house to house and her final betrayal when he ran out of money—rather than the one he had concocted for the sake of his pride. He swallowed his shame.

'If other ladies think one has not made the proper effort to conform to accepted standards they can be quite unpleasant, I am given to understand.'

'Given to understand by whom?' he asked.

'By Mrs Robins, naturally. She is the arbiter of all things regarding ladies' fashion.'

'She's certainly a bit of a battleaxe when it comes to your wardrobe,' he muttered, his voice a bit more gravelly than he intended. 'Had Lewis in a fine old fuss when she thought someone had put the hatboxes beneath your trunk.' He tossed the stays on top of her skirt and turned her about by the shoulders.

Breathing faster than normal, she gazed up at him with the light of desire in her lovely amber eyes. Little puffs of air caressed his jaw.

Unable to resist, he bent and kissed her lips, brushing his mouth gently back and forth across hers, loving the velvety feel of plush lips against his own. He deepened the kiss. Tasting the sweetness of her mouth, feeling her body arch against his.

Over two weeks they'd been wed and he suddenly realised he wanted her so badly his eyes were crossed.

Julia met her husband's heavy-lidded, seductive gaze with breathless anticipation. A drugging glance to a woman who thirsted for that particular look and seen little to nothing of it since the day of her wedding.

Her heart drummed in her chest, not a warning, but the rhythm of a deliciously sensual melody. Julia had never felt so alive as she did at that moment. Her blood was singing in her veins. Her pulse setting the rhythm for a dance she wasn't sure she knew the steps to.

But if she stopped now, he might turn away. She remembered how bold she'd been during their first encounter and reached for the courage to be so again.

Her fingers untied the knot at his throat, without her consciously thinking about it. She tossed it aside and started on the buttons of his waistcoat, his shirt.

'You would play the valet,' he said, his voice husky in her ear as he nuzzled at her throat.

'If you would allow?'

Buttons undone, he eased out of his coats. He pulled his shirt free of his waistband and pulled it off over his head.

A breath caught in her throat at the sheer male beauty of the man. She'd forgotten how muscular he was beneath his clothing. How defined his arms and shoulders and how the smatter of springy golden hair across his chest gleamed in candlelight. Her husband. Hers. And she was his wife. Finally, they were free to indulge their every desire.

And yet a blush rose in her cheeks. A sudden feeling of shyness. She hesitated, gazing up into his face. The heat of passion in his eyes, the softening of those lips gave her courage.

She lifted up on her toes and pressed her mouth to his. His mouth was warm, tenderly wooing. Seductively soft, yet demanding. She leaned into him, sliding a hand around his neck to curve against his nape, pulling him closer while her other hand explored the magnificent width of his shoulders.

Strong arms encircled her. He exuded strength and restraint, for he did not seem in any sort of hurry. The press of his chest against her breasts caused her nipples to tighten. His tongue licked along the seam of her mouth. A dart of dark pleasure low in her abdomen made her gasp.

She'd forgotten the sharpness of desire.

A heartbeat later he dipped his tongue into her mouth, tasting, exploring the delicious slide of tongue against tongue, sending cascades of thrills down her back. Her insides fluttered wildly.

Until now, she had not realised how hot her desire for him had burned. The glowing embers of passion sparked to wicked flame with the feel of his body flush with hers.

She raked her fingers through his silky hair. It felt so good to hold this man, this husband, whom she had feared did not want her. The evidence of his desire was a hard ridge against the swell of her stomach.

He broke the kiss, holding her close, his forehead to hers, his heart a strong steady beat against her ribs, his every breath a statement of male lust under rigid control. She longed to see him let go and become as undone as she was herself.

His warm palm cupped her jaw. Raised her head. Gazed down at her. 'Julia.'

Assurance. The man wanted to know if she was all right.

'I want you,' she said softly.

His eyelids lowered, his expression so sensual she could hardly breathe.

'It is your turn to undress,' she gasped.

Heat flared in his eyes. A slow sensual smile

curved his lips. He lifted her up on to the bed and she scooted backwards, up against the pillows. She licked her lips and his gaze fixed on her mouth.

Slowly, he unbuttoned his falls.

The jolt of pleasure that had zipped up his spine at her boldness had almost brought him to his knees.

In tamping down his desire for this woman, Alistair had also buried his memories of how passionate this wife of his truly was, how lusciously she responded to him when kissed and touched. He prided himself on his ability to arouse desire in a woman to such a fever pitch she would forget her own name. Now he was undone by the need to make Julia respond that way again, over and over.

Given his current view of long silken thighs, and a hint of her femininity through her shift, not much of his mind was capable of thought, but feral instinct remembered her deep sighs at the sight of him naked.

In moments, he stripped down to his bare skin and despite the urgency of his roaring lust, he waited beside the bed while her gaze roamed his body. Her moistened lips parted. The way her eyes stroked along the length of his shaft made blood the temperature of molten metal race through his veins. His heart pounded against his ribs and echoed in his ears.

'Mmm...' she said.

He grinned at the moan of pure pleasure. 'I hope you've seen enough, because I am going to bite and lick and savour every inch of you until you beg for mercy.'

She opened her arms. 'Now there is a pleasing promise.'

He climbed on to the bed, crouching over her, straddling her hips. She leaned forward to kiss his mouth.

Gently he pressed her back against the pillows. 'Now it is my turn to play.' He glanced down her length, practically salivating at the sight of her nipples standing out beneath the filmy fabric of her shift. 'Here, I think.' He licked at first one, then the other.

She shuddered and reached for him.

'Not yet, little one,' he murmured.

He backed down the length of her until his face was level with the apex to her parted thighs. He gave her a wicked glance from beneath his lashes. 'Like to tease, do you?'

She raised up on her elbows, her expression sensual and her eyes slumberous. 'As much as you do.'

'Hmm. Too bad we forgot to bring your mask.'

She sucked in a breath, as if the reminder of that night was not one she welcomed. A glance at her face showed a flash of embarrassment before she got it under control and her expression calmed to the point of reserve.

'I was sure it had a couple of feathers left,' he continued as if he had not noticed her discomfort, though he filed the reaction away for future consideration, when he was capable of thought. For future discussion, too, because the game they had played with the feather had been one of the most sensual experiences of a life filled with hedonistic games.

The playful words seemed to ease her tension and he leaned forward on his knees and took one rosy peak in an open-mouthed kiss. She arched her hips upwards in an attempt to increase the pressure of his erection against her, showing him with her body what she wanted while clutching at his shoulders to hold him in place.

He easily slipped from her grasp, ducking down to blow a hot breath into the valley between her thighs.

She gasped. 'Alistair. Please.'

A tingle ran up his spine. Hades, he was too close... He drew in a deep breath and rode out the pulses of pleasure until like ripples caused by a stone dropped in a pond they diminished at the edges of his consciousness.

Sitting back on his heels, aware of her greedy gaze touching that male part of him, yet distancing himself by willpower alone from the urgency she incited, he pushed her shift upwards, baring her fully. She lifted her hips to help in the process, drew the whole thing up over her head and tossed it away.

He did not see where it went, he was too focused on the lovely shape of her, curvaceous calves encased in stockings to just above the knee, pale thighs, softly rounded yet long and elegant, chestnut curls, the flare of her hips, the dip of her waist, the flatness of her belly, the fragile ribcage supporting her deliciously full breasts topped by tightly furled dark rose tips.

No artist could capture the warmth, the subtle scents of her perfume and the musky scent of arousal that spun him into her orbit as if he were no more than a falling star.

Twining her arms about his neck, she brought her mouth and lips and tongue down to dance with his. Tendrils of desire curled around him, drawing him in, her sensuality surrounding him until reason slipped from his grasp. Her kisses were heavenly. Seductive as hell.

He wanted to be inside her, to drive himself

deep, to claim her in the most fundamental way. And bind them together on some deeper level. A rush of something tender and fragile swamped him. Tenderness. Hope.

He froze. He would not let emotion take control. That way led to disaster, weakness. This was all about pleasure. Nothing else.

As if sensing a change in him, she drew back, her gaze puzzled.

'Alistair. Please,' she moaned and wrapped her legs around his waist in a primal invitation.

This, *this*, he understood.

He bent his head to lick first one breast, then the other, while his fingers danced over her, teasing and stroking until he could sense she was close to her climax. At last, he entered her, finding her natural rhythm, listening to her sighs and sensing what pleased her most. And still without warning, her inner muscles tightened and pulsed around his shaft. A glorious heart-stopping climax that shook him to the core.

A storm of sensual pleasure raced along his veins. The urge to follow into bliss was nigh overwhelming.

Fighting to hold back the primitive need, he jerked away, collapsing to one side of her before he unravelled. The pain of denial had him clenching his jaw and breathing hard while coherent thought escaped his command, but he sensed her confusion.

He pulled her close, his heart thundering in his chest, his body a jangle of anger and disappointment.

Her hand cupped the side of his face. 'Alistair?' The question was little more than a breath of air across his cheek.

He swallowed rawness in his throat. Only once in recent memory had he forgotten himself entirely during intimacy. With her. That time, he had been assured all precautions had been taken and they had not been married. This time the risks were too great, yet he'd almost forgotten, he'd been so overcome.

He blew out the candles and drew the covers up to her chin. 'Sweet dreams.'

In the dark, he sensed her uncertainty. 'Alistair, why—'

'Sleep,' he whispered against her hair. 'I have quite worn you out.' He pushed away from the bed and returned to his chamber. He didn't have a choice. He did not trust himself not to want her again.

And that was troubling.

Chapter Eight

When Julia arose the next morning, to the annoyance of Robins she hurried her *toilette* in hopes of meeting Alistair at breakfast. She wanted to see for herself whether what had happened the previous evening augured a new beginning in their marriage. Or whether he'd be back to his cold reserved self.

Doubts pecked at her hopes. Sharp claws tore them to shreds like raptors at a kill. Their lovemaking had been lovely. Extraordinary. And yet… She'd felt as if Alistair, the man, had removed himself from the equation and left her with the dissolute Duke. A man whose emotions were uninvolved and only physical pleasure held sway.

And then he'd walked away as if it had been no more than a handshake.

Was it something she had done? Had she been

too bold? Too wanton for a duchess? A chill ran
down her spine as she entered the breakfast room.

Empty apart from Grindle.

'His Grace?' she asked hating the hesitation
in her voice.

'He left earlier, Your Grace. A meeting with
Mr Thackerstone, the land steward. Some issue
with a tenant.'

Her heart sank. Could it be he'd left to avoid
her? He'd certainly avoided her attempts to talk
to him before she fell asleep.

She pushed the fear aside, vowing to face him
when he returned. Somewhat disgruntled by her
solitary state in the breakfast room, solitary apart
from two footmen and Grindle, Julia wondered
if she might just as well have taken her breakfast
in her chamber.

Grindle poured tea from the pot that Alistair
must have drunk from. It was still hot. And it
was Oolong. Apparently, she had only missed
him by minutes.

She added more sugar than usual. 'Did His
Grace indicate when he might return?'

'It is a fair distance to the Mollet holding, Your
Grace, a good morning's ride. I doubt we will see
him until late this afternoon.'

So what was she to do with herself all day?

There was one duty she had not yet performed.

'Then I will meet the staff, if you would be so good as to have them assemble in the hall in one hour's time.' Allowing them time to finish their morning duties. 'After that I think a tour of the house would be in order.'

Grindle looked pleased. 'I will let the housekeeper know, Your Grace.'

After breakfast, Julia spent the remaining time before meeting with the staff in the library trying to choose a book. She could not keep herself from glancing through the window, wondering if Alistair might return earlier than expected. How could she be missing him already? They had been together last night. A ripple of warmth went through her at the memory.

Yet miss him she did. She missed him and worried. She had the odd feeling something was wrong.

'The staff are ready, Your Grace,' Grindle announced. 'The indoor staff. I think we will leave those employed outside for another day, if that suits you?'

'I am happy to abide by your advice.'

He led the way to the hall, where some twenty people were gathered in order of importance. She walked down the line meeting everyone from the tweeny, who cleaned the fireplaces before the family were awake, to the jolly cook and the fear-some housekeeper.

Everyone seemed pleased to meet her and she managed a few words with each. The house-keeper then led her on a tour from attics to kitch-ens where Grindle took over her education and proudly showed off what were the finest wine cellars in the country, according to him.

'There was a time when things here were not so well run,' Grindle said lowering his voice. 'After the old Duke died and this here one was declared dead, the Dowager Duchess nigh on sent the Duchy to the poorhouse.'

Wait! What? 'His Grace was declared dead?'

Grindle frowned. 'By his stepmama, he was. Did he not mention it? It is old news now, I sup-pose. He went off to France during the false peace. He was caught there when war was de-clared and nothing was heard of him. Sent the old Duke into a decline, it did, and 'tis my be-lief he died of guilt for sending his heir away in a fit of temper.

'After that, the Dowager Duchess badgered the House of Lords to have him officially declared dead and Lord Luke made Duke, but Parliament is slow to move when there's no corpse.' The old man gave a little shiver of distaste.

Julia knew she should not be gossiping with

the servants, but these were things Alistair should have told her and had not. *More* things he should have told her. 'If not dead, where on earth was he?'

He gave her a piercing stare. 'Your Grace, to my knowledge he has never said where he was, but whatever happened, His Grace came back a changed man. Older. Well, he would be. But older than his years. More reserved. But he worked day and night to turn the Duchy around.' He grimaced. 'Well, that and other things.'

He was hinting at Alistair's reputation for debauchery, no doubt.

His brow cleared. 'For a while I thought he might never marry and provide the next heir, but now it seems all is well on that front, too.'

Pain clutched at her heart. He had said he did not want to rush having children. He'd proved it with his actions the previous evening, but she hadn't admitted to him the full truth. Her shame of being barren. He might not want children now, but surely he would, eventually.

Even the servants were getting their hopes up. Shame filled her. And guilt. She must tell her husband.

The old man's eyes twinkled with a pleasure that seemed to make her pain worse. 'Is there anything else you would like to see, Your Grace?'

She fought back a sudden rush of tears. 'Thank you, no, you have both been most thorough.' The housekeeper had also made it clear that everything was so well run, there was no role for Julia, apart from approving the menus for the week.

Grindle escorted her back to the drawing room, where she took out her needlework. She glanced at the clock. It was barely ten. Perhaps she should leave this for later and go for a walk. Visit Bella in the stables.

She went to the window. The day was cloudy, threatening rain, but perhaps it would hold off for a while. A carriage coming up the drive gave her pause. Who on earth would be calling at this hour of the morning?

A few minutes later, Grindle announced the Dowager Duchess of Dunstan.

A strikingly beautiful woman with black hair and an olive cast to her skin swept in. Her eyes tilted upward at the corners, adding to her exotic allure. She looked familiar. Of course, her son, Lord Luke, was the masculine version of this very feminine woman. Alistair was not going to be pleased that his stepmama had come to call when he was out.

Julia rose and curtsied. 'Your Grace.'

The woman swooped across the room and embraced Julia. 'My dearest daughter, no need for ceremony between family, surely?' She turned back to the butler. 'Grindle, bring the tea tray and some of Cook's lovely little cakes. I declare I am famished.'

Grindle looked none too pleased, but bowed. 'Yes, Your Grace.'

'Sit down. Sit down,' the Dowager Duchess said, waving Julia to a chair and taking the one in which Julia had been seated. She picked up Julia's embroidery and inspected it. 'Very nice, my dear. Where is my stepson?'

'Visiting a tenant, Your Grace.'

'Call me mama, my dear. A tenant? On his honeymoon? How very odd? But then he was always cold, even as a boy.' She gave Julia a kindly look. 'But perhaps he has changed.'

Julia scrambled to catch her breath. 'It is a pleasure to meet you at last.'

The Dowager's smile lit her face, making her look even more beautiful. Her gown was of the richest purple silk Julia had ever seen and fit her slender figure to perfection. Her jewels were worth a king's ransom. 'How lovely you are to say so. I know my stepson would not agree, since he did not invite me to his wedding.'

Guilt assailed Julia. 'It was a very small affair. I apologise.'

'No matter. The deed is done.'

Grindle and a footman entered with the tray. The Dowager Duchess signalled them to set it down on the little table beside her. 'Now, Julia, how do you take your tea?'

Julia flinched. She had been remiss, first in not ordering the tea for her guest and then in not arranging things properly. Now the poor Dowager was forced to act as hostess. 'With milk and a little sugar, please.'

The Dowager smiled, her dark brown eyes warm and friendly. Julia could not imagine why her husband had taken her in dislike. 'Perhaps you could move your work, in case I spill.'

Flustered, Julia leaped up. 'I beg your pardon.' What on earth was the matter with her? Perhaps it was the Dowager's forceful personality making her wits go begging. She put the embroidery in its linen bag and tucked it in a drawer before taking her cup from the Dowager.

The Dowager took a sip of tea and gave a small sigh of pleasure. 'Now, tell me all about yourself.'

Julia sipped her tea. For once the tea tasted as tea should. Perhaps her illness had made things taste strange. 'My father was an earl. I was widowed three years ago.' What else could she say that would not have this woman turning up her nose?

'A widow? And how on earth did you manage

to catch the most elusive bachelor in London? You are to be congratulated, my dear.'

Heat flushed all the way to Julia's hairline at the recollection of how she and Alistair had met. 'Dunstan and I met at the house of a friend.' If one could call the owner of a brothel a friend. 'He offered and I accepted.'

The Dowager's brow furrowed. Something flashed in her eyes. 'A love match, then.'

If only it were. She looked down at her hands. Pride did not allow her to reveal the truth and if this telling sounded romantic, perhaps it was better left at that. If more explanations were to be made, those would be left to her husband.

The Dowager raised her cup as if in toast. 'I must say, I was surprised. All the family were.'

'It came as a surprise to us, too,' Julia said, wishing she did not sound quite so defensive.

She winced as the other woman's eyes narrowed and fell to her waist. She barely prevented herself from clutching her hands across her stomach.

The Dowager lifted her cup in toast. 'To the happy couple, then.'

Julia took another sip of refreshing tea. 'Thank you.' She put her cup down. 'We met your other son, Lord Luke, when we were out riding yesterday.'

Her face lit up. 'Luke. Such a dear boy and so good to his mother. It is too bad…' She sighed.

'You and my husband do not get along well.'

'I do not know why. I did everything I could when I first married his father.' Another sigh. 'Alistair did not take to me once Luke came along. Sibling jealousy, I suppose. Like father, like son. The old Duke also had little warmth in him, though one must not speak ill of the dead. I did my best to be a mother to Alistair despite the way he pushed me away.'

The Dowager reached for the teapot. 'Do drink your tea before it is cold.'

Julia bit back the urge to remind the Dowager that this was her house now. It must be difficult to find oneself replaced.

'Foolish boy, he resented his father marrying again,' the Dowager said sorrowfully. 'He can be shockingly nipfarthing. He hates spending a guinea on anyone but himself.' Narrow-eyed, she glanced at Julia over the rim of her cup. 'He won't even have the dower house made ready for me. Instead I am forced to squander my small portion on renting a house in town.'

Somehow this part of her description of Alistair did not ring true. Cold as a winter's frost he might sometimes be, but he had been generous to a fault in every other regard. 'The dower house?'

'On the outskirts of Sackfield. It is quite unfit for habitation. If I could live there, I would be able to see my grandsons more often. Luke has no room for me in his tiny cottage. And that is a disgrace, too—his father would have been most displeased. Alistair's lack of family feeling...' She closed her eyes. 'Forgive me. I should not speak ill of your husband and you so newly married.'

It seemed Alistair did not treat his family at all well. It wasn't the first time she had noticed his lack of familial feeling. 'I am not sure how I can be of assistance.'

The Dowager drew her handkerchief from her reticule and dabbed at her eyes. 'Foolish of me. I do beg your pardon. But perhaps a word with your husband...'

'I will try.' She sipped at her tea, embarrassed by the woman's show of distress.

The woman tucked her handkerchief away with a frown and a piercing look at Julia. 'And what about you?' She cocked her head on one side. 'You look a little pale. You should get out in the fresh air, my dear, instead of sitting indoors tiring your eyes.'

'I have been a little unwell. The journey did not agree with me.'

The soft brown eyes sharpened. 'You are not—'

'No,' Julia said. 'No happy event expected as yet.'

Oddly, the Dowager seemed to relax. 'I hope your husband is treating you as he should? Dunstan has a reputation for breaking hearts. Nor is he known for consideration or kindness.' She paused as if waiting for Julia to speak. As if expecting Julia to gossip about her husband.

The Dowager's voice lowered, she leaned closer. 'If you ever need help, come to me.'

Alistair had been kind to her recently. And there was something about his stepmama that made her feel uncomfortable, yet the woman was being perfectly sweet.

The Dowager finished her tea and pulled on her gloves. 'I really must not linger, I promised a friend I would call on her this morning, but I simply couldn't resist the opportunity to meet you.'

And in a flurry of kisses beside each of Julia's cheeks and mutterings about time, the Dowager departed, leaving Julia feeling strangely exhausted and in need of fresh air.

Alistair stared at the waterlogged field and its drowned crop. He turned to his steward. 'I thought we agreed to clear the ditch.'

His steward glared at the red-faced tenant, Mollet. 'I relayed your orders, Your Grace.'

'And so he did, Your Grace, but see the trouble ain't here. It's run-off from Beauworth's land. River's choked.'

An excuse if ever he heard one. Mollet was lazy. Always had been. Thackerstone knew this. He turned to his steward. 'Ask Beauworth's man to take a look.' That man would be Luke. He lowered his brow at the smug-looking Mollet. 'After *you* check the ditch.' Beauworth would haul him over the coals if he started making false accusations.

Mollet removed his pipe from his mouth and spat.

Alistair had the sudden urge to get home to his wife. To feel her softness in his arms, to bury himself to the hilt, to feel the wonder of her as she came apart. He could have had that, had he remained in her bed. Instead, he'd galloped off on the flimsiest excuse. His steward could have handled this without any help.

It was this very desire he felt to be with her that had him traipsing around his estate at this ungodly hour. He wanted her too much.

He kept thinking about how ill she had been on their journey. First queasy. Then violently ill. And then…perfectly fine. Hungry.

As if she was… But she could not be. They'd taken every precaution.

Doubt roiled in his belly. She could have been carrying another man's child before he found her in that accursed bordello. Had that been her plan all along? To find some rich fellow to take responsibility for an unwanted brat.

The idea revolted him. And infuriated him. And surprisingly he was saddened by the thought. He did not want to think ill of his wife. He wanted… More.

He cut the thought off. 'Where next?'

His steward gave him a considering look. 'How about we take a look at this year's crop of lambs? That should take us 'till dinner time. We can stop off at the Wheatsheaf after that if Your Grace wishes.'

Hearing something in his tone, Alistair eyed him askance and saw a knowing curl to the man's mouth. Had the man heard gossip and thought to help him avoid his duchess? He'd certainly been avoiding her in town and news of that sort travelled fast.

Thackerstone had been in the family's employ for many years. No doubt he thought it gave him the right to be impertinent. Or helpful.

'No urgency about seeing the lambs, is there?' He glanced up at the sky. 'Jaimie said it would rain this afternoon. Let us leave them for another day.'

'No urgency, Your Grace.'

'Then I'm for home.' And a cup of tea with his wife. And perhaps to assure himself these new suspicions were groundless.

Julia had set out on a walk with the intention of visiting the orchard and discovered it was at a greater distance on foot than she'd assumed. After half an hour, she'd felt unusually tired and had been caught in a shower on her way back. Not a successful outing at all.

Robins appeared the moment she entered the sitting room beside her bedroom.

'You are soaked through, Your Grace.' The woman tutted. 'Shall I send for a tea tray?' She relieved Julia of her hat and spencer.

'What I would really like is a bath,' Julia said. 'After the ride yesterday and the chill of the walk this afternoon, I think a soak would do me good.'

Robins pressed her lips together as if she guessed the real reason Julia felt sore. Heat flushed her skin as the woman helped her into her dressing robe. 'As Your Grace wishes. Shall I bring tea as well?'

Thank goodness she wasn't offering chocolate. And as always she seemed to be trying to please. 'Tea would be lovely. Not Oolong though, please.' She smiled at the woman and received a stiff little grimace in reply.

'Right away, Your Grace.'

Julia sank on to the *chaise* and picked up a book to read while she waited. A few moments later she heard voices in her dressing room, Robins relaying her orders.

Soon the chamber next door was bustling with servants bringing the bath and traipsing the water in. It was such a chore. She wondered if Alistair had ever thought about installing a system of piped-in hot water. It would make it so much easier for the servants. But when one was as rich as a nabob, perhaps he didn't need to care about his servants' travails.

'Would you like your tray in here, Your Grace, or would you care to sip it while you soak?'

Tea in the bath. The idea sounded heavenly. While she had enjoyed every moment of Alistair's attentions, her body was aching from the unaccustomed activity. 'While I soak, thank you.'

'Your bath is ready, then, Your Grace.'

Divested of the rest of her clothes, Julia stepped into the tub perfumed with oil of her favourite jasmine and took the cup and saucer from Mrs Robins. 'Thank you, Robins. You have been very thoughtful.'

'My very great pleasure, Your Grace.'

The woman actually sounded as if she meant it. Perhaps she was mellowing. Perhaps she had realised Alistair did not like her and was trying to recover some ground. Whatever it was, it was a whole lot better than her previous officiousness.

Julia sipped at the tea. A little too strong, a great deal too sweet. She sniffed at it—not Oolong, but something familiar. She felt too tired to care.

'I will come back in a while, Your Grace.' The woman bustled away.

Julia set the cup aside. She leaned back against the edge of the tub and luxuriated in the heat sinking into her bones. Images from the afternoon flitted through her mind as she daydreamed about the return of her husband. And what she would tell him about his stepmother's visit. Some of what the woman had said had been...disturbing.

'Julia!' The deep voice sounded urgent.
She dragged herself from the haze of sleep.
Sleep?
She sat up, chilly water sloshing around her, to find her husband staring at her in shock. She covered herself with her hands. Her head spun ominously. She closed her eyes briefly. It didn't seem to help. 'Alistair?'

'I came to see if you were going to take tea in the drawing room this afternoon.'

She swallowed, feeling suddenly very ill. 'I— I'm afraid I have already had my tea. Oh, dear heaven, I feel dreadfully unwell. Ring for Robins.' She tried to stand.

He cursed under his breath. The next minute she was in his arms, dripping wet and entirely naked. He lifted her out of the water and set her on her feet, quickly wrapping her in a towel before carrying her across the room to the privacy screen. While she knelt over the chamber pot, he held back her hair. Water dripped from his coat sleeves on to the carpet.

She swallowed hard and her stomach seemed to settle. She groaned. This was dreadful. What on earth was going on? 'I'm all right. I simply felt a little dizzy upon awakening.'

'You should not have gone walking today,' Alistair said, helping her to stand.

The servants must have told him. 'What has that to do with anything?' she gasped, leaning against him.

'Clearly, your constitution is not strong. In your condition—'

'My condition?'

A muscle in his jaw flickered. 'You do yourself no favours by lying about it, madam.'

She pushed back from him. When she saw the direction of his gaze, she pulled the towel higher. 'What condition?'

She shivered and this time it was from cold. He strode away and returned with her robe, pulling it about her shoulders and sweeping her up in his arms. It ought to feel good to be so cherished, but he was furious. What did he think was wrong with her that made him look at her so coldly? He lay her down on the *chaise longue* at the end of the bed, his face expressionless.

Panic fluttered in her breast. 'Tell me, Alistair, what condition?'

'Your being with child.'

For a moment the words made no sense. Then they did. A feeling of hope fluttered in her chest. But why was he furious? And how would he know when she did not?

The nausea.

Was it possible?

'You seem so sure, when the idea never occurred to me once,' she said. Not given how many years she had hoped and been disappointed. It would be nothing short of a miracle.

Her heart felt too full of joy for mere words. While he seemed unmoved.

'You aren't pleased?'

His thin lips curled in a smile that had an

edge of cruelty. 'I am delighted to have cuckoo in my nest.'

It took a moment for the words to sort themselves into meaning. 'A— What?' Despite a wave of dizziness, she shot to her feet. 'How dare you?'

Surprise widened his eyes. 'Dare? An interesting turn of phrase when I know very well Mrs B. took precautions as did I, *ergo*…'

Now the man was spouting Latin in the same breath as he was speaking of that place? *'Ergo,'* she snapped, 'I must have been with child prior to our first meeting. Is that what you think?'

She wanted to throw something at him. Too bad she could not reach the soap. Or the rinsing water.

He inhaled a breath through his arrogant nose. 'Precisely.'

'Well, you are wrong. I am not with child. I cannot be with child. I am barren.'

At the sight of his stunned expression, she sank down on the sofa. She closed her eyes against another wave of dizziness. 'I am sorry,' she said dully. 'I should have told you.'

'You are sure of this?' His voice was arctic and she could not meet his gaze.

'My husband dragged me from one *accoucheur* to the next. The best money could buy.' One humiliating interview after another accompanied by nasty inspections and questions. And ever-increasing fury from her husband. It made her shudder to recall it. 'Each and every one of them agreed that there was no hope.' She wanted to cry and she wanted to rage against fate. But most of all she wished she had told him right from the beginning.

After a few moments' silence, she risked a peep. He was staring down at her with sympathy. 'Julia, I'm sorry. But it doesn't concern me all that much. I have an heir.'

'Not an heir of your body,' she muttered, relieved at his reaction, but unable to rejoice in it.

An odd look crossed his face. Chagrin? Disappointment? And then it was gone as he crouched down beside her. 'Really. It doesn't matter.'

She did not believe him, but she was grateful for his kindness. 'I'm useless as a wife.'

'Julia.' The note of command in his voice had her looking up. There were white lines around his mouth, his lips were a straight line. 'You need to rest. We will talk of this later, when you feel better. I will send your dresser up to you.' He bowed and left.

Chapter Nine

Alistair pounded his fist into the wall and welcomed the pain in his hand even as he winced and shook it out. He needed to get a grip of his feelings where his wife was concerned.

Seeing her in the tub, her skin white, her lips tinged with blue, for one awful moment he'd thought she was *in extremis*. Devil take it, he could barely speak the words in his head, let alone out loud and in English.

How could anyone sleep in water so frigid? Likely only a woman exhausted first by riding all around the countryside and then his carnal needs overcoming good sense even though he knew she'd been ill. But she wasn't expecting a child. A tremendous relief flooded his veins. Something he'd tried not to show, as he could see it made *her* unhappy.

Barren. What a surprise. If it was true. What

reason would she have to lie? Had she guessed he did not want children and sought to trick him? It hardly seemed likely. And the sadness in her eyes when she told him did not lie. She wanted a child.

A throat cleared behind him. 'Your Grace.' The voice was male and tentative.

The study wall looked no worse for wear, but his knuckles were bruised. He turned to meet the worried gaze of his amanuensis. 'Lewis.' He clasped his hands behind his back, ignoring the flush of heat in his cheeks. A duke did not explain himself to anyone. 'You found one?'

'No, Your Grace. I took the liberty of ordering one from the jeweller.'

'Thank you.' He wasn't sure he'd give her the gift. It smacked of a kind of sentimentality any man of sense should find distasteful. He glanced at the mess on his desk. At last now with Lewis's help he'd be able to catch up.

Lewis's face took on a strained expression. 'I beg your pardon, Your Grace, but I must hand in my notice effective immediately.'

'What the devil?' He reined in his temper and looked closely at his secretary. He had never seen Lewis looking so dejected. 'Something has happened.'

'My father is ill. I must go.'

'You hie from somewhere in the west, do you not?'

'Devonshire, Your Grace.'

'You should have sent me a note and gone straight there.'

'Sackfield is not far out of my way and I wished to tell you in person. Also…' he lowered his voice '… I gather the Dowager Duchess has left town for the summer. Visiting family, I understand.'

The only family who would invite her to visit was Luke, who had already imparted the news as a warning, or a threat.

'It is good of you to take the time to let me know, Lewis. I appreciate it. You will stay here tonight and be on your way first thing in the morning, refreshed.'

'Thank you, Your Grace.'

'Since you are here, I wonder if I might impose on you for an hour or two. There are matters among my correspondence that would benefit from your assistance.' Not to mention that the man looked as if he needed the distraction. As did Alistair. Or he'd be dwelling on what this latest development with his wife might mean for their future. All sorts of possibilities fired his imagination and his blood. 'If you don't mind?'

'I would be glad to help, Your Grace. I cannot tell you how badly I feel at deserting the ship.'

'We are not sinking yet, Lewis. You will join the Duchess and me for dinner, I hope?'

Usually, when he was in the country, he and Lewis dined together. Lewis was, after all, the grandson of an earl and a gentleman. He was also good company. Just because Alistair had a wife, there was no reason to change things. He grimaced at his cowardice. Using Lewis to keep him from lusting after a wife who apparently was the perfect choice for a man in his situation, once she recovered from her illness.

He couldn't help wondering if the fates had finally decided to be kind. If so, he had better beware. In his experience, their generosity never came without a price.

'It will be my pleasure, Your Grace.'

He was not surprised by the puzzlement on the younger man's face. What bridegroom wanted a chaperon? One who should never have married in the first place.

It sounded like the last line of a really bad joke.

Julia almost cried off from dinner, after Alistair's accusation. He must have thought her the worst sort of woman, if he thought she would pass another man's child off on him. Even worse than she had thought herself, to tell the truth.

But she wasn't going to hide in her room looking guilty, even if a duchess who could not provide her lord with an heir really was guilty of a crime.

What man would be content for his brother to be his heir? Perhaps he was one of those men who disliked babies. Or worse, would become jealous of a wife's attention to her children. If so, she was better off being barren. It would be better for the children. Or it would be, if the thought of never having a child didn't continue to ache in the centre of her chest.

Head held high, she descended the stairs to the drawing room.

One of the footmen opened the door.

Two men were waiting. Alistair and one with his back to her. He turned.

Ah, Mr Lewis, back from his mysterious errand. She pasted a cool smile on her lips to encompass both men.

'Your Grace.' Alistair came forward to welcome her with the air of a perfect gentlemen. Clearly they were going to pretend all was well. 'Look who has returned to us.'

She held out her hand. 'Mr Lewis. How are you? Quite recovered from your journey, I hope.'

'Indeed, Your Grace.'

'Lewis is only with us tonight. He leaves tomorrow.'

She arched a brow. 'You have been and will be missed, Mr Lewis.'

The man looked surprised and pleased, though surely he knew how indispensable he was to the Duke.

'Dinner is served,' Grindle announced.

Alistair escorted her to the table in the adjoining room. She sat on his right while Lewis sat to his left. Despite his modest attire and retiring manner, Lewis was a handsome young man with the sort of face that would set the hearts of many a maiden fluttering.

Not hers, though. There was not even a flicker of interest in her chest. Beside Alistair's fallen-angel golden looks, he faded into the background. It would have been better if she was not so attracted to her husband. It might have been easier to cope with his obvious distrust.

The footmen served them a consommé. Hopefully that would sit well with her badly behaving digestion.

Silence descended. A hostess needed to make her guests comfortable as well as make sure they were included in a conversation no matter how unsettled she felt within herself. 'I hope your journey to London was successful, Mr Lewis?'

A strange glance passed between the two men, a frowned warning from Alistair to say nothing.

Her heart stumbled. Did Lewis's return to London have something to do with her?

'It was a most uneventful journey, Your Grace,' Lewis said.

'It was fortunate the weather has been fine these past few days.' Heat rushed through her as she recalled one activity the lovely warm weather had allowed. She risked a glance at Alistair, but his expression remained coolly polite. And his voice silent.

She struggled on. 'And you return to town tomorrow?'

Lewis's expression changed. 'I go west. My father is ill.'

Why hadn't Alistair mentioned this instead of letting her blunder about? But then she hadn't yet mentioned his stepmother's visit, either. 'I am so sorry to hear it. You will give your family our hopes for a speedy recovery?'

If anything the young man's face grew darker. 'Thank you, Your Grace. The prognosis is not good, but we can hope for the best.' His heavy tone made it clear he did not expect a favourable outcome.

'I am sorry.'

'I heard from Beauworth this afternoon,' Alistair said. 'We are invited to tea the day after tomorrow. If you are well enough, that is.'

She gritted her teeth at his chilly tone.

'We can decline, if you wish,' she said.

'I have business with the Marquess. Your presence is not required, but Beauworth did say his Marchioness would be glad to make your acquaintance.'

'May I suggest we ride over?'

His mouth tightened. 'Are you sure your health will allow?'

'I will do better on Bella than in the carriage.'

He looked far from convinced, but shrugged. 'As you wish. We are invited for afternoon tea and must leave here by two.'

She turned to their guest. 'Where in the west does your family reside, Mr Lewis?'

'Near Plymouth, Your Grace.'

'Near the sea. How lovely.'

A sad expression filled his gaze. 'Beautifully wild, Your Grace.'

And so dinner continued. While careful not to appear to be prying, she had the feeling Mr Lewis wanted to talk and she learned a great deal about his family, while Alistair, occupied with his own thoughts, rarely spoke unless addressed directly.

When it came time to withdraw after dinner, she pleaded tiredness and forwent tea in the drawing room. As she left the gentlemen to their port, the prickles at the back of her neck indicated someone was watching her closely, and she did not think it was Mr Lewis.

Alistair's coolness hurt far worse than she could have imagined. Was it possible that he would, despite his assurances to the contrary, send her away now he knew she could not bear his children?

Once he had seen Lewis to bed, Alistair, wearing only his dressing gown, hovered at the adjoining door to his wife's bedroom. The sorrow in her eyes at dinner was eating at his conscience. Whereas he was relieved, she likely thought herself a failure. It was quite clear in her face that she thought herself less of a wife.

She was the sort of woman who wore her every thought on her face. And he did not like to see her unhappy.

He cursed beneath his breath.

Was his need for his wife to be happy so out of control he was actually prepared to believe she wouldn't betray him at the first opportunity—if it suited her needs? Would he really risk his son's pride for the sake of her smiles? If past experience had taught him anything, it was that women had no concept of the meaning of honour.

Julia was different. Wasn't she unlike any

other woman he had known? Wasn't that her irresistible allure?

Or was he once more allowing a naïve longing to have someone care about him override common sense? Bitterness entered his soul as he realised he had found his answer.

Then he was a fool indeed to stand here dithering outside his wife's door when her bed was the one place where they were in perfect accord.

He knocked lightly on the door and walked in.

She was sitting in bed with a book. She glanced up as he came in and put the book aside. 'Alistair?'

'Julia.'

'I was expecting Robins with a glass of milk. To help me sleep.'

'Feeling restless, were you?'

She tilted her head in enquiry. 'A little.'

'Me, too.' He locked both doors.

'Oh, but Robins—'

'You prefer milk to me?' He kept his voice light. Teasing. Shrugged out of his dressing gown and slid into the bed.

She stared at him open mouthed. He kissed her, long and hard. He felt her melt against him, heard the soft little sounds in the back of her throat and experienced the strangest feeling. A sense of coming home.

'Snuggle down, my dear,' he whispered against her mouth. 'Before you catch cold.'

Being cradled in one's husband's arms had to be one of the nicest things in the world.

His warmth surrounded Julia like the glow from a blazing fire. The scent of his cologne mingled with soap dizzied her senses. Her body tingled with anticipation.

His arms encircled her, one hand cupping her breast, the other splayed possessively on her belly, while he nuzzled at her nape, sending shivers down her spine.

Desire shimmered hot through her veins, warming her skin, pulsing low in her belly. She moaned with the pleasure of it and rolled to face him.

The light from the candle on the bedside table cast shadows over his face, hiding his thoughts, but showing her the gleam of a smile as he stroked the back of his fingers over her cheekbone, along the curve of her ear, across her jaw, to rest the pad of his thumb against her lower lip.

A shudder of pleasure ran through her. A simple touch and she melted.

'Warmer?' he asked softly.

He knew the answer, the wicked tease. She was on fire from the inside out.

'Much,' she managed to whisper breathlessly against the pressure of his digit.

In retaliation for teasing, she opened her mouth and licked, tasting the slight flavour of salty skin, then bit down hard enough to cause him to hiss in a breath.

He flexed his hips and she felt his hardness against her thigh. 'Do that again and I may have to devise a punishment,' he murmured, his voice low and deeply erotic.

Her insides clenched at the prospect of what such delicious punishment might entail. She grazed his thumb with her teeth. 'You should know better than to dare me, Your Grace.'

He rose up on his elbow. 'Always a surprise,' he said, amusement in that dark velvety voice. His mouth descended upon hers, wooing, gentle, when her primal urge demanded a show of strength.

She nipped at his lower lip.

On a sharp indrawn breath, he came over her, pinning her hands beside her head and taking her mouth with the ruthlessness she needed. He slid one thigh between hers, pressing down on the place where her body ached for his touch.

Their mouths melded. Their tongues duelled, the silken slide sending stabs of pleasure to her core where the pressure he applied only served to drive her need higher.

Slowly, teasingly, he withdrew his tongue, encouraging her to follow into the hot recess of his mouth. He tasted of toothpowder and promised bliss. She fell into the darkness of heady sensation. Teasing him, leading him to taste her once more. As her tongue retreated, he closed his teeth gently. She stilled, expecting the pain of a bite. He suckled.

Sparks of sensation shot through her body, pleasure so painful it left her weak. She moaned and writhed beneath his weight, trying to capture the beckoning climax.

Lingeringly, he raised his head, gazing down into her face, his eyes hot and wild and slumberous. 'More?'

She groaned. 'More.'

'Ah,' he said, smiling. 'Is it not manners to say please?'

He was tormenting her on purpose. Her fists clenched, but while his grip was not painful on her wrists, it allowed her no freedom of movement and right at that moment she felt the need to dig her fingernails in those powerful shoulders, or bite the chin just out of reach.

'Please,' she gasped, grinding her hips against that blissfully hard thigh.

He avoided the movement and grinned. 'No cheating.'

A growl rose in her throat. She bared her teeth, reduced to little more than a feral creature by his teasing. 'Please,' she managed to say again.

He hastened to remove her nightgown. Then he dipped his head and licked up the valley between her breasts, nuzzling his nose against the fullness, circling her nipple with his tongue, first one, then the other, sensations that drove her wild, while she gazed at the beautiful gold of his thick hair, not sure if she wanted to run her fingers through the silken strands or tug them out of his head for teasing her so.

His mouth closed, hot and wet, over her nipple, his teeth grazed the sensitive flesh, biting... almost but not. Promising pleasurable pain, but not quite...delivering.

Her inner muscles clenched wildly, gentle ripples of pleasure spreading outwards, teasing tormenting little flutters that were a prelude to the grand finale.

'Alistair,' she gasped.

He suckled on her nipple.

The bond holding her down stretched and tightened. 'I need you,' she begged him, restlessly churning beneath him, trying to get his attention with her hips, with her voice. 'Now. Please, Alistair. I need you inside me.'

He turned his attention to the other breast, leaving her gasping and melting and wanting.

Somehow she lifted her head and closed her teeth on his shoulder.

On a hiss of breath he raised his head, his eyes dancing with fire. The flames of lust.

'Now, Alistair,' she demanded.

He shook his head at her. 'Oh, no, my dear.'

She swallowed at his sensual tone.

His lips curved in a smile. Still holding her hands in his large one, he moved off her body, denying her his weight, and kissed his way down her ribs and her stomach, amid the crisp triangle of curls.

She gasped in shock at the strangeness and the delicious searing pleasure of the feel of his warm breath against her most private place. 'Alistair, you cannot—'

He blew out a breath that caused her hips to jerk. He came up on his knees, pushing her thighs apart, his erection hard against the ridged muscles of his lower stomach.

She smiled at him as he looked at her with raised brow. Now he would enter her. She let her eyes flutter closed in anticipation of that beautiful hot hard length pressing into her.

He released her hands and, leaning forward, he licked.

Panting, breathless, she could not move for the shock of it.

The soft wet slide of his tongue was a sensation like no other. His tongue circled that spot at the source of her pleasure, the rasp of his stubble against her inner thighs a counterpoint to his tongue, circling and licking in swift little passes that caused her hips to buck and her limbs to go boneless. He toyed with her until there was nothing left but that hot sensation of his tongue. And then his lips pressed against her, his tongue stroking with delicious delicate little tastes that racked her body and drove her out of her mind.

A little pause. She inhaled a breath. He suckled.

She shattered.

Hot darkness enveloped her for long, long minutes, her breathing rasping in and out of her lungs, her blood a rapid thump in her ears, her body suffused with heat.

He held her against his chest with such tenderness wetness pooled at the corners of her eyes.

Gradually, her brain began to function. Awareness stole into her mind and she realised that not only was he holding her sweetly, he was still aroused, the hot blunt head of his erection pushing at her hip.

'Alistair,' she said, trying to look over the broad forearm holding her close. 'You did not…'

A deep breath filled his lungs, lifting her, and he slowly exhaled. 'Do not be concerned.'

'But surely—' She frowned. While he had not moved, the hardness she had felt was no longer there.

'Sleep,' he said.

She didn't want to sleep. She wanted to give him pleasure.

He stroked her head and down her back. Soft sweeping caresses that sweetly lulled her. This man was beautiful. Loving. Gentle.

But he was also the dissolute Duke.

Which was real?

Sleep pushed at her mind, dragging her down into warm darkness. She opened her mouth to object, but yawned instead.

'Shh…' was the last sound she heard.

The tenderness Alistair felt for the woman in his arms was dangerous in the extreme, yet he continued to hold her while her breathing slowed and her body relaxed.

And still he did not move, needing to ascertain her sleep was real and deep. Finally, her laxness, the evenness of her breathing, told him she truly had succumbed to Morpheus.

He shifted to ease the ache in his groin.

He would not take chances with his son's future, but if he was careful they could have a decent sort of a marriage.

He breathed through the dull pain, the same way he had breathed through the need to join her in pleasure. The only purpose of their intimate play had been to remove some of her worries. Her bliss was all the satisfaction he required, along with the pressing need to ensure no child resulted from their intimacy.

He closed his eyes and breathed deeply.

Hours later, surprised at the realisation he had slept, he drifted awake to the feel of a slender body snuggled close to his side. He opened his eyes to see the grey light of day peaking in through the open curtains and the awareness that he once more desired her. Badly.

Times when he spent all night in bed with a woman these days were rare, though Donatella, the Italian courtesan who had hidden him from the French soldiers for months, had always been in favour of waking up to his lovemaking. She'd taught him all she knew about the carnal arts. She'd been a generous lover, an amazing teacher and in some aspects a friend.

Her final betrayal had hurt at the time, but he

should not have been surprised when she was tempted by the price on his head.

Julia stirred, opened her eyes, blinked. 'Oh.'

'Hmmm,' he replied noncommittally, looking into her lovely eyes as they squinted in puzzlement, unsure what to make of her surprised little syllable.

She smiled. 'It is indeed a good morning, Your Grace.'

All at once things were right with his world. And his body was once more demanding he give in to the seduction of her sumptuous softness.

The only other time he recalled falling asleep with a woman after Donatella was with Julia on their first night together. Was that what had led him into this morass of a marriage? This needing to belong to someone? To have someone need him?

If so, he was hiding from the truth. Julia, like all the women in his life, needed his wealth and position for protection—not him. Given how badly he'd failed his son, he was lucky to have that much. Wanting more was a recipe for disappointment.

Inwardly he cursed. He could not allow himself to give in to this weakness. This marriage would only work if he maintained his detachment.

He rolled away from her and reached for his dressing gown, shoving his arms into it and wrapping it around himself. He stalked to the window, looking out, fighting to get himself under control and decent enough to face her. 'I should get back to my room before your woman arrives with your tray.'

The sounds of her leaving the bed were almost more than he could resist. A moment more for her to be suitably swathed in that frilly thing she'd worn the night before and he turned around.

Relief and disappointment in equal measure battered at his mind. She was indeed well covered. Frilly though it might be, it was also demure, covering her from her throat to her ankles.

The scent of her invaded every pore of his body and left him wanting to hold her, kiss her one more time.

In his mind, he opened the door between their chambers, moved through it. Shut her out. In reality, he reached out for her, brought her hard against him and took her mouth in a kiss so wild, so all encompassing, her gasp of shock filled his mouth. Then she leaned into him and kissed him back with equal fervour.

When they broke apart, they were both breathing hard.

'Join me at breakfast?' he managed.

Eyes slumberous, lips full and rosy from his kiss, disappointment filled her expression, but she nodded her agreement.

Somehow, he managed to close the door between them.

The day was gloomy and rainy and after breakfast Julia was confined to the drawing room and her needlework. She kept thinking about the visit from the Dowager Duchess and the fact that she had not mentioned it to Alistair last night. She'd had so many chances it was now a mountain instead of a molehill. Would not Grindle have told him? Coward.

As if conjured by her thoughts the butler bowed his way in. 'Shall I bring tea, Your Grace?'

'Yes, please. Grindle, did you mention the Dowager Duchess's visit to His Grace?'

His brow wrinkled. 'I did not, Your Grace. Should I have?'

'No. I wondered, that was all. Would you send word to the Duke to see if he would care to join me for tea?'

After Grindle left she walked to the window and looked out, plucking up her courage to admit her lie by omission. Beyond the glass, little could be seen of the magnificent vista this morning, the rain obscuring all but the closest objects.

She straightened her shoulders. There really was nothing to fear, but given his suspicions, his talk of cuckoos, would he think this was another attempt to deceive him?

Thank goodness he hadn't changed his mind about visiting Beauworth. She felt the need to get out of doors, to see other people. Hopefully this rain would be over by tomorrow. If not, they would be forced to go by carriage—or postpone the outing. She glanced up at the sky. Naturally it looked as if it might rain for days.

She sighed and prepared herself to spend a few days drinking tea and plying her needle. Perhaps she'd work on a set of cushions for this room. Something bright and cheery.

The tray arrived with a message that His Grace would take his tea in his office, though the kitchen had included a second cup on the tray. Disappointed, she tucked her embroidery away and poured herself a cup. The steam brought with it the distinctive scent of Oolong and something else. Dash it all. Had they added a small amount to the pot for flavour or had they brought her the wrong tray? She poured herself a cup and added milk and sugar. When she lifted the brew to her nose and breathed in the scent her stomach re-belled. Oolong, certainly, but it was that other underlying sickly smell that turned her stomach. She

sniffed again. Deeply. And the smell hit the back
of her throat in a way that was familiar.

Laudanum.

Of course. It was what she had been tasting
and smelling all along.

In her tea? Why? In disgust she poured what
was in her cup back in the pot and put the lid on,
to keep the smell enclosed.

Her chest constricted. This was the reason for
her illness these past many days. Certainly not
what Alistair had accused her of. What she had
barely dared hope. Laudanum must have been
what she had been tasting in her morning chocolate, too. She shuddered. A dose of the poppy had
made her violently ill as a child and the doctor had
told her parents she should never take it again.

Why would anyone do such a thing? *Who*
would?

No one else knew of her intolerance. There had
been no reason to discuss it. She simply never
used it, not for a headache or her monthly pains.
So if it was not being given to make her ill...

She pressed her fingers to her temple, trying
to reason it out. As far as she knew, laudanum
made people sleepy. Took away pain. Some people also gained a penchant for daily usage. Cold
fingers crawled down her spine. Could that be it?

But why?

Trembling, she covered her mouth with a hand, trying to stem her rapid breathing, the panic. Should she say something to Alistair?

This was his house, his servants, his everything. He could arrange for such a thing. Could he have done so? To what end? To make her compliant to his every wish?

Or because he regretted marrying her and wanted rid of her one way or another? And now he knew she couldn't give him children would it make him all the more determined to see her gone? Her conversation with his stepmother had revealed a man who was ruthless in obtaining his own ends. A man who seemed to care for no one but himself.

If he discovered the laudanum did not work, what next should she expect?

Blinded by dread, she wrapped her arms around her waist.

Chapter Ten

Alistair took the stairs up to the second floor two at a time. He'd done his best to stay away from his wife. To assure himself he was not a slave to his desires. He was not. But after his overwhelming terror at finding her comatose in her bath, if he wanted to get any work done, he was going to assure himself she was well at regular intervals during the day.

And likely through the night, too.

Odd behaviour indeed.

Outside the door, he schooled his face into polite friendliness.

Julia gasped at his entrance, her gaze flying from the teapot she had been staring at, to rest on his face. A hand flattened on her throat. 'Alistair. You startled me.'

She looked afraid. 'You invited me for tea.'

She visibly pulled herself together. 'You declined the invitation.'

The way she stood up to him was something he liked about her, but seeing evidence of the courage it took to overcome her fear of him was a bitter pill.

'I changed my mind. Will you pour me a cup?'

She stared at him, her hand hovering near the pot, but not touching it.

He frowned and reached to take it for himself, noticing that she had not yet poured for herself.

'You cannot,' she said breathlessly, pressing her palm to the lid.

He froze. 'What? Am I not permitted to change my mind?' He kept his voice even, an indifferent drawl, but her refusal pained him more than he would have expected.

'No. I mean yes. It is not that.' She sounded flustered. Looked flustered. Anxious.

'What is wrong?'

She stared at him as if he had spoken in a foreign language.

How exceedingly strange. Once more he reached for the teapot.

She sat bolt upright. 'Stop. I didn't think you were coming. It is full of the stuff you like, but I cannot abide. I am sorry. I tipped my cup, milk and all, into the pot.'

He frowned. 'You were supposed to let the kitchen know this.'

Her eyes filled with worry, she twisted her hands in her lap. She sagged back against the couch. 'I—I forgot.' Miserably, she gazed at him.

Did she fear he would be angry she had spoiled the tea? Would her last husband have been angry at such a small thing? Punished her for such a transgression?

Did she expect him to be similarly inclined? Guilt racked him. His distance had been designed to protect her, but he wanted to offer comfort. At least she should understand that she was safe from him in that way.

'Get your coat and hat,' he said, inwardly shaking his head at yet another strangely spur of the moment idea.

She stared at him and then out of the window at the rain. 'Where are we going?'

'To find you a cup of tea you can drink. Meet me in five minutes at the bottom of the stairs.'

It only took Julia a moment to pull on her cloak. Why she had chosen one of the few things remaining from her old wardrobe she wasn't quite sure. Perhaps because it was familiar and comfortable when everything else about today seemed confusing. Worrisome in the extreme.

Or…it was because it was raining. Nothing

else she owned was suitable for wearing in a downpour.

Already waiting for her when she reached the hall, Alistair tucked her hand beneath his arm. 'This way.'

Instead of going out of the front door, he led her out of a side door no doubt used by servants. A path circumnavigated the stables and various outbuildings and arrived at a small thatch-roofed cottage she had not noticed before.

At first, when he knocked on the door, she thought no one was home, then she heard the sharp rap of quick footsteps and the door swung inwards.

A small bird-like lady, with a thin face and a pair of spectacles perched on a formidable nose, peered out at them. A smile changed her appearance from stern to welcoming. 'Crawfy! Come in, come in. Do not stand there getting wet. And you, too, young lady. Oh, my goodness, I mean, Your Grace.'

Alistair, leaned in and kissed her thin cheek. 'Here we are at last, Digger. Julia, this *grande dame* used to be my governess, Miss Digby.'

'Crawfy?' Julia whispered over her shoulder as Alistair ushered her in. 'Digger?'

He took her cloak, whispering back as he did so, 'Childhood pet names.' He hung their outer raiment on hooks beside the door. He waved her into the room where their hostess had disappeared only moments before. It turned out to be the kitchen. On every available surface teetered a pile of books.

'Sit down. Make yourselves comfortable.'

Miss Digby bustled about taking a teapot to the water already boiling on the small range on the other side of the room. She peered at Julia over her spectacles. 'I hope you are not expecting that horrid Oolong stuff Crawfy is so fond of. I cannot bear it.'

'Nor me,' Julia said with heartfelt relief.

Alistair made a face. 'I came for the biscuits.'

'Foolish boy. They make them in your kitchen and bring them over here.'

The tea was soon made and shortbread fingers set out on a blue-patterned plate. They ensconced themselves around the kitchen table with full cups deliciously laced with cream.

Julia closed her eyes with pleasure at the lovely taste and the sense of being welcome.

'So, Crawfy, what brings you to my door?' She smiled at Julia. 'These days he only comes to see me when he has something on his mind.'

'We came for the tea,' he said.

Her lips folded in as she tried to repress a smile. 'What troubles you, Your Grace?'

'Uh-oh. If dear old Digger is getting formal I know we are for it.'

'Dear old Digger' gave him a stern look. 'Confess.'

It seemed that the elderly lady still held the power of a governess to keep her unruly charge in line. Julia repressed a smile of her own. She could not have been more grateful to Alistair for bringing her here. The woman made him seem much more human. More approachable than the Duke who had been sitting in her drawing room only a few minutes ago. More approachable even than the man who had made love to her so delightfully.

His eyes sparkled with mischief. 'My wife thinks someone is trying to poison her.'

Julia froze.

The woman's eyes sharpened behind her spectacles. 'Gracious me.' She glanced at Julia. 'Is this true?'

'No, no,' Julia said, realising too late that Alistair was joking. 'They brought me Oolong, that is all. It doesn't agree with me.'

Especially when laced with laudanum, but she was not going to mention that. Not after Alistair had spoken of poison. 'They must have confused our trays.' She wished it was that simple. She really did.

'Are you sure it is not the antics of this young scamp upsetting your digestion?'

Julia almost choked on her sip of tea.

'Now, Digger,' Alistair said. 'Do not be giving away my secrets. I need my wife's respect.'

Miss Digby chuckled. 'Respect is to be earned, young man.'

'How many times have I heard that quote?' His gaze was fond. Almost tender.

Julia felt as if she was looking in on something precious. As if Alistair had allowed her to see part of him he never exposed to the world. Something wrenched at her heart. She didn't want this. Didn't want to be lured in when she knew that most of the time he barely remembered she existed. If she relaxed her guard, when next he turned all cold and distant, it would hurt too much. She was tired of the pain of rejection.

'Have you always lived here at Sackfield, Miss Digby?' Julia asked, hoping to put the conversation back on a more comfortable footing.

'Dear me, no,' Miss Digby said. 'I left when it was time for a proper tutor.'

The hardness returned to Alistair's jaw. 'I was seven. My stepmother feared Miss Digby was too lenient.'

'Well, I was a little,' the elderly lady said regretfully. 'I never could bring myself to cane small children.' She smiled sadly. 'More is achieved with honey than with vinegar in my experience. But you were quite the handful, even for me.'

'If I had known Isobel was going to send you away, I would have been a model of good behaviour.' His voice was bitter. He looked up and caught Julia watching him. His expression cooled. The illusion of being let in dissipated as if it had never been.

A pang pierced her heart. 'But here you are now?'

'Yes, here I am in my own little cottage just as I always wanted, thanks to Alistair. He came and found me once he reached his majority. When he was little we joked about living in a little cottage in the country and doing nothing but reading books. He loves books as much as I do.'

'You do?' This was something else she had not known.

'I do not have time for reading,' he said. 'Being a duke requires all my attention.'

The old lady's eyes twinkled. 'As well as your new duties as a husband.'

Julia blushed.

Miss Digby looked at Julia. 'You must convince him to take some time for himself,'

As if she had any influence on the man. Although he had spent more time with her here than in Richmond. 'I will try.' What else could she say? The woman was small, but she had a powerful will.

The older woman's lips pursed, creating a concertina of wrinkles around her mouth. 'I hear you hired on a number of new servants, Crawfy. Brought some of them with you, too.'

'A married duke needs more than a skeleton household,' he mumbled. 'Both here and in London. Especially here, since Her Grace will no doubt be receiving callers.'

The old lady nodded. 'Sensible. What about this dresser of yours, Your Grace? Mrs Robins. I have heard a few grumbles. Not a woman who is inspiring of warm feelings amongst her peers.'

Julia blinked at the directness of the question. 'Robins has been with me for three weeks. I agree, she is rather strait-laced, but came highly recommended.'

Alistair narrowed his eyes. 'Recommended by whom?'

'I am not sure. Mr Lewis didn't say.'

'Hmmph,' Miss Digby muttered.

A look of significance passed between her and Alistair.

'What is it?' Julia said.

'The Dowager Duchess,' Alistair and Miss Digby said in unison.

'She sometimes tries to plant spies among my staff,' Alistair said. 'She likes to poke her nose into my business.'

Julia's jaw dropped. 'Oh, my goodness. Really?'

Alistair shrugged. 'She keeps an eye on me for some reason, the idiot female.'

Perhaps she worried about her stepson. She had implied that she did. Still... 'But why would you think she would spy on me?'

His expression hardened 'To cause me trouble. If she could find some unpleasant gossip...'

Her stomach dropped as she thought of the gossip that could never be revealed, of the night they had met.

She swallowed. If she said nothing about the Dowager's visit now, he might think she was colluding with the woman. She gathered her courage. 'I d-did not tell you, but your stepmother visited me yesterday.'

Alistair glowered. 'The devil she did. No doubt she came knowing I was out.'

'She hinted as much.'

'Why did you not mention this before?'

Julia stiffened under his piercing gaze.

'Crawfy,' Miss Digby said. 'You know you are not the most approachable of men. Especially not on the topic of your stepmama.'

'Quite honestly,' Julia said, 'I forgot about it yesterday, with so much going on.' Forgot for a while and later was hesitant as to how to approach the matter. 'She wanted me to support her request to move into the dower house.'

'Do not bother. My father's will provided for the dower house at Balderston. Never again will she set foot on Sackfield soil, so please don't invite her here.'

'Her Grace is not partial to Yorkshire,' Miss Digby said, looking at Alistair, but Julia was not sure if it was censure or support she offered. 'Too many sheep.'

'Too far from London, more like,' Alistair said. 'I'm surprised she didn't ask you to return the Dunstan rubies. She acted as if they were her personal property. They belong to the Duchy, to be worn by the sitting Duchess.'

Her face burned red as she recalled exactly what they had done when he had draped those rubies all over her naked skin that first night. Her inner muscles clenched at the memory.

A glance at Alistair told her he remembered, too. Heat blazed in his eyes. For once, he did not look anywhere near indifferent.

She folded her hands in her lap, clenching them together until it hurt, trying to get those visions out of her mind.

Should she tell him about the laudanum? But with the awful possibility that *he* was responsible for doctoring her tea. If so, it would be foolish to let him know she had found him out.

Julia felt ill. First laudanum in her tea, then a dresser who might be working for his stepmother. Had she, by marrying Alistair, jumped from the frying pan into the fire?

Alistair must have sensed her disquiet for he reached over and gave her hand a brief squeeze. 'Don't worry about Robins, I will write to Lewis and find out just who she is.'

She only wished she trusted him enough to believe he wasn't trying to mislead her.

Dinner had been strangely quiet, Alistair as seemingly preoccupied as she was herself. Miss Digby had talked about what a lovely little boy he had been. Happy. Sweet. Intelligent. Only the last of those epithets seemed applicable now, yet he had occasionally been sweet to her. More than sweet, kind. And generous. Was she wrong to suspect him?

'Tea is served, Your Grace,' Grindle announced, having been informed earlier that they would both remove to the drawing room after dinner.

Alistair held her chair while she rose and escorted her to the drawing room. He lifted the lid of the teapot and inhaled. 'No Oolong. I had a word with them in the kitchen and asked them not to send it up any more. I told them it didn't agree with you and to only use it when they serve it to me in my office.'

Julia leaned close to him and breathed in the fragrant steam. 'It smells lovely.' Not a whiff of poppy.

Alistair grunted.

'I agree. It *is* perfectly horrid when one has to do without something one likes for the sake of another.'

He gave her a sharp look, but a small smile pulled the corners of his mouth upward. 'It always amazes me how much information you glean from little more than a sound.'

Seeing that smile gave her courage. 'I have brothers who rarely did more than grunt or order one about.' It was one of the reasons she had been so willing to accept her first husband's marriage proposal. She had thought nothing could be worse than a house full of brothers. She'd been so utterly wrong.

Alistair winced.

Of course, he had a brother, too, from whom he was estranged.

She set about pouring them both a cup of tea.

'You are ready for our visit to Beauworth to-morrow?'

'I am looking forward to it. Do you plan to see your brother while you are there?'

He took a deep breath. 'Quite the opposite.'

His dark tone did not encourage her to ask for elaboration.

He finished his tea and placed the cup and saucer on the tray. 'I have some correspondence to finish. I will escort you upstairs.'

In other words he was tired of her company.

She finished her tea and he helped her to rise.

Always so gentlemanly, so observant of the rules of polite society, but there was no warmth in it. In him.

Most of the time. Yet on occasion he'd let her glimpse the seductive man she'd been attracted to that first night. And then there was the man he'd been with Miss Digby. Boyishly enchanting. But which was the real Alistair? The man was as elusive as a drop of quicksilver.

Was he someone who could put laudanum in an unwanted wife's tea? The only thing stopping her from fleeing was the recollection of him being ready to pour himself a cup of the tea that afternoon. If he had been responsible, surely he would not have done so.

Unless he was really, really clever.

They walked up the stairs, she with her hand on his arm, he with his gaze set firmly ahead. He stopped when he reached her chamber door and gazed into her face with a questioning look.

Air that a moment before had been cool crackled with tension. The line of his lips softened to sensual as he gazed at her mouth.

Her heart picked up speed and her breath shortened as if there was not enough air left to breath. His eyes widened a fraction. Awareness sparked between them. Despite all of her doubts, she found him wildly attractive.

'Would you care to come in?' She sounded breathless. Hopeful. Pathetic.

And to her great chagrin, fearful.

He opened the door to the bedroom, gazed down at her for a moment and then straightened his shoulders as if coming to a decision. 'It has been a long day and it will be a longer one tomorrow. I would not have you overtax your strength. I will see you in the morning for breakfast.'

He ushered her in and walked away.

The smile on Alistair's face when he greeted her at the breakfast table gave Julia a warm feeling in the region of her heart. The expression on his face was sweet and even a little bashful. He actually seemed pleased to see her.

'How are you feeling today?' he asked as she took her plate to the table and he seated her. So gentlemanly.

'I feel quite myself again, thank you. Is our visit to Beauworth to continue as planned?'

He cast her a brief searching look as if assuring himself she had spoken the truth about her state of health. As if he didn't trust her to know. Or didn't trust her to tell him the truth. The hard line of his mouth softened. 'The weather looks to be holding fair. Do you still prefer to ride?'

'I do.' Knowing now what it was that was making her ill, she really did have a choice. The carriage would not upset her, but riding was a pleasure and a privilege she had been denied for years. Fortunately the rain of the day before had swept away as quickly as it arrived.

'Then I will see you at two. I have quite a bit of paperwork to get through before we go.' He got up and left, taking his newspaper with him.

She frowned at his half-full plate. Was it her putting him off his food? Did he perhaps suspect her of colluding with his stepmother because she had failed to tell him about the visit?

She lifted the lid of his teapot and inhaled. Oolong. She lifted the lid of her teapot. Laudanum. Her blood ran cold. A very real urge to run left her feeling breathless and her heart pounding.

A footman stepped forward. 'Shall I pour for you, Your Grace?'

'Thank you, no.' What on earth was she to do? Trust Alistair and tell him, or keep her own counsel until she uncovered the culprit? The latter was the wisest course, even though her heart told her he ought to know—if she believed he was innocent. Somehow the day no longer looked quite so bright.

To keep her mind busy with something other than fretting, she spent the morning inspecting the linens with the housekeeper. At the midday meal, Alistair did not join her and she drank only water.

At two, they met at the stables, he coming from the steward's office where according to Grindle he had been sequestered all morning and she from the house. He gave her one of his searching looks before they mounted up. 'Everything all right?'

'Of course,' she said, hoping her smile did not look as false as it felt.

They rode at a swift trot that was not conducive to chatter, but at the fork in the lane that led to the orchard, she could not resist a glance at Alistair, wondering if he, too, was recalling the intimacy of their time in the apple tree.

He lifted a brow and there was that little quirk to his lips again. He was remembering all right. Heat rushed to her face as she smiled back.

She decided. She was going to tell him about the laudanum the moment they returned home. She had to bite her tongue to stop herself from saying something about it right then. She had no wish to be in the middle of such a discussion when they arrived at Beauworth.

The road to Beauworth required them to once more pass through the hamlet of Boxted.

Alistair straightened in the saddle and turned to look back as they passed by the village green.

She followed the direction of his gaze. 'Someone you know?'

He frowned. 'I'm not sure. A woman. She had her back to me, but there was something familiar about her and the fellow she was with.' He grimaced. 'Never mind. It is not important.'

'How much further is it?'

'A few minutes. Boxted is on the edge of the Beauworth estate.' He glanced at her. 'Are you tiring?'

Quite the contrary, having made her decision she felt a great deal lighter, freer, as if a weight had been lifted from her shoulders. 'Not in the least, but it is kind of you to ask.'

He nodded his acceptance of her compliment.

'You will like Beauworth House and the grounds are extraordinary. There have been Le Cleres in this part of Hampshire for centuries. Their ancestors go back further than mine. Vikings or some such.'

'He does not appear very Viking-like. I thought they were all blond giants, though he is large enough to be sure.'

'Takes after his mother, I gather. She was French.'

'Did you know each other as boys?'

'Not really. I was away at school. He remained here with his tutors. He and Luke are closer in age.'

His face had hardened at the mention of his brother.

Another person in his family with whom he was at odds.

'Have you met the Marchioness?'

'I have met her, although she rarely comes up to town. You will like her, I think. Beauworth was at our wedding ball only because he had Parliamentary business requiring his attention.'

'He is a devoted husband, then.'

'Apparently so. He spent years fighting the French.' He hesitated. 'There were rumours that he was a traitor at one time, but now the war is over it seems it has all been forgotten in the interests of peace.'

A gatehouse appeared beside a gap in the hedge and a sweep of drive up to a lovely Palladian house of golden weathered sandstone. When they arrived at the columned portico over the front door, grooms came at the run to take their horses.

By the time they had dismounted, Beauworth and his lady were walking down the steps to greet them. Clearly a duke and duchess merited a proper formal welcome, but their smiles were warm. Lady Beauworth's gold hair glinted guinea bright in the sunshine. Though small of stature, her presence was commanding and her dove-grey eyes gleamed when they rested on her large handsome husband.

'Welcome to Beauworth,' the Marquess said, escorting Julia indoors and leaving Alistair to accompany the Marchioness. He did have a tinge of French in his accent. It was very slight and perhaps only noticeable if you were looking for it.

The drawing room was beautifully appointed, painted in a pretty blue with white moulding and cornices. The tea tray arrived in short order. It wasn't long before Julia felt an immediate liking for the vivacious Lady Beauworth.

'Call me Ellie, please,' she said, 'for I am hoping we will be good friends since we live so close.'

'I am Julia and would like that very much.' It would be wonderful to have a friend. Though there was much in her past she could never discuss with a lady as fine as the Marchioness of Beauworth, they must surely have some things in common. 'Your house is lovely.'

'Hah. You would not say so had you seen it when we were first married. Garrick's uncle had turned the place into a haven for bachelors.' She shuddered. 'Fortunately, my husband was only too glad to give me a free hand in making it livable.' She poured tea for them all and the two men wandered off with the cups to look out of the window while they chatted in low voices.

Julia could not quite imagine Alistair giving her a free hand in anything. 'Did you hire an architect?'

'We did for the larger projects, but you know simply adding a few flowers and changing the curtains and furniture made a huge difference.'

'Perhaps more flowers are what Sackfield needs.' It needed something to turn into a home instead of a mausoleum.

'The gardens there are lovely, so I am told.'

'They are.' As was the apple orchard. And the bedchambers. She quelled the memory, but something must have shown in her face because Ellie gave a delighted little chuckle.

'Oh, you newlyweds. I suppose you will soon be thinking about setting up your nursery.'

A weight descended on her chest. The weight of her failure as a wife. More hot blushes scalded her cheeks.

Ellie chuckled wickedly, completely misinterpreting her embarrassment.

Beauworth glanced over at his wife with a fond smile, his expression changing in an instant from stern to loving. Alistair's expression, on the other hand, remained coolly aloof.

'Why not take Her Grace up to the nursery when you have finished your tea?' the Marquess said. 'I am sure she would like to meet our chicks.'

Ellie looked at her doubtfully. 'Would you indeed? I am a terribly proud mama. Utterly boring on the subject, if you must know. We have two little lords and one very demanding young lady in our nest.'

Julia couldn't remember the last time she'd been among any little ones. 'I would love to meet them.'

'You are not saying that to be polite, I hope,' Ellie said, frowning.

'No. I mean it, quite sincerely. Since we are to be friends, I promise you, I will never lie or pretend.'

'Nor will I,' Ellie said, nodding firmly. 'How

splendid.' She glanced over at her husband. 'Can you manage without us?'

The Marquess bowed, but there was a twinkle in his dark eyes. 'With difficulty, my love. I gather the Duke and I have a matter to discuss.'

Chapter Eleven

What had once been a bachelor domain positively reeked of feminine influence. Fresh-cut flowers cluttered a table. The scent of beeswax and lemon permeated the air. Embroidered cushions overflowed the sofa beside the hearth. Clearly the Marquess of Beauworth was firmly beneath the cat's paw.

As Alistair was fast becoming. There had been a bouquet in the middle of his breakfast table, he now recalled.

Beauworth's piercing gaze levelled on his face. 'Now the ladies are otherwise occupied, have a seat and tell me your concerns about my employment of your half-brother.'

Thank the deities for a man who got straight to the point. Alistair took the armchair. Beauworth, shoving a couple of floral cushions out of the way, sprawled on the sofa.

'I don't trust him,' Alistair said. 'To have him within a hundred miles of me or mine is a hundred miles too close.'

The Marquess frowned. 'You have evidence that he means you ill?'

Ah, hell, what did one say? Old wounds knotted his gut. He had no proof that his brother had tried to kill him. Or that he was in any way involved with his mother's schemes. 'He's my heir.' It was as far as he would go, but too many things had happened in the past to make him comfortable with members of his family living close by. Or visiting.

Beauworth leaned back and rested one long arm along the back of the sofa with a grimace. 'You think he wants the title.'

'If I die first it is his.' Whatever happened, the title would ultimately go to Alistair's supposed nephew. In the meantime, he was keeping the estate safe from his stepmother's tendency to pillage. Something Luke would never manage. The woman was his mother, after all.

Beauworth scowled. 'You would do well to follow my maxim. Keep your friends close and your enemies closer. In the meantime get yourself a son and solve the issue.'

Simple for Beauworth to say. That would never happen. Not that he was going to air his family's dirty laundry to his neighbour. 'Running into him is awkward in the extreme given our past disagreements.' As was meeting his nephew, who looked nothing like his legal father. The last thing he wanted was for Julia to put two and two together. And seeing the boy himself was always a wrench. A reminder of what he could never have. 'I can only presume he feels the same way.'

It was not stated as a question, but Beauworth got the point and shook his head. 'Not that I know of. I did ask him why you did not make use of his talent. He intimated that you did not work well together.' The Marquess shot him another of those piercing glances. 'And thus your loss is my gain.'

'You will keep him on, then? Over my reservations?'

'Why would I not? I haven't come close to finding anyone with his expertise. The man is an excellent steward. And also a friend.'

Alistair bit back the temptation to demand. He was Duke after all. But Beauworth would not take kindly to orders. Nor did he wish to arouse the Marquess's curiosity any more than he had. 'Very well. We shall not speak of it again, but I do not want to find him wandering on Dunstan property at any time, day or night. I assume you will make these wishes known.'

Beauworth's eyes narrowed. 'If you could give me one good reason—'

Alistair raised a hand. 'My brother is not worth us falling out.' He had few enough friends as it was. He would simply keep Julia and Luke apart. He put down his cup and saucer on the tray and rose to his feet. 'Perhaps we should go and find my Duchess. I praised your gardens to the skies and she was looking forward to seeking your advice on some horticultural matters.'

For a moment, Beauworth looked as if he might press Alistair further, but he must have thought better of it. He stood up. 'It will be my very great pleasure, Duke.'

'Lord and Lady Beauworth are a lovely couple,' Julia said, as they passed the last of Boxted's cottages on the Sackfield side of the village. A woman working in her patch of garden straightened to watch them pass. She hesitated, not sure how he would react to what she had to say. Dash it, she was not a mouse to shiver in a corner waiting for the cat to pounce. 'Lady Beauworth invited me to join a committee raising funds for a new church bell. It meets once a week.'

'Is that something you would like to do?' Alistair sounded non-committal.

'I would. It will help me to get to know our

neighbours.' She waited, breath held. Her first husband had rarely let her go out of the house.

'There are great many who would like to get to know you.'

Again he gave her no clue as to whether he deemed this a good or bad thing. She decided to take his lack of opinion as approval.

'We should invite the Beauworths to dine with us before the end of the summer,' she said. 'His lordship gave me a great many ideas with regard to the gardens and I would like to show him the results.'

'Good idea.'

'Their children are delightful.' She smiled brightly.

'I will take your word for it.'

She wanted to shake him. He responded politely, but he did not converse. He had withdrawn again. It was most annoying. And worrisome.

A sigh escaped her when she had sworn she would not let him see how much his reserve troubled her. It was his nature. She could not expect him to change to make her happy. It was she who had to suit him. That was the way things were.

A little beyond the village, Alistair gazed around him. 'I suggest we take a shortcut across that field,' he said. 'Thor needs to run.'

The meadow to their right did indeed look inviting, nearly as inviting as the apple-tree house. Alistair opened the gate, when she knew he and his horse could easily have jumped it. And would have, had he been alone. Jumping in a lady's saddle was always a risk, so she could appreciate his gentlemanly consideration, even if she did not appreciate his cool nature.

The field rose in a gentle incline and the horses, once given their heads, did indeed show their eagerness to be stretching their legs in a full-out gallop to the top of the hill and over a log in the break in the wall that Thor hopped with ease. Beneath her, Bella gathered for the jump. Julia relaxed and the little mare took it easily. When she lifted her gaze to see which way Alistair had gone, she was shocked to see him crumpled on his side on the grass. Thor stood a little way off, trembling, his saddle slipped around beneath his belly.

Julia kicked free of her stirrup and slid carefully down. 'Alistair?'

She ran and knelt at his side, touching her fingertips to his neck to find his pulse a strong, steady beat. With some effort, she pushed him onto his back. He remained pale and unconscious with a trickle of blood running down his forehead.

Gently, she ran her fingers over his scalp, sifted through the thick silk of his golden hair and found a lump sticky with blood just above his hairline. She parted his hair to see a still-swelling bump already turning blue. His head must have hit a rock when he'd landed. 'Alistair.' She shook his shoulder and wildly looked around for help. Not a soul in sight.

Now what was she to do? She could not carry him, nor could she leave him here alone. She sat down beside him cross-legged and eased his head into her lap, gently stroking her fingers across his forehead, praying he would wake up, praying someone would pass by and see them.

He groaned. Brought a hand to his head.

Relieved he was coming to his senses, she captured his hand in her own. 'Careful, you might make it worse.'

His eyes fluttered and opened. 'Gads, that hurts.'

He blinked several times, then squeezed his eyes shut. 'Everything is blurry.'

She glanced over at Thor. 'You came off your horse. Bumped your head.'

He frowned. 'Where?'

'We were taking a shortcut.'

He pressed his fingers to his temple. 'We were going to Beauworth, last I recall.' His voice trailed off. 'No, we were there.' He squeezed his eyes shut. 'What happened?'

'You showed me a clean pair of heels and jumped a log. By the time I reached the other side you were down. Your saddle slipped.'

'My saddle?' He made as if to sit up, groaned and lay back down in her lap. 'Devil take it, I feel dizzy.'

'You hit your head. Lay still for a moment or two.'

'Thor?' He tried to turn his head, but closed his eyes immediately.

'I told you, lay still.'

'Bossy little thing, aren't you.'

Only a man as large as Alistair would call her little. 'It is for your own good.'

He gazed up into her face, the grey eyes not cold any more, but the frown creasing his brow speaking of pain. 'Do that thing with your fingers in my hair. It felt nice.'

'Close your eyes, then.'

He did as she bid and she combed her fingers slowly through his hair, careful not to touch his scalp near the bump. His sigh was long and soft through parted lips that looked softer and fuller than usual. Her heart gave a little clench. Why couldn't he always be this open? He was so handsome. And protective. But so aloof.

He was not aloof now. He was permitting her to care for him. A feeling of great tenderness filled her chest. She closed her eyes briefly, not wishing to admit how much she also wished he could care for her.

'Better?' she asked.

'Much.' Eyes squinting, he peered around. 'Thor?'

'He is all right. A bit twitchy about the saddle being almost below his belly, but calm enough.'

He frowned as if trying to make sense of her words. With a groan he came up on one elbow. He shook his head. 'Hades, if only the ground would stop heaving.' He rolled on to his knees and pushed up. 'I must see to Thor.'

Even in pain, he worried about a creature unable to care for itself.

'I will see to him. Lay back.'

He collapsed on his side with a soft moan. 'I feel as if I have drunk a gallon of brandy.'

Sick and dizzy and his words were slurred. Worry gnawed at her stomach. How on earth was she to get him back to the house? 'Wait here. I will not be long.'

He rolled over on his back and flung his forearm over his eyes, huffing out a breath through his nose. 'Not going anywhere.'

Fortunately, Thor was a gentleman and after only a bit of a struggle she got his saddle off. The horse eyed her in puzzlement as she removed his bridle. There was only one way she could think of getting help that did not involve leaving Alistair. She whacked Thor on the rump and he took off at a gallop.

Hopefully heading back to his stable. With a bit of luck someone would realise there was something wrong and come looking for them, though it might take a while.

Bella, who had tossed her head when Thor took off, fortunately didn't attempt to follow her equine friend. Julia made her comfortable, too. If only there was a stream nearby, she could give her and Alistair a drink of water.

She went back to where Alistair was stretched out on the grass to tell him she was going looking for water.

He didn't move at her approach or open his eyes. 'Alistair?'

No answer. He was lying so very still. And so very white.

Her heart missed a beat. 'Alistair?'

Alistair's head was pounding fit to burst. He risked cracking an eyelid and squeezed it shut at the glare. What the devil had he done? Drunk a barrel full of brandy? And if so, why?

Or was it something worse? An old haunting nightmare of his past?

Something cool and damp glided across his forehead.

'You are awake.'

His wife's voice. Full of relief.

The acid of dread eating at his gut faded. 'Close the curtains. Please,' he added in afterthought. No need to get her back up when he couldn't raise a hand in his own defence.

There was the sound of dragging fabric. The light on the other side of his eyelids dimmed.

Again the cool damp cloth caressed his face.

He licked his lips. Found them parched.

'Would you like some water?'

'Thank you,' he croaked. He swallowed against the dryness. He peeked from beneath his lashes, glad to discover opening his eyes was not nearly as painful as the last time.

A luscious pair of breasts appeared inches from his face and a hand curled around his nape, propping him up, while pillows were pushed behind his head and shoulders. Despite the delicious view, he closed his eyes against the odd way the room distorted.

The glass pressed to his lips was cool, the water cooler and sweet to his gravelly throat. He leaned back against the pillows and once more braved fully opening his eyes. This time the room remained steady, if a little blurry.

'What happened?' Damn, he sounded like a whiny child.

Julia's face came into focus, smiling uncertainly. Worried, then. He waited for her explanation.

'You fell from your horse.'

That sounded unlikely. He frowned, trying to recollect the event. He remembered a field and his head resting in her lap and something about his horse. 'Thor?'

She tutted. 'What is it about you and that horse? He is fine. Indeed, we can thank him for our rescue.'

'How so?'

'Well, I am not sure I believe it, but I scared him off, hoping he'd run for his nice comfortable stall, and Jaimie swears he led them back to where you had fallen and he, being a very smart stable lad, brought a wagon along.'

'Did I misjudge a jump?' It would be the first time he had been thrown since the age of eight, when Isobel had put him up on a half-broken colt.

She smoothed the pillows each side of his head, bringing those deliciously plump breasts close enough to kiss. Beneath the sheets his body hardened. Well, even if his head was unusable, one part of him was in perfect working order.

Unfortunately, that was the part he would rather went to sleep.

She straightened, her face serious. 'Your girth gave way.'

He stared at her blankly. He would never ride out with a loose girth. 'Gave way?'

She gave a little grimace. 'One broke and the other slipped. You were lucky it did not happen during the jump.'

The jump would have likely been the cause of the break, yet his equipment had been in perfect condition. He'd checked it himself before they rode out. His and hers. 'I see.'

'More water?'

'Thank you, but I must get up—'

A hand flattened on his chest, a light touch but commanding. He froze, hauling back on the reins of a surge of anger.

'The doctor said you are to remain in bed until the dizziness passes.' she said. 'It might be a day or so.'

'The doctor came? When?'

'Yesterday afternoon.'

He glanced toward the now covered window. 'What time is it?'

'My, what a great many questions. It is late afternoon. Almost dinner time. Are you hungry?'

He grinned. 'I'm not the only one with questions.' Much as it went against the grain, and he certainly was not going to admit it, he was enjoying her fussing. He had no memory of anyone fussing over him in quite this way. Ever.

Reality came rushing in. Recollections. 'How are you?'

'I am well. No sign of any illness.' The relief in her voice was odd. Too intense. 'I took afternoon tea with Miss Digby, by the way. She was worried about you.'

'I hope you set her mind at rest.' He did not like to worry Digger.

'As much as I was able.'

A scratch at the door and Grindle entered, his face anxious. His lips twitched in what might be described as his version of a smile when his gaze rested upon Alistair. 'You are awake, Your Grace.'

'It would seem so,' Alistair replied.

'McPherson begs a word, if you feel so inclined.'

'I expect he wants to apologise about the broken girth,' Alistair said. 'Show him up.'

Julia rose to her feet. 'While you lecture Jaimie, I am going to see about some broth since you haven't eaten since yesterday.'

Lecturing was also a wife's privilege. 'I would prefer bread and a few slices of roast beef.'

'Broth first. Doctor's orders. You do not want to be ill again.'

He vaguely remembered casting up his accounts. 'I apologise if—'

'No apology required. After all, you were exceedingly kind to me when I was ill. But we do not know if your stomach can handle anything more than broth, especially if you continue to feel dizzy.'

When he made as if to argue she raised a brow. 'Now you wouldn't want to set me a bad example, would you?'

He let go a sigh. 'Broth it is. Show Jaimie up, will you, Grindle?'

Julia slipped out and the butler closed the door behind them both. Alistair pushed up a little higher on the pillows and cursed as the room took a slow circle around his head.

A moment or two later, Jaimie entered the room with a collection of leather straps. 'How are you feeling, Your Grace?'

'As if I fell off a horse.'

Jaimie grinned. 'Excellent. You'll soon be up on your feet. Quite a blow to the noggin, the doctor said. It is a good thing you are a hard-headed man.'

Those were likely the most words he had ever heard Jaimie McPherson utter at one time in the year since he'd come to work for Alistair. He dropped his gaze to the tack. 'What happened?'

The grin faded to grimness. 'The girth was cut.'

Was this an excuse for bad management of his stable? Oiling a girth would result in stretching, which would result in it slipping. But Julia had said it broke. 'Cut, you say?'

'Cut.' Jaimie lay the straps on the bed and showed Alistair a clean break on one girth and how the other was holding by little more than a fraction of leather. 'If this one had torn through. I am thinking you would have landed far harder than you did. Someone intended you should be badly injured or worse.'

'Someone did not place the rock right where my head landed.'

'You might have broken your neck.'

Jaimie was right. The damage to the saddle was too clean to be normal wear and tear. A deliberate act that must have happened while the horses were at Beauworth. There was only one person who benefitted from his death and that person was now employed by the Marquess. Something about the thought stirred a memory. It slipped away again. 'It might have caught on something right before being placed on Thor.'

The eye Jaimie gave him was none too complimentary. 'You did bang your head, didn't you? I am riding over to Beauworth—'

'No.'

Jaimie's eyes widened. 'Surely—'

'No.' This required careful handling if it was deliberate. Perhaps Luke and Isobel had decided they'd waited long enough. Or had heard about Alistair's attempt to have him removed from his position. Or something else entirely.

Julia entered with a tray which brought with it the scent of beef tea.

Alistair nodded at Jaimie, who instantly understood their discussion was over and gathered up the tack.

'I'll be out to take a look at Thor as soon as I am able,' Alistair said.

'Dinna worry. The lad is feasting on oats and feeling very much the hero.' He neatly bowed to Julia and her tray and left the room. There was more to Jaimie than a stable master. Occasionally, he forgot his lowland brogue and sounded more like a landed gentleman. And his manners were far too nice. He bore watching. After all, who had more contacts among stable hands at the other estates than he?

And then there was the matter of his wife. She was looking as pale as a sheet, when she'd seemed perfectly calm before she left.

'Is something the matter?'

She bit her lip, her gaze dropping to the contents of the tray. 'No, nothing.'

Once more he had the feeling she wasn't telling him the truth. He thought of asking her to trust him with whatever was causing her worry. How could he, when he honestly didn't trust her?

Or he shouldn't.

'Now,' Julia said, hoping the rapid beating of her heart caused by yet another pot of laudanum-doctored tea was not obvious, 'drink this broth and we will see how you do.' She had intended to tell him about the laudanum the moment they returned, but now she was not sure she should bother him at a time when he should be resting.

He made a face, but took the tray on his lap and sipped cautiously at the soup. She watched for any signs that his stomach might be rebelling. All seemed to go well.

She rubbed at her aching back. She had sat all night in the chair by the window and it had left her sore.

'May I pour you some tea?' she asked, hoping he would not take a pet and throw it at her head in the way of a wilful child. Men were like that when they were ill. Her last husband had been anyway. 'It is a tisane recommended by the doctor to settle your stomach.'

He eyed the teapot suspiciously.

'It will do you good. I made it myself.'

Alistair frowned.

'You don't believe me?'

He leaned back against the pillows. 'Of course I believe you. What is in it?'

'Herbs, mostly,' she said. 'Something for the pain. I will drink some, too, to ease my aching muscles. I haven't ridden so much for years.'

The wary look on her husband's face eased, but still he waited until she had taken more than one sip before he tried his.

'Gads,' he said, finally putting down his empty cup. 'I am exhausted. And the d—I beg your pardon, the blasted room is still lurching about like a drunken pig at a party.'

She giggled. His surprised look caused her to put a muffling hand over her mouth. 'I beg your pardon. The image took me by surprise.'

He grinned at her. 'You don't suppose it is the tea making us silly.'

'No. I think it is the relief.' She was extraordinarily relieved that her husband hadn't died out there in that field. 'You need to sleep.'

'As do you, I think. Go. Seek your bed.'

His words were a kindness she had not looked

for. The idea was tempting. 'The doctor said you must not be left alone.'

'Ask one of the footmen or my valet to—'

She shook her head. 'I am your wife. It is my responsibility.'

A smile touched his lips. 'You are a very dutiful duchess, are you not?'

'As is right, Your Grace.' After all, he had taken her in out of the goodness of his heart. She kept telling herself that, because having done so, why would he then turn around and try to harm her? If only she could be sure. It seemed odd that only the tea or chocolate she drank alone was ever touched. Except for that one day when he had changed his mind about joining her. He had definitely intended to drink that tea. She was sure. Almost sure.

If only she could stop her thoughts from going around and around and out and say what was on her mind. 'Jaimie looked upset when he left.'

'He was angry about the ruin of a good saddle.'

She blinked. 'He surely did not blame you?'

'Wear and tear,' he said, but his voice was harsh.

'You blamed him?'

'Julia, let it go.'

She inhaled a sharp breath, then let it go with a nod. She would not argue with a man whose head must be aching.

'Let us get you comfortable for sleep, Your Grace. You are sure to feel better in the morning.'

He gave a long-suffering sigh. 'So, we are back to your gracing each other to death. You, too, need to rest. You spent last night sitting up with me, did you not?'

Back to that argument. A smile escaped from her at his tenacity. 'Do not worry about me. I will lie down on the *chaise* over there by the window.'

His bark of laughter came as a surprise. 'Good try. You will climb up here and lie beside me in comfort.'

Shock rippled through her. 'You cannot think to...'

Pinpricks of light danced in his eyes. 'Think to what? Importune you? When I am completely at your mercy, drinking all manner of nasty concoctions?' He huffed out an irritable breath. 'Hardly. But if you insist, sleep on the *chaise*...' He eyed it. 'Be uncomfortable, for I swear it isn't long enough to permit you to stretch out.'

It wasn't. It was more chair than bed, she had discovered last night. And for some reason he seemed to be insulted. 'As long as you don't think I will disturb you, I am more than content to join you on the bed.'

She picked up his tray and busied herself putting it outside the door and ringing for a servant to collect it, quite undone by his teasing.

'Turn the key in the lock, Julia.' His voice had hardened. 'If anyone should come at us, I doubt I could stand, let alone mount any sort of meaningful defence.'

Her heart stilled. Was that why he wanted her close? 'Come at us?'

'Put it down to a ducal thing. Pull up the drawbridge, down with the portcullis and all that rot. I do not like feeling helpless.'

She could understand that, having been helpless more times than she liked to think about. The idea that he wanted to protect her made her feel cherished.

Having locked the door, she climbed the steps up on to the bed which was more than large enough for two. She lay down on the dark blue counterpane sporting the ducal crest embroidered in gold thread.

'You will be warmer under the covers,' he commented wryly. 'And more comfortable out of your gown and stays.'

Unable to face any sort of battle in her present state of exhaustion, she undid the tapes at the neck and waist of her gown and wriggled out of it. He made short work of her stays when presented with her back. It felt intimate and comfortably familiar. Something she had never expected to feel with this man.

She dived beneath the covers in her shift and lay on her side. 'Happy now?'

He rolled over to face her. 'Not quite. Lay on your front and I will massage your poor aching back.'

He'd noticed? 'Your head,' she protested.

'I'm not going to be using my head.' He rose up on one elbow.

She knew better to argue with a duke, and his strong skilful touch on her lower back was heavenly. She groaned her pleasure. But then the man was a renowned seducer of women.

'Alistair?'

'Relax, love.'

Love. So casually spoken. It could mean nothing. It could also be a sign of growing affection. A sign he was not the one she should fear. She wanted to believe it. With all her heart.

Her head warned her to be careful.

Chapter Twelve

They were seated at breakfast when an out-of-breath Grindle poked his head into the room. 'Your Grace, you have a visitor.'

'Who is it?'

Grindle looked uncomfortable, when he rarely showed any expression at all. 'Lord Luke, Your Grace. I told him you were not at home as you instructed, but he barged in and said he would wait. I put him in the green drawing room, but he is threatening to come looking for you, if you won't go to him.'

'It is all right, Grindle,' Julia said, soothingly. 'We are finished here. We will go at once.'

'There is no reason for you to see him,' Alistair said.

The hurt in her expression was almost more than he could stand. 'Come if you wish, but he won't be staying long so there is no need to offer him refreshment.'

Wide-eyed, she stared at him, then nodded. 'If that is your wish.'

He wanted to curse that look of disapproval when they had finally seemed to reach some sort of balance but instead offered his arm and escorted her to the drawing room.

Alistair froze at the sight of the blond, blue-eyed boy standing beside Luke. What new ploy was this? Since coming in to his title, the only time his family showed up on his doorstep was when they wanted money or to use his influence to their benefit. But bringing the boy? Was this his brother's way of reminding him of his duty to his heir? 'Luke. You want to see me?'

The boy gazed at him warily and then his gaze flicked to his father. His legal father.

'Good to see you, too,' Luke drawled.

'How kind of you to call, Lord Luke,' Julia said, stepping forward, holding out her hand. Alistair gritted his teeth at the warm smile she bestowed on his brother and, in his turn, the lad. A punishment, no doubt, for his rudeness. Holding his breath, he waited for Julia to really look. To see.

'Your Grace, it is a pleasure.' Luke bowed and the boy followed his lead.

Alistair drank in the sight of the boy, so young, yet trying so hard to be the perfect gentleman. A pang pierced his heart. A longing to know more of the boy. To have some hand in his upbringing. Luke was teaching him well, but Jeffrey did not look particularly happy. Still, it was understandable. What boy wanted to call on curmudgeonly uncles on a bright sunny day?

'Please, do sit down,' Julia said sinking on to the sofa.

'Thank you, Your Grace.' Luke took a seat on the sofa. The boy hopped up beside him, close enough to touch, as if seeking protection from his wicked ducal uncle. Bitterness rose in Alistair's gullet.

'Please, won't you call me Julia since we are family? And, Jeffrey, how are you today?'

Alistair sat beside her, keeping a careful watch on his brother. Not that he thought the man would pull a pistol and shoot him in broad daylight before a witness. But he wasn't taking any chances.

Luke ran a glance over Alistair. 'I see the reports of you at death's door were wrong.'

His brother didn't look particularly well either. Far too skinny for his large frame. 'Came to commiserate, did you? Or were you hoping to dance on my grave?'

Bleakness filled his brother's face. 'The latter, naturally.'

The boy squirmed.

'This is the first day since the accident that Alistair has risen from his bed,' Julia hastened to intervene, her face mirroring distaste at the awful things being spoken and those not spoken. 'He received a bad blow to the head.'

'Then I am surprised he suffered any ill effects,' Luke muttered. 'Being the most hard-headed individual of my acquaintance.'

Julia, curse her, smothered a smile.

He glared at his brother. 'Tell me, Luke, exactly why you are here? And be quick about it. I am a busy man.'

'I would prefer we discuss it in private.'

Ice filled Alistair's veins. 'Need money, do you?'

Julia gasped.

The boy on the sofa cringed and gazed up at Luke, his face pale.

'Jeffrey,' Julia said, her smile brittle, 'would you care to show me your pony? We did not have time for proper introductions when we met the other day. I assume you left him at the stables?'

The look of longing on her face as she gazed at the child was like a blow to the solar plexus. This was all his fault. His guilt. Which was now visited upon a wife he should never have married.

'May I, Papa?' What a good job his brother

was doing with the lad, despite his lack of a wife. He ignored the pang the thought gave him and retained his cold expression with effort.

'You may,' Luke said, his face as grim as Alistair envisaged his own to be.

He and Luke rose as Julia led the boy out of the room.

'Well?' Alistair said.

Luke glowered. 'First, I'd appreciate you not insulting me in front of my son.'

Alistair's fists clenched. He relaxed them and curled his lip. 'Your son.'

Luke flushed. 'Damn you, Alistair. I did not come here to argue. But when your stable master curses my name at the local watering hole, it is beyond enough.'

Alistair stared at him, recognising anger and frustration and genuine bewilderment.'

'What did McPherson say?'

'Only that your accident might not have been an accident and there is only one person who will benefit from your death.' He threw up a hand when Alistair opened his mouth to speak and went to the window to look out. 'Oh, he didn't say it in so many words, but the meaning was clear enough. Are you trying to get me dismissed?'

Alistair pulled in a deep breath at his brother's genuine distress. 'I did not put McPherson up to his mutterings, if that is what you are suggesting. But my girth was cut.'

Luke blanched. 'It could have happened here.'

Jaimie could be trying obfuscate the truth in other words.

'It might also have been an accident.'

Luke looked worried. 'As you say.'

'I'll have a word with Jaimie.'

Luke huffed out a breath. 'Actually, that was not my sole reason for calling. It is about Mother.'

Saints preserve him. '*Your* mother.'

His brother's lips tightened. 'From what I gather she's close to being done up.'

Money. It was always about money. 'She called on my wife, uninvited.'

Luke winced. 'I know. Your steward blabbed in the Wheatsheaf as how he was going to be escorting the great Duke of Dunstan around the estate the other day. Gossip travels fast in the country.'

Especially when the Dowager had eyes and ears everywhere. The thought struck a chord of memory he could not quite capture. Curse his knock on the head. 'I have no plans to renovate the dower house at Sackfield, Luke. She has a perfectly good house in Yorkshire. And I will not have her under my roof.'

'Damnation, Alistair, she wishes to visit her

grandsons and I have no room at my cottage. You could—'

Alistair swung away to look out of the window and to avoid the quiet rage in his brother's eyes. Was that rage deep enough to lead Luke to kill? 'I could not. I am on my honeymoon. I do not intend to spend it with *your* mother. I will have my man of business send her an advance on next quarter's allowance, but she needs to rein in her expenses.' Bitterness filled him. 'What about you? No funds required?'

Luke muttered a soft curse. 'I have everything I need.'

He gritted his teeth and turned to face his brother. 'Jeffrey does you credit.'

Luke's eyes widened. 'Thank you. I try. I brought him because I thought you should have some knowledge of your nephews.'

He enclosed himself in ice. Nephews. Even when they were private they continued the pretence. Luke's way of keeping Alistair at arm's length from his son. He glared at his half-brother. 'Because they are my heirs, after yourself, you mean.'

Luke's mouth twisted. 'That is not likely, now you are married.'

Was that enough of a reason for Luke to consider murder? 'My man of business tells me you refuse to use the allowance your mother set up for you while she was my guardian.'

'I don't need your money. Beauworth pays me very well. He at least appreciates my skills.'

His brother had stewarded the Duchy after his father's death, when Alistair had been otherwise occupied abroad. Luke's grasping harridan of a mother had run riot with the estate's income. It had taken Alistair years to refill the coffers. But that was old news and not worth getting into.

'I believe it is time to rescue my wife.'

Luke heaved a sigh. 'Then I bid you good day, Alistair.'

'I will walk you out to the stables.'

'Making sure I don't steal the silver on my way.'

The words were spoken loud enough for Alistair to hear and softly enough for him to ignore.

'The Duke doesn't like my father,' Jeffrey said, feeding another carrot to his pony, Rascal.

Out of the mouths of babes... 'Siblings often don't get along well.' She hadn't got along well with her older brothers after her parents had died.

'Father said they used to be good friends when they were my age.' He reached out and rubbed his pony's nose. The horse nuzzled his palm, looking for another treat. 'I'm not to fall out with my brother. Father said. Ever.'

'What is your brother's name?'

'Daniel. He's two years younger. His pony is smaller than Rascal. We usually ride out with Papa together, but Danny broke his arm two weeks ago.'

'Oh, I am sorry.'

'He followed me up the ladder. Now he can't do anything fun.' His face crumpled.

'And you feel partly to blame.'

'Danny flew the kite up on the roof of the barn and Ben, our man, was too busy mucking out to fetch it down. I should have waited.'

What a handful it must be with two lively boys and no wife to add a civilising influence. 'Did you ask him to follow you?'

'I told him to wait at the bottom, but Danny always follows me. I know this.'

'That is what your papa said?'

He swung on the stall rail, pivoting in a half-circle of drooping misery. 'I stayed indoors for a week.'

Relief shot through Julia. There were more severe punishments fathers visited upon their sons. Some visited upon wives by husbands also. 'To help you remember.'

He gave her a shy grin. 'Papa said he was proud of me for taking my punishment like a man.'

She gave him an encouraging smile. 'Shall we return to your papa?'

Jeffrey let go of the rail. 'I read to Danny every day after my lessons.' These were the tones of a long-suffering older brother. Had she seemed like such a burden to her own older brothers?

They headed up the aisle towards the stable entrance. A change of subject was needed. 'I expect you will be going away to school soon.' It was normal for boys of his age to board at a public school.

'School is expensive,' Jeffrey said in lowered tones. 'I go to the Vicar for lessons twice a week and then study at home. Danny is to start next year.'

Really. They were nephews of a duke. As head of the family, Alistair should be making sure they had a good education. If the father didn't want to send his boys away, they should at least have a proper tutor. The reason why Alistair was not helping seemed obvious. Male pride. On both sides. But why?

Outside, the sunshine dazzled her for a moment. 'Would you like to go away to school?'

'And leave Papa and Danny?' Although he

tried to hide it there was a touch of longing in his voice. 'Papa would be sad. More sad.'

Children understood a great deal more than adults gave them credit for.

He squinted. 'Papa!' He waved.

Two tall men strode across the courtyard. Alistair was taller and broader than his brother, but not by much. They were both handsome men, in their prime, one fair, one dark, and as unalike as brothers could be, but only the sight of Alistair made her heart give that funny little hop.

Strangely, Jeffrey was more like his uncle than his father.

A groom emerged from the stable with their visitors' horses in hand.

The farewells were awkward with Alistair barely unbending enough to offer a stiff bow.

Side by side she and Alistair watched them trot down the drive. 'Is everything all right?' she asked, since none of the tension she'd felt in him when his brother arrived had dissipated.

'He was concerned for my health.' Ice coated Alistair's voice.

Why would that not please him? She sensed there was more to it, but clearly he did not want to speak of it. 'A brotherly concern, then...' She hesitated.

'Hardly.'

'What on earth happened between you and your family?'

'It is not something I wish to discuss.'

He was shutting her out, the way he always did. 'We are married, Alistair, like it or not. You need to tell me—'

'I do not *need* to tell you anything. If you will excuse me, I have an appointment with my steward.'

He strode off in the direction of the estate office.

A feeling of loss welled up in her chest. What on earth had she said now?

The pain in her chest intensified as she walked back to a house where she felt like a guest. It wasn't good enough. She deserved more. If not love, then at least respect and affection. And she wasn't talking about what they got up to in the bedroom. She was, after all, for better or for worse, his Duchess.

If only she didn't suspect it was for worse. Perhaps the news of her barrenness having sunk in, he was after all regretting his choice.

'We generally meet here at Parsings,' Ellie said, emerging from her carriage to join Julia waiting in the lane where her own coach had dropped her a scant two minutes before. 'Poor

Lady Wiltshire and her rheumatism.' She glanced up at a sky full of threatening clouds. 'That is not going to help.'

They turned and walked arm in arm up the front path. 'Thank you for inviting me,' Julia replied. 'I have been looking forward to this all week.'

Looking forward to getting away from Sackfield and Alistair. Not that she'd seen much of him since he'd recovered from his accident. He'd been preoccupied, busy with his business affairs in Lewis's absence.

The butler admitted them and took them straight through the house to the conservatory, where three other ladies were already gathered. Ellie performed the introductions to Mrs Retson, the Vicar's wife, a pleasantly plump middle-aged woman; Lady Finney, the Squire's wife, with iron-grey hair and a gimlet eye; and Lady Wiltshire, a fashionable lady in her fifth decade and clearly a widow of means.

'That is everyone,' Lady Wiltshire said. 'Please, ladies, take a seat, let me pour you some tea.'

The butler bowed himself out.

'Have you thought any more of my suggestion for an assembly?' Ellie said over the rim of her cup.

'I think it is a brilliant idea,' Mrs Retson said,

her eyes bright. 'We haven't held an assembly since before the war. We are bound to draw quite a crowd with so many of our neighbours here for the summer. Everyone has been bemoaning the lack of a bell at St Agnes's for three years, I am sure they will be supportive.'

Lady Finney frowned. 'It will require some organisation. We will need a dedicated committee.'

'I take it you are in agreement,' Ellie said, smiling. 'What do you think, Your Grace?'

'I have not had the opportunity to help organise such an ambitious event,' Julia said, 'but, given the cause, I think it a worthy endeavour. While I do not feel qualified to lead the charge, I would like to offer to help with the decorations.'

Given her title was by far the highest in the room, if she had insisted on running the whole thing, the other women would have accepted it without demur, no matter their private opinions. But she was being honest with them. The only event she had arranged had been her eldest brother's wedding breakfast.

'I will take charge of tickets,' Mrs Retson said, her eyes gleaming.

'I will speak with Prosser about the catering,' Lady Finney said. 'He will want some watching, that one. Finney is sure he waters his ale, the scoundrel.'

'You will take charge, then, Marchioness?' Lady Wiltshire asked.

'Not at all,' Ellie said, smiling at the older woman. 'You know all the great families hereabouts. I would defer to your superior knowledge of who can be engaged for what role. I will deal with the music and the dancing.'

Julia relaxed as the ladies began discussing the merits of one day over another, one nurseryman over another, whether or not waltzing would be permitted and how many tickets should be sold without turning the affair into a terrible squeeze. This was what she had always wanted. To be part of something useful. To make a difference, in some small way.

'It seems we have our next steps laid out,' Lady Wiltshire finally declared. 'We will meet again in two weeks' time, if that will suit everyone?'

She used her cane to push to her feet and crossed the room to ring for their carriages.

Another woman entered the conservatory and stopped as if startled. Lady Dunstan.

'Oh,' the Dowager said. 'I do beg your pardon, Elmira, I was sure your company must have left by now.'

Lady Wiltshire raised a brow. 'We are just concluding, Isobel. I believe you know everyone?'

She turned to the room. 'Lady Dunstan is visiting me for a few days.'

Isobel smiled generally at the company, but her gaze rested longer on Julia's face. 'I do indeed know everyone.' She made a gracious movement with her hand. 'Please do not let me interrupt your meeting.'

Ellie rose to her feet, her expression polite but not warm. 'Our business is finished, Lady Dunstan. We were about to leave.'

The Dowager's warm brown eyes turned from Julia and for a moment her eyes hardened a fraction and her lips stiffened, but then in an instant the warmth was back. 'Lady Beauworth, how is your family? I gather it is growing apace since I saw you last. Congratulations on your heir and a spare.'

'Thank you,' Lady Beauworth said, buttoning her gloves.

Julia offered her hand to her hostess. 'Thank you for your kind hospitality and your invitation to join your committee.'

'Thank *you*, Your Grace,' the woman said warmly. 'Your participation is most welcome.'

The other ladies added their farewells, but when Julia made to leave, the Dowager Duchess touched her arm lightly. 'A word, Your Grace.'

Lady Finney, who had been speaking to her,

cast an enquiring look at Julia. Clearly to ignore the woman would be offering a snub that would have the county gossiping for weeks.

Ellie cast her a questioning look and Julia smiled at her. 'Please, do not wait for me, but tell my coachman I am on my way.'

Lady Wiltshire eyed her guest. 'If you do not mind, Isobel, I will see the other ladies off.'

'Please, do not trouble about us,' Lady Dunstan said. 'I won't keep Her Grace but a moment or two.'

The other ladies left the room.

Lady Dunstan gestured for Julia to sit down.

The Dowager gave her a sharp look. 'I heard the Duke was thrown from his horse. How is he?'

'He is well.'

The slanting eyes narrowed. 'Recovered, then?'

'Completely.' There was something about the woman's reaction that gave Julia a sense of unease, made her not want to mention his continuing headaches.

'Did you speak to him about the dower house?'

'I mentioned it.'

'And he refuses his aid.' She made a dismissive gesture with an elegant hand. 'It does not surprise me in the least. He has no family feeling at all or he would not have disappeared the way he did. *Travelling*, he said.' She made a scornful sound. 'You can imagine how that made us feel, after leaving us to believe the worst. My poor husband had an apoplexy when he turned up missing when the peace broke.' She patted Julia's hand. 'Well, well. It is all in the past. I am simply glad to have made your acquaintance even if Alistair would keep us apart. Let us continue our friendship, despite him. Come for tea in a day or so. Elmira will not mind. We will have a long and comfortable coze.'

Discomfort slithered down Julia's spine. Strange to have such a feeling, when the woman was so friendly. She ought to feel sorry for the woman's feeling of exclusion instead of uncomfortable. 'I will send you a note and let you know when it is convenient.'

'Wonderful. Let me see you to the door.'

The Dowager put her arm through Julia's and they strolled down the corridor leading to the front door.

A young man walking down the stairs stopped short at the sight of them. 'Aunt,' he said, 'there you are. There is something— Bless me! It is you, Your Grace.'

'You two know each other?' Lady Dunstan asked.

'We met in Hyde Park,' the young man said. 'Percy Hepple, your cousin, Your Grace. You do remember?'

'I do.' She held out her hand. 'How lovely to meet you again, Mr Hepple. What are you doing in Hampshire?'

'Serving as my escort,' Lady Dunstan said, her voice dry. 'Percy is rusticating. As far from his papa as he can get.' She lowered her voice. 'In Dun territory, you know.'

'Aunt,' Percy said, colouring up, 'no need to set rumours about. It is a minor setback, is all. I shall come about when next quarter rolls around.' He winced. 'I might drop in on His Grace later this week. See if he might be willing to sport a bit of the ready. Put me dibs in tune again.' His smile was rather forced.

Julia could only imagine Alistair's response at this young man applying to him for money.

'Nonsense,' his aunt answered before she could say anything. 'You know very well Alistair will only lecture and prose on about budgeting.' She gave a light laugh with a brittle edge. 'It is your father you should approach.'

But Percy wasn't listening. He was looking at Julia with an odd light in his eye. Indeed, his gaze wandered over her, coming to rest briefly in the area of her chest before returning to her face.

'You know, Coz, I thought it when we were introduced in the park and I think it again now— we have met somewhere before.'

Aghast, Julia froze. He could not have been at Mrs B.'s the night of the auction. Please, no, not that.

'I do not believe so,' she said, horrified by the tremble in her voice.

Percy frowned. 'I am sure of it. I will think of it, you will see.'

She prayed not.

'Enough of your flirting,' Lady Dunstan said lightly, but her eyes were fixed on Percy as if she sensed an underlying truth in his words.

She turned her narrowed eyes on Julia. 'Come, Your Grace, before your coachman frets about his horses. Please give my regards to my dear step-son, will you not? Tell him a call here would be most welcome. For Percy's sake, if not for mine.'

Julia's heart sank. She could already hear the ice in Alistair's reply when she imparted that message. And dare she ask him if Mr Percy Hepple had been anywhere near Mrs B.'s on the night of the auction?

She shuddered.

Chapter Thirteen

Alistair looked up as his wife entered his office. *His wife.* Why did his mind keep lingering over those two words as if the sound of them now gave him satisfaction? A sense of comfort when everything about their marriage was wrong and was set fair to get worse. Guilt rode him hard.

He frowned. Something was wrong. There were shadows in her eyes.

He got up and came around to lean against the front of his desk, removing at least the physical barrier between them. 'How was the meeting?' Even as he asked, his sense of her unease, her anxiety, intensified.

'Your stepmother was there.'

He hissed in a breath, swallowing a curse. 'At Beauworth's?'

Julia wandered the room, touching the spines of books on the shelves, a china dog on the table, a pile of papers on the corner of his desk. Her fingers were long and elegant and the memory of them stroking his flesh made desire a heavy beat in his blood. He desired her too much, but more than that he wanted her happiness. The one thing that it was not in his power to give.

'The meeting was held at Lady Wiltshire's house,' she said over her shoulder. 'It usually is. Did I not say?'

She had not. Nor had he asked where the meeting was to be held, come to think of it. He'd simply assumed it was at Beauworth.

'Lady Wiltshire is one of my stepmother's cronies.' Something Julia would not have known. Not that knowing would have made a jot of difference.

She turned to face him, her teeth sinking into her bottom lip in a way that made him want to bite it, too. 'Alistair, she is very cordial.'

A black widow spider might seem cordial upon first acquaintance. He shrugged.

'Your cousin, Percy Hepple, is also visiting Lady Wiltshire,' she continued. 'It seems your cousin is hopeful of speaking with you.'

He groaned inwardly. Though harmless, like all family, Percy was a royal pain in the buttocks. 'Rusticating, is he? Hiding out from his creditors.'

A small smile curved her lips. 'It would seem so.' The smile disappeared, replaced by a frown.

'He's a wastrel and a fribble. Pay him no mind.'

The frown did not disappear. 'Should we perhaps invite them to dine?'

She sounded so hesitant. So unsure.

How could he ever explain that the last thing he ever would want was to spend time with any member of his family and particularly not his stepmother? A woman who seemed cordial. Entertaining her would only serve to encourage her, then lead to accusations, tears and duns for money while she bludgeoned him with what she called his cruelty in going against his father's wishes.

All because she refused to live within her means. Within the unbelievably generous settlement his father had put in place and that Alistair had struggled to maintain each and every quarter when he first returned to England. And while his cousin Percy was harmless and would be happy with a few guineas in his pocket, Percy's papa would resent the interference. 'I will send her a note. Did she say how long she was staying?'

'No. She invited me to call on her again.' She flushed. 'She invited us.'

So that was the crux of the matter. The reason for her hesitation. 'No.'

Her gaze shot to his face and away again.

'You disagree?' he asked, gritting his teeth.

'I can have no opinion one way or the other, Alistair. She is your family.'

Ice filled his veins. His stepmother was working her wiles again. This time trying to turn his wife against him as she had done with his father. 'She is no relation at all. It is my most fervent wish that you have no more contact with her or Percy for that matter.'

The anxiety in her eyes increased. 'As you wish.'

He hated that she sounded so crushed. But he had no intention of starting down the road of confidences, of telling her the reasons for his antipathy, some of them founded on instinct rather than fact. One confidence might lead to another. The idea that she would learn just how badly he had betrayed his family, and her, made him physically ill.

As did the sight of her unhappiness. Hell and damnation. Things had been going along quite well between them these past few days. Why could she not simply accept that he wanted nothing to do with Isobel? If she could do that, then there was a chance this marriage could work reasonably well for them both.

They could even perhaps continue to make

love. Surely, if any man could give her only the pleasure of his body, it was he.

Robins came in from the dressing room, carrying a tray. 'I sent down for some warm milk.' Robins's voice was full of sympathy. And something else. Sadness? She placed the glass on the bedside table. 'This will help you sleep. And I have rewarmed the hot water bottle His Grace sent up earlier.' She tucked it in between the sheets.

'You are very kind.' Julia eyed the tumbler with misgivings. Robins had taken delivery of the tray through the servants' door tucked away in her dressing room. A way of staff coming and going without disturbing their employers. The question was, did it contain laudanum? And did it arrive at the door already laced, or had Robins added it before she brought it in? Whichever it was, the question of why and on whose behalf continued to torture her.

Robins gave her an encouraging smile. 'Drink your milk while it is warm.'

Unwillingly, Julia picked up the drink and cradled it in her palms. The idea of warm milk was indeed comforting. She lifted the glass and sniffed.

Laudanum. The scent stronger than usual.

She wanted to hurl the glass across the room. Instead she watched Robins gather up her gown and shawl and carry them off to the dressing room. As quick as she could, she disposed of the milk in the chamber pot she had placed beneath the bed. Robins smiled when she returned. 'Sleep well, Your Grace.' She carried the glass away, closing the chamber door behind her.

Julia snuggled deeper under the covers. How did one sleep well with the grinding ache of fear in one's belly and nagging away in one's brain. A fear that made it almost impossible to eat or drink anything.

Despite her struggle to keep her eyes open, exhaustion claimed her. She felt herself sinking into darkness. A nap. She would nap for a bit.

It was hard to breathe.

Something was pressing down on her chest. Something soft was covering her face. She tried to sit up. Too heavy. She fought against the weight flailing. Her hands tangled with her attacker's hair. She tugged.

A screech of pain. The weight shifted. She grabbed a bony wrist and twisted hard. A yell. Something, or someone, landed on the floor.

Panting, she shot out of bed.

The door between her room and Alistair's

banged against the wall. 'What the devil is going on?'

Alistair, candle in hand, wearing his dressing gown, his hair dishevelled, stared at first at Julia and then at Robins, who was hunched up on the floor, weeping. A pillow lay next to her on the carpet.

'Julia?' he said. 'Are you all right.'

Julia swallowed.

Alistair stepped towards her. Instinctively, she backed away. His eyes widened. 'It is all right,' he said softly, holding out a hand, as if gentling a skittish horse. 'Tell me what happened.'

She glanced down at Robins. 'She attacked me.'

'What?' He seemed so absolutely stunned, so horrified, she could not help but take comfort in it.

Alistair pulled the weeping Robins to her feet. He shoved her into a chair when she seemed unable to stand unaided. 'Is this correct?'

The woman cried even harder.

'Robins,' Julia said sharply. 'Answer His Grace.'

The woman hiccupped.

Julia fetched a glass of water from the washstand and shoved it at her. She was so angry she didn't know why she didn't throw it in her face. 'Drink it and calm yourself.'

The woman drank.

'What the devil is going on?' Alistair's voice crackled with ice.

When the woman took in the rage in his face, she shrank away. 'He said he would kill my daughter.'

'He?' Alistair said, his quiet voice far more menacing than a shout.

Robins flinched. The glass trembled in her hand. 'A man.'

'What man?' Julia asked, more gently, controlling her own anger, her sense of betrayal by this woman who looked ready to collapse.

'He came to my last position and told me I would be offered a place with Her Grace. I was to take it if I wanted my daughter to reach her next birthday. She's only five.' She burst into tears.

Threatening a child. The height of cruelty. Julia shook her head at Alistair, who looked ready for murder. 'Tell us everything, Robins.'

Robins burst into sobs again. Julia wanted to shake her. 'Calm yourself. Who is this man you speak of?'

'I do not know,' she said, gasping for breath. 'Please. He told me I would never see Minnie again if I did not do exactly as I was told.'

Julia felt sympathy, but also anger. The woman should have trusted her instead of…

'You have been putting laudanum in my tea and chocolate. To what end?'

The woman started sobbing again. 'I'm s-s-sorry.'

Alistair cursed softly. 'You said nothing of this.'

Julia looked up from the woman hunched in the chair and squared her shoulders. 'How could I? I did not know who was doing it.'

He looked horrified. And cut to the quick. He inhaled a deep breath. 'We will talk of this. Right now we must discover who means you harm. How did you know…?'

'The poppy in laudanum makes me violently ill. It has done so ever since I was a child. It took a few days for me to realise why I did not like the chocolate I was given each morning. And why I was so violently ill. I stopped drinking the chocolate. It then turned up in my tea.'

Robins looked up, her eyes red and swollen. 'That is why you were ill? I thought it was the travelling.'

And her husband had suspected she was with child. Julia glanced at Alistair. He looked shame-faced.

'I knew you were bringing the stuff to me, Robins, but I did not know if you were part of the plot. Or someone's dupe. Or what exactly the laudanum was supposed to accomplish.' She took a deep breath and looked at Alistair. 'She tried to smother me with that pillow.'

'Dear God...' he breathed. He glared at Robins. 'Is this true?'

She nodded miserably. 'He said I was taking too long. His employer wanted it done with.'

A shudder went through Julia at how cavalierly the woman spoke of her death. Yet if she had a child, would she not do anything to protect it? Anything at all. Even murder?

Alistair's fists clenched as if he would strike the woman. 'And once she was dead? What then?'

Robins shrugged. 'Minnie would have been safe.'

Alistair paced away as if he could not bear to be near her. He kicked at the logs in the fire, sparking them to life.

'This man,' Alistair said, swinging around suddenly. 'Did I see you speaking to him in the village the other day?'

She nodded. 'I didn't think you saw us.' She gazed at Julia. 'Your Grace, I am so sorry. I had to do it. I couldn't let them hurt my little girl. And now...' Sobbing, she buried her face in her hands. 'They will kill Minnie for certain,' she wailed.

'What would you have done if my wife had

been in bed with me tonight?' Alistair asked, his voice full of ice.

Robins struggled to breath. 'Waited for another night, I suppose. It isn't as if you come to her all that often.'

The coldness of the words stung Julia like a slap to the face. The woman's betrayal hurt so much, she did not want to be near her. She rose to her feet, anger making it hard to think clearly.

'When do you meet this man again?' Alistair asked, the menace in his voice making Robins shrink back. 'And where.'

The woman wrung her hands. 'He finds me. Or sends a note. I never know when to expect him.'

She sounded resigned.

'What are you thinking, Alistair?' Julia asked.

'I am thinking you need your rest.' He glared at Robins. 'Give me the key to your room.'

The woman fumbled in her pocket and handed over a key. 'What will you do with me?'

'I will decide that in the morning.' He walked over to the door. 'For tonight I am going to lock you in your room where you can do no more harm.'

'Please, Your Grace,' Robins said, looking at Julia, her eyes wide. 'Don't hand me over to the magistrate. My daughter...' She started sobbing again.

'Do as His Grace ordered,' Julia said, but pity for the child made her soften her tone.

The woman scuttled from the room followed by Alistair, who returned a few moments later.

'Alistair—' Julia said. Her knees felt suddenly weak. Fear, anger, even relief all warred with each other for attention.

'Hush.' He picked her up in his arms and carried her into his bedroom. 'It is all right. She's safely locked away. She cannot hurt you.'

He gazed down into her face and she saw he was worried. For her? All at once she felt safer than she had for days. 'It is so hard to believe that someone wants me dead.' She shuddered.

He nodded tersely. 'You've had a shock. You need to rest.'

Tenderly he lay her on his bed and pulled the covers over her. 'Sleep now. We will talk in the morning.' He snuggled in beside her and held her close, gently running his hand over her back in circles.

She felt cherished. And strangely happy. As if she had drunk too much champagne, something she had done only once as a girl at her very first house party.

She lifted her head and kissed his cheek. 'Thank you for coming in time.'

'Sleep,' he said and his voice was gruff.

* * *

Alistair put the breakfast tray on the end of the bed and leaned over his wife. Pride filled him as he saw she slept soundly. Trust. It was a heady thing, even if he hadn't truly earned it. The idea that she had feared he might be the one causing her harm had been a bitter but not undeserved blow. He struggled with his sudden urge to tell her the truth, expose his guilt, yet it wasn't his secret to share.

'Wake up, sleepy head,' he said, jostling her shoulder.

She opened her eyes. The moment her gaze focused on him she beamed. The beauty of her smile went straight to his groin, robbing his brain of all but lust. Now was not the right time, for so many reasons. He forced himself to focus on the task at hand.

'Sit up. I brought breakfast on a tray so we can talk without interruption.'

Once they were settled with the tray between them and she had a cup of tea in her hands, Alistair took hold of his courage in both hands.

'I sent Robins away,' he said.

Her teacup rattled in the saucer and he steadied it, letting go only when he saw she had pulled herself together.

'I put her in my carriage at four this morning

and sent her off with Jaimie to collect her family. Jaimie will hide them away until we discover who is behind this plot to have you harmed.'

She frowned. 'Why?'

He hadn't slept a wink all night, thinking about this very thing. 'One thing I know for certain, if we involve the magistrate it will create a great scandal. A blot on the family escutcheon.' Not to mention bringing Julia into the limelight where her past might be revealed. 'Her child is an innocent in all of this and she would suffer greatly if the mother was convicted of a crime.'

Her eyes widened in surprise. 'That is generous of you.'

'No matter what people say of me, I am not completely heartless.' He wondered if she believed him but suspected she did not and that hurt more than he liked to admit. 'Jaimie will get them away before the people involved realise what happened. He'll spread some rumours at the local watering hole of a death in her family.'

Julia sipped at her tea. 'And so you pre-empt any strike at the child they might make in retaliation.' She sighed. 'As angry as I am with Robins, I would not like the child to suffer. But we still do not know who *they* are. Or why they are doing this.'

Shadows of doubt remained in her eyes. Did

she doubt him? How much more could he say to assure her he meant her no harm? That her welfare was important to him.

His mind went back to the deliberate sabotaging of his saddle. He could not help surmising that whoever was behind this attack was using his wife as a means to destroy him. Who, other than him, would have been accused of her murder, if Robins had succeeded?

Whatever the case, he would bet his title that his brother was involved, possibly with the help of his stepmother. And, Alistair admitted, with an arrow of pain that pierced his soul, his brother had good reason to hurt him. However, coming after Julia was a huge mistake. An act of aggression he would not tolerate.

He toyed with the idea of telling Julia his suspicions. Of easing her suspicions about him, but then he would have to tell her the whole story and she'd know exactly how badly he'd misled her. How shameful he really was. Self-disgust roiled in his gut. If she ever learned the truth he would likely lose her entirely.

'I think we should talk to Digger. She might have some ideas.'

Chapter Fourteen

Seeing Julia and Digger together, talking like old friends, did something to Alistair's insides. He rubbed at the strange ache behind his sternum.

But for the folly of his youth, this sort of camaraderie with his wife might have been his. 'Might' being the operative word. A man with a lofty title was a target for every matchmaking mama in the kingdom. More likely he'd have married for power and position and never known Julia at all.

As a man, he counted for nothing. There was only his duty to the Duchy. Especially after what he'd done. He knew it in his mind, yet there was this aching loneliness inside him for something more, something better for them both, but especially for Julia.

While she had married him as an escape—a choice between transportation, life in a bordello or him—with all this going on, he wasn't sure she had made the right choice in choosing him.

They had both gone into this marriage with open eyes. No illusions of sentiment. But now he knew her better, the dissembling left him feeling horribly guilty.

'So when before you said someone was trying to poison you,' Digger said after hearing the entire tale, 'you were not joking?'

'Not poison,' Julia said. 'Put me to sleep so soundly I would not awaken at the attempt to smother me.'

Digger shook her head and tutted. 'How awful. Do you suspect who might be behind this terrible deed?'

Alistair quelled the urge to smile at the dear lady's excitement at being presented with a mystery to solve. It really was no smiling matter, but he could see Digger was thrilled they had brought her their problems.

Julia shook her head and looked at Alistair.

'My brother. He is the only one who gains.'

Digger looked pained. 'I can't believe my dear little Luke would do anything so mean.'

She might believe it if she knew how badly Alistair had betrayed his brother. Plus the fact that someone at Beauworth had tampered with his saddle. Not to mention that a ship sent by

Alistair's father to bring him home from Italy had sailed off without him and the captain fled to America. She might. But Digger was steadfast in her loyalty to both him and Luke.

'Once they realise Robins is gone,' Julia said, 'are they likely to try another tack?'

'Highly likely.' But not one which would involve Julia if he had any say in the matter.

'Perhaps I could lure them out into the open,' Julia mused.

'Leave yourself exposed?' Digger said, looking shocked, but also intrigued.

'No!' Alistair almost shouted. 'Categorically not,' he said more calmly. The thought of it made his blood run cold.

Julia frowned at him.

'Then how do we ferret them out?' Digger said, pursing her lips. 'Do we know yet who recommended Robins to Julia?'

'We do not. I wrote to Lewis a few days ago, but he has a great deal on his plate. I know he will reply at the first opportunity.'

'You don't suspect him?' Julia asked. 'Mr Lewis? He did leave the moment things started happening.'

Admiration for his wife's quick wit assaulted him anew. Why hadn't he thought of Lewis as a suspect?

He considered the idea. 'Honestly, I cannot believe it of him.' Whereas he could believe it of his half-brother. 'And besides, what would it gain him?'

Silence descended.

'Then we do nothing,' Julia said. 'And wait to hear from Lewis.' She sounded upset.

He reached across the table and took her hand. 'I will make sure nothing untoward happens in the meantime.' Even if he had to lock her in her room and stand a guard at the door.

Hell, talk about the need to protect his own. It had been there all along, of course, or he would never have married her. He could only hope he could keep her safe. Failing was not an option. It was his fault she was in danger.

Fortunately, the look on her face said she drew comfort from his words and that pleased him far more than he would ever have believed possible a few short weeks ago.

And he realised he would protect her with his life if need be.

He released her hand and sat back. 'Julia, you will not go anywhere without me or one of my handpicked men.'

In the meantime, *he* was going to see if he could lure his enemies into making a mistake.

Digger was looking at him from beneath lowered grey brows. 'Alistair, is there something you are not telling us?'

He should have guessed Digger would see through him. He gave her a smile of complete innocence. 'Nothing at all.'

She narrowed her eyes. 'Then I suggest you write to your Mr Lewis again and tell him an answer is needed sooner rather than later. We must know as soon as possible who it was who recommended Mrs Robins to him for Her Grace.'

'I agree.'

'I wish you would call me Julia,' his wife said to Digger, albeit a little hesitantly, but with a very sweet smile for a lady Alistair held in great affection. Julia went up another notch in his esteem. If he wasn't careful he would soon be putty in her lovely elegant hands. Chill settled over him like a blanket. While she might mean a great deal to him, for her sake he could never let her get too close.

He glanced at the clock on the mantel. 'I hate to spoil our tête-à-tête, but my bailiff is due to see me shortly.' He rose. 'Julia?'

'She can stay a little longer, Crawfy dear. We have such a lot to talk about.'

Inwardly he groaned, guessing who would be the topic of their conversation. Fortunately, not even Digger knew all his secrets or even she might not look on him so kindly.

One thing he knew for certain, he was a danger to anyone around him, so the further he kept away from them the better.

Loneliness weighed down on his chest. The accompanying dark empty space inside him made breathing a chore. As usual he ignored the feeling. Buried it in ice. 'I'll have Matthew come for you in half an hour and see you back to the house.'

Julia was staring at him oddly. 'Is that really necessary?'

'For now.' It was if he was not going to go mad with worry.

He bowed and left.

Julia paced her bedroom. She knew she was safe—Alistair was only a few steps away, within earshot of her call despite the closed doors, but she could not convince herself to get into the bed.

She should have said something before they retired for the night. Asked him to stay, but in truth she feared his rejection. As wanton as it sounded, even in the depths of her own thoughts, she dared to believe he desired her as much as she desired him.

The night they first met, their lovemaking had

been spectacular, passionate and exceedingly naughty. The games he'd played with her had been shocking and wonderful. She'd seen little of that playful man since their wedding. Occasional gleams of amusement in eyes usually icy cold, the odd crack of laughter, and those nights that he'd come to her... The wicked side of him was still there, hidden, kept rigidly under control by the Duke.

She came to a halt at their adjoining door. Stared at the door handle. If he turned her away...

She took a deep breath and quietly opened the door. Silent as a ghost she glided through the dressing rooms, hers and his, that separated their rooms. In the old days, their servants would have slept on little cots in these commodious chambers that now contained only presses full of clothes. Thank goodness they now slept in the attics. She paused at the final door.

Straightened her shoulders. If he was asleep, she wouldn't wake him. She might, however, cuddle in beside him, the way she had on the night of his fall.

She eased the door open and peeped inside.

The great four-poster bed was empty.

Disappointment hollowed a place near her heart. She'd been so sure she'd heard him moving around in here after he'd escorted her to her chamber after dinner.

About to turn away, she became aware of a shadow partially blocking her view of the banked fire in the hearth. A shadow too bulky to be simply an armchair. The shadow moved. Rose.

'Julia?'

She could not retreat now. She stepped closer. 'Yes. It is I.' He was wearing his dressing gown. He had a tumbler in his hand. There were a great many things this man could do with his drink that had nothing to do with imbibing.

'Are you unwell?'

'I couldn't sleep.'

He led her to his chair and sat down with her on his lap. She rested her head on his broad shoulder and inhaled the scent of soap and husband laced with the fragrance of brandy.

'You neither, I assume,' she said.

He settled her more comfortably in his lap and lifted his glass to her lips. 'Drink?'

She took a tiny sip and let the liquid burn a path down her throat. She sighed.

He tightened his grip about her shoulders. 'You are perfectly safe. I have two men I trust in the corridor. Not even a bat could come through the windows.'

'It isn't that.'

He dipped his chin in enquiry. The low light from the fire cast his face in a series of planes and dark hollows. Gave him a demonic look. She cupped his cheek, felt the faint prickle of new stubble against her palm. 'Oh, it is part of it.'

'And the other part?'

'I was missing you.' She held her breath. Would he admit to missing her too?

'I am here.'

Clearly not. 'And so am I, now.'

His lips twitched, displaying for the briefest moment that elusive smile.

She smiled back. 'I know. A bit obvious, but sometimes I feel as if you need to be reminded.'

'I apologise. I will be more attentive in future.'

A flicker of anger coursed through her veins at his politeness. 'Please, if it is another duty, another responsibility to be added to your long list, do not trouble yourself.'

Time to go. She pushed away from him.

'Stay,' he said softly. 'I am in need of your company.'

Thank the stars in the heavens. At least he could admit to needing something. 'You are worried.'

'Not only worried. I am angry. Someone tried to cause you harm and very nearly succeeded.'

He gave her another sip of his drink and for

long minutes they gazed into the fire. His heart-beat was a steady rhythm against her cheek, each inhale and exhale lifting her a fraction. Unsure whether or not she should stay, she toyed with the ribbon at the end of the plait she wore to bed.

'You are quite recovered from the shock of last night?' The deep rumble of his voice was comforting. As was the squeeze of her shoulders and the feel of his breath against her neck.

A pleasurable shiver zipped down her spine. 'Completely,' she said softly. 'How is your head?'

'Cured.'

'I'm glad.'

From this angle she had an excellent view of an expanse of pale gold skin where his silk dressing gown gaped in a deep vee. A dark flat male nipple peeked out from a swirl of crisp golden hairs. Did he have any idea how much the sight of that tempted her tongue and teeth and lips?

She experimentally flicked it with the soft hairs at the end of her braid.

He hissed in a breath. His nipple furled up into a tight little point, the same way hers did when he touched them.

Fascinated, she did it again. This time he groaned softly, a dark sensual sound.

'You like that,' she said, delighted with her discovery.

'I don't like it.'

She froze.

'I adore it.' He flexed his hips and she felt the hard ridge of his arousal against her hip.

Oh, yes, he liked it, a lot. 'In that case…' She did it again, feathering the brush-like end around and over his chest, up his throat and across his lips.

He bared his teeth in a feral sort of smile and snapped his teeth. She whisked it away before his teeth closed over it. She explored his reaction to its touch on his manly nose, across the straight golden brows and across the sharp angles of cheekbone and jaw. He closed his eyes in pleasure at the soft sweeping stroke, but sucked in a breath when she traced the curvaceous shape of his ear. The sound set off little flutters low in her abdomen. Delicious.

She resisted the urge to squirm against his erection. Instead she teased her own lips to see how it felt.

His eyes grew heavy, watching the little tuft waft lightly back and forth. Not as soft as a feather, she decided. A bolder, more assertive sensation. Tingles tightened her nipples.

She gave him a naughty smile. 'I think it would make a fine paint brush. I could paint you pretty colours.'

'Could you now?' He gave her the lazy smile of a male who was charmed and entertained.

She tilted her head and stroked her braid brush across each cheekbone. 'Blue here.' A dab at the end of his nose. 'Red.' A feather-light stroke across an eyelid. 'Purple.'

He grinned. 'You would have to catch me first.'

She tickled his ear and a deep laugh erupted from his chest.

Unable to resist, she leaned forward and kissed his smiling mouth. He caught her by the nape, angled his head and deepened the kiss. She turned into him, pressing her aching breasts against his hard chest, resting her hands on his shoulders, her tongue sliding against the slick heat of his. Heat pooled between her thighs.

While their lips clung together, he rose effortlessly to his feet and carried her to his bed. He untied the belt of her dressing gown and drew it off. A moment later he laid her out naked on his bed.

His wife was a pagan goddess. Comfortable in her skin. Glorious in her nakedness with a glint in her eyes that was an invitation he could not have resisted, even if he wanted to. She looked good enough to eat, sprawled in abandon on his bed. Irresistible.

'I think we need to be rid of that braid,' he said,

eyeing the powerful weapon that had driven him nearly mad. 'May I?'

Teeth nipping her lower lip, she nodded her assent. His shaft twitched at the seductive sight of her lush mouth. Her gaze dropped to where the fabric of his robe jutted away from his groin. She licked her lips.

'Do not worry, it will still be there when needed.'

She smothered a laugh with her hand, her eyes dancing. He gazed at her beautiful body, with its lovely swells and hollows and long slender limbs. She was so lovely, he really didn't deserve such loveliness in his bed. But here she was and he would not disappoint.

He leaned over her and stroked the long rope of her hair, neatly plaited for sleeping. 'Such a pretty colour.'

She made a face of disagreement. 'It's brown.'

'Caramel. Toffee with a glint of gold in the sun.'

'Yours is gold,' she scoffed.

'Believe me, to me it is glorious.' He freed it from its ribbon with a quick tug. Slowly, he unravelled the plait from tip to root and stroked his fingers through the long, soft waving tresses, arranging them around her on the pillow and pulling them forward over her breasts. He caressed the soft strands with his fingertips. 'This is how Godiva must have looked.'

She chuckled. 'It feels thoroughly debauched.'

'My speciality.' He shed his robe and lay down alongside her. He buried his face in the fragrant mass of silk. Jasmine.

A moment later, she rose up and leaned over him, her hair gliding delicately across his shoulders and forming a veil around them both.

She lowered her head and kissed him so sweetly, his heart ached. He enfolded her lithe body in in his arms. This woman was special, precious. And she deserved so much better than him.

With gentle hands she stroked his hair back from his face and looked down into his eyes. 'You are a lovely man,' she whispered. 'Beautiful.'

He couldn't speak for the lump in his throat. Longing.

She didn't seem to notice as she returned to kissing her way down his body, pausing to nip his chin and lick at his nipples. He burned for her, his body on fire, his mind focused only on the feel of her tongue and lips and teeth. Finally she straddled his shins and sat back to admire his erection with a particularly arousing smile.

His breath caught in his throat at the idea she might...

She glanced at his face from beneath her lashes. 'Oh, I nearly forgot.'

He blinked, startled by her words. She reached back and felt in the pocket of the robe she'd been wearing and brought forth… The necklace from the Dunstan ruby parure, glowing gently in the soft light of the fire and the candle beside the bed.

'Julia?'

Her smile grew as artfully she arranged it just above his erection, the stones shockingly cold against his stomach at first. She drew back to take in the results of her handiwork. 'Tit for tat,' she said, her face full of mischief.

'Naughty.' He'd made love to her the first night they met with her wearing the full complement of rubies, the bracelets circling her breasts, an ear-bob in her navel and the necklace draped across her mons. A picture he would never forget as long as he lived.

He raised his head and gazed down at himself. 'They looked better on you.'

'That is your opinion, sir. To me you look good enough to eat.'

He groaned.

She leaned forward, gently cupping him, and delicately she licked up his shaft, circling her tongue around the crest.

Against his will, his hips rose up and he fisted

his hands in the sheets to keep himself still. When she took him in the warm wet heat of her mouth his mind went blank and his body rigid with desire. Tenderly, she swirled her tongue around the head. His spine tingled.

He croaked a warning.

Slowly, she released him and raised her head. Her eyes had a wicked gleam, her smile was teasing. 'Still ready, I see, Duke.'

In an instant he had her on her back.

'Now, Alistair,' she said, her voice husky with need.

A gentle touch confirmed she was ready and he pressed home to the hilt.

Her ecstatic sigh had him moving, setting a rhythm tied to each nuanced expression of pleasure on her face.

He thrust harder. Nails scraped his back. A hand kneaded his buttocks. Her legs came up around his waist.

'Yes…' she breathed. 'Alistair, yes.'

He drove into her and she moved her hips, setting the pace and the depth of penetration. Her inner muscles stroked him the way her mouth had and he lost all sense of self. They were one. He felt her body tighten as she approached her climax.

His own roared along his veins with unstoppable force. He couldn't… He must…

Then she shattered with his name a soft cry on her lips. He fell apart.

Never had he felt such an incredible feeling of pure joy. A sensation that went far beyond pleasure. An intimacy of the soul.

Longing filled him for something he had sought all his life, yet never dared to hope for until now. Warming a heart he'd thought frozen out of existence. He drifted on the warm tide of pleasure.

As bliss waned, so did the inexplicable emotions. When he finally came to his senses, he realised with dawning horror that he had not withdrawn from her body. His stomach fell away. The loss of control shook him to the core of his being.

Idiot! What on earth had been going on in his head? This was a physical connection, nothing else. He did *not* need it, though he had enjoyed it immensely, as had she. He certainly did not want ridiculous feelings cluttering up his mind or messing with his plans.

Anger at his stupidity filled him, and an odd sense of loss. Too bad. This must never happen again.

He rose and went for water and a cloth.

Julia raised her head, and regarded him with a sleepy gaze. 'Alistair, is something wrong?'

'Nothing.' His tone sounded harsher than he had intended, colder.

She frowned.

'It is all right, Julia.' He stroked her hair back from her face, where it had stuck to her cheek. He gave her lips a brief kiss. 'Everything is lovely. You are lovely.'

A smile and her eyes slid closed. If only he could believe she would not betray him the way everyone else had. He couldn't. In the end, they all did. Bitterness filled him. And loneliness.

He rose from the bed and dressed. For a moment he gazed down at her lovely face. Drank in her expression. Inhaled her scent.

The sight of the rubies tangled with the bed-sheets made him smile sadly. He picked them up, arranged them on the dressing table, and went downstairs to his study. To work.

Two days later, Julia went in search of the husband who had set her about with footmen, then set about avoiding her by riding out in the morning with his steward and sending apologetic notes about being unable to get home in time for dinner each evening. And when he did arrive home, after dinner he promptly went off to play billiards or chess with some neighbouring Squire, the same way he had avoided her in London.

She'd had quite enough. They needed to talk.

If not for Grindle whispering in her ear, she would not have known to find him in his estate office this morning.

He looked up from a pile of papers that looked higher than when she had been in here the last time. For a second or two a smile of welcome hovered on his lips. It disappeared so fast she wondered if he'd been expecting someone else. His face was thinner than it had been. His eyes were shadowed and weary.

'Julia. How unexpected.' He looked as if he'd lost a sovereign and found a penny.

Reaching for calm, she forced herself to gaze past him to the desk. 'No word from Mr Lewis?'

'Not as yet.' He remained behind his desk, keeping distance between them.

'I see Jaimie McPherson has returned,' she ventured. 'I assume Mrs Robins is settled.'

His lips flattened. 'She is. How are you?'

'Well enough for anything.'

He raised a brow. 'How may I be of service?'

The vision his words conjured in her mind caused a pulse of pleasure that had her squeezing her thighs together. A flicker of the muscle in his jaw made her think he had noticed her response.

She inhaled and straightened her shoulders,

moving away, seeking courage. 'I wanted to discuss our marriage.'

His fair brows drew down. 'In what regard?'

'The lack thereof.'

He gestured for her to sit. 'Shall I call for the tea tray?'

'Perhaps afterwards.' She wanted this over with. She perched on the edge of the chair in front of the desk. 'Alistair, I cannot blame you if you think marrying me was a mistake, but we are stuck with it.'

He frowned. 'I am not sure I understand your meaning.'

'For one thing, you are now avoiding my company as if I have the plague.'

His expression became more remote. 'There has been a great deal of business requiring my attention. Things that Lewis—'

'Even you do not work all night.' Oh, there were the longings again pressing to the fore. Heat scalded her face. 'I hear you late at night.' Through doors he now kept locked.

His lips thinned. Deep lines bracketed his mouth. 'You have been ill. I thought it best—'

'Alistair, please. Do not lie to me.'

He rose to his feet and leaned over the table hands planted flat on the surface. 'How dare you, madam?'

She flinched at the ice in his tone, but rose to face him. 'When I told you I was barren, when you said not to worry, I thought you were being kind. That you were offering comfort. But that wasn't it, was it? The other night when you—' She made a circle with one hand. 'You don't want to even try for a child with me, do you?'

He shook his head. 'I do not.'

She sank back on her chair, the pain in her heart making it hard to draw breath. 'Why?' she whispered. 'Is it because of what I did? Where you found me? You are ashamed.'

He looked shocked. Stunned. 'Certainly not.'

The pain eased a little. 'Then what?'

He closed his eyes briefly, then stared up at the ceiling. 'I already have an heir of my body.'

The words made no sense. Nor did the anguish in his gaze. 'You have an heir? You were previously married?' Why had he never mentioned this? Why not so much as a hint of having had a child? She frowned. 'My child would not supplant your previous issue.'

He gazed at her, his face a mask of bitterness, his eyes like shards of ice. 'I have never been married. Any son of yours would supplant Jeffrey.'

'Your nephew?'

'My son.'

Her stomach fell away in a sickening lurch. The dissolute Duke. No woman had been safe from his seduction. All the rumours battered at her mind. He'd played his own brother false. 'That is…awful.'

She struggled out of the chair, stumbled blindly for the door. How could he? She turned back. 'You never intended to wed.'

He held himself rigid. 'No more than you did.'

What a fool she had been to hope that this marriage could be better than her last. 'I wish I had never met you.'

His lip curled. 'I suppose you would have preferred old Lord Pefferlaw to have won the bidding that night?'

A low blow. She straightened her spine. 'It might have been a whole lot better than ending up with you. At least I would have known where I stood. At least he wouldn't have pretended to care.' At least he wouldn't have stolen her heart and then walked all over it.

She stalked out where she ran the gauntlet of three hovering footmen and a worried-looking Grindle. They must have heard the anger in their voices, if not the words.

Finally, in her chamber, she gave in to the anger coursing through her veins. And the despair.

She threw herself on to the bed and struck

her pillow with her fist. Damn him. All the time she'd had this faint little hope he was beginning to care for her the way she cared for him, that perhaps caring might make a difference to her ability to conceive. What a joke. He cared only for the rights of another woman's child.

Worst of all, how could she blame him for trying to do his duty by his son? Jeffrey was an innocent in the whole horrid mess.

Reality lay heavily on her chest. They were married and there was no way out.

For either of them. Bleakness filled her heart.

The old adage, be careful what you wish for, certainly seemed to hold true in Alistair's case. He'd started off wanting to keep his wife at a distance and now she barely spoke to him. Day by day what little accord they'd found in their marriage was withering on the vine.

And while he'd hedged her about with the footmen he trusted, he'd been riding around the estate day in and day out in hopes of flushing out his enemy.

He handed his reins over to Jaimie, who gave him a look of exasperation, but since the man's previous admonitions about overdoing things after his *accident* had gone unheeded, the man merely shook his head and went off to walk the horse out.

Once indoors, Grindle met him with an envelope. He didn't recognise the seal. Something ornate with a ship in the middle and cherubs blowing trumpets. He did, however, recognise the return address.

At last! Word from Lewis. Now he would know the identity of his enemy.

He broke the seal with his nail, cursing when his own letters, both of them unopened, dropped to the floor. He picked them up and wandered into his study. A quick scan of the note from Lewis's mother had him grinding his teeth. His first missive had arrived the day after Lewis's father's funeral. The same day the man had left the family estate for parts unknown.

He sank into his chair. This was the worst possible news. He wanted to have it out with Luke, but without any evidence, he was handicapped.

He pressed his fingers to his temples. The headaches returned when he was tired. Perhaps he should heed Jaimie's warnings. Certainly, Julia no longer cared where he went or what happened to him. As he deserved. Indeed, the further he kept from her, the more likely she was to be safe because with Robins out of the picture, he was certain the attacks were primarily aimed at him.

He eyed the rectangular box in the middle of his desk. The hand delivery from a jeweller. He knew exactly what it contained. Rather than open it, he shoved it in the bottom drawer of his writing table.

Wearily he dragged himself up the stairs to change for dinner. Not that there was much point. Julia wouldn't join him. Since his revelation about Jeffrey, she preferred a tray in her chamber.

If she knew she filled his thoughts for more than half of his waking day and most of his dreams at night, would she feel even a little in charity with him? Likely not.

He hated that she'd turned away from him, but he felt some relief that she knew the truth, even if her hurt did not lessen his determination to do the right thing.

What would he do if she sought solace with another man? His fists clenched at the idea. Marrying her had been utterly selfish. Wrong.

Every day, he fought the urge to seek her out. He'd tried to make himself believe she was no different than all those other women who had merely wanted him for the title and money. That he couldn't trust her. He tried to hang on to the resentment that had kept him single all these years.

But time after time he found himself picturing her smiles. Remembering how she'd held his head in her lap in that field. Seeing her courage when faced with a murderer and experiencing the fear all over again for her safety. No matter how he wished things were different, wished that he had never met Elise, the past remained set in stone.

Since Robins's departure there had been no more incidents of laudanum in her drink. He'd had a word with Cook, who ensured no one else put a hand on anything Julia ingested. Only a handful of his most trusted servants, people who had known him since he was a child, were permitted to handle her tray and to guard her night and day.

He'd talked his plan over with Digger privately and she had agreed it was the best way to proceed. Against her better judgement, she'd agreed to say nothing of his worry to Julia. She'd remonstrated, of course. Vigorously. She always did, but in the end she'd given in.

As for the state of their marriage, there was little he could do. There was no marriage. He'd made sure of it by staying away from her.

The gossips among the servants would soon spread the news that the Duke and Duchess were at outs and there were no heirs in the offing.

The hurt he'd caused Julia was a bitter ache in his heart, but hopefully, it would keep her safe from the threat of his brother until he had the proof he needed to face Luke with his crime. Lack of word from Lewis was an unexpected hitch in his plan.

Julia might be safer if he sent her away.

Such a draconian step would end any hope of making a go of what little marriage they had left. He rubbed at his sternum, trying to ease the ache knowing it might be the only answer.

After breakfast in her chamber, and having ascertained Alistair had left with his steward, Julia descended to the drawing room.

Disconsolately, she stared at her needlework. Another handkerchief for Alistair, to be embroidered with his initials. Was there really any point? But she had to do something to pass the time and the cushions were finished.

It was sad that she and Alistair had arrived at this impasse. Heartbreaking, if she was honest. The few times their paths had crossed these last few days she had the feeling he also was lonely. Perhaps another woman might have reached him. One with more sophistication. Or a less-chequered past. A lump rose in her throat.

And since it was out in the open that he didn't need a wife, he would no doubt go elsewhere for pleasure. If that happened, she would leave. She swallowed the lump in her throat.

* * *

'A note has arrived for you, Your Grace,' Grindle said an hour or so later, offering her a silver salver.

Putting aside her hoop, Julia broke the seal. The note was from Lady Wiltshire. Apparently an emergency meeting of the committee had been called for that afternoon and her presence was required.

At least someone had some faith in her abilities as a duchess. Could she be bothered? She ought to go. It was her duty, after all. Doing something constructive might serve as a distraction from the miseries of her marriage. At least she'd feel useful, since her husband had no use for her at all.

'Can you have the carriage brought around, please, Grindle?'

'Most of the staff are off this afternoon, Your Grace. I only have one footman available to go with you. Mr McPherson took one of the horses to the blacksmith, I understand.'

'One should be enough, surely?'

He looked worried. 'His Grace asked that two men accompany you at all times.'

So she was left housebound? Irritation prickled along her skin. 'I will have two. John Coachman and a footman.'

Grindle bowed and looked relieved. 'Yes, Your Grace.'

* * *

At two o'clock she was admitted to the Wiltshire house by a puzzled-looking butler. 'Her ladyship is in the conservatory, Your Grace.'

'Julia,' a female voice said.

She looked up at the imperious note in the voice of the woman walking down the stairs into the entrance hall.

Bother. The last person she wanted to see. Alistair's stepmother. She was no doubt going to have to explain why Alistair had not called or why Julia had not invited her for tea. 'Good day, Lady Dunstan.'

'I apologise for the subterfuge, but I had the feeling I would not be admitted to Sackfield a second time.' The other woman offered an apologetic smile. 'Nor was I sure you would answer an invitation from me.'

Julia stared at her. 'Are you saying there is no committee meeting?'

Lady Dunstan had the grace to look chagrined. 'Is it too terrible of me? I desired words with you in private. I could think of no other way.' She glanced at the hovering butler. 'Come, we will go into the library.'

The butler opened the door to an adjacent room. When Julia stepped inside she was more than a little disconcerted to find Percy Hepple standing beside the hearth with his hands behind his back and a smirk on his lips.

She turned to object, but the door was already closed. 'You may very well look dismayed,' the Dowager Duchess said, sadly. 'My nephew has told me all about you.'

The blood drained from her head. Her knees trembled. She forced herself to remain standing, though the nearest chair looked terribly inviting. 'I have no idea what you mean. If there is no meeting, I will leave my card for Lady Wiltshire and depart.'

'I wonder what that dear lady would say if she knew you had posed naked before most of the men in London who then bid on your favours. How dare Alistair bring such disgrace on the Dunstan title?'

Her stomach fell away. She collapsed into the chair.

'Well?' the Dowager Duchess said, glaring. 'Will you deny it?'

Julia glanced at Percy, at the knowing smile on his lips. 'My past has nothing to do with you or Mr Hepple.'

The woman glanced at Percy and drew in a deep breath. 'So it is true. What is the matter with my stepson? Offering marriage when he had to know the scandal would ruin us all? For you may be assured, if this dunderhead recognised you, others will, too.'

'I say, Auntie,' Percy whined.

Julia pulled herself together. 'What is the point to this? There is nothing to be done. I am married to Dunstan. If he does not care, I do not see why you should.' Though if the truth got out Alistair would likely be mortified. And despite everything else, his rescue had been a kindness.

The Dowager flinched. 'Doesn't care?' Her brows drew down. 'Does my stepson know you are also a criminal? A thief?'

Julia's heart clenched. 'How do you—?'

'My stepson was a confirmed bachelor. The speed of your marriage, the circumstance Percy revealed to me, made me suspicious. I looked into your background. Someone had to.' Her voice softened, her face expressed sympathy. 'My poor dear, I don't blame you for marrying him, given the trouble you were in, but I am worried for you as well as for the family name.'

Julia repressed a start at the change in the woman's demeanour. 'You may save your concern.'

The woman shook her head. 'I don't suppose he told you he got my son's wife with child and then fled the country?'

Hepple looked pained. 'Auntie, you should

not say these things about the Duke.' He glanced around. 'Or at least keep your voice down. Someone might hear.'

Julia stiffened. 'I know about Jeffrey.' It still hurt to think about it, but it had happened long before Julia had appeared in his life. 'Everyone makes mistakes. He is trying to do the right thing.'

The Dowager glared at her nephew. 'Percy, leave us. I have things to discuss with Her Grace in private.'

Percy pouted. 'If you upset Dunstan, he won't pay my debts.'

The Dowager waved his objection aside. 'Your debts are a trifle. A mere bagatelle compared to the family's good name. Go. We will talk later.'

With a huff of impatience, Percy bowed and departed.

The moment he closed the door, the Dowager lowered her voice. 'My dear, once this information becomes public I fear what Alistair may do. Gossip is already spreading that he is tiring of you.' She pursed her lips. 'You would not be the first woman he has cruelly cast aside.' She shook her head. 'Though you would be the first wife.' She patted Julia's hand. 'Perhaps you have nothing to worry about, after all. I cannot imagine Alistair going through anything so crude as divorce. Until death do you part.' She inhaled a sharp breath and her eyes widened. 'He wouldn't. Not even he would dare such a dastardly deed.' Sympathy filled her expression. 'I am sure of it.'

Chilly fingers walked across Julia's skin. Her stomach roiled. Her heart clenched. She could not believe it. Would not. 'What did you mean about him casting a woman aside?'

The Dowager frowned. 'You did not know that before Luke married her, the woman he got with child was his fiancée?'

'They were engaged?' This was not exactly what she had imagined. From the way Alistair had spoken she had assumed he'd had a fling with his brother's wife, not that he had abandoned her before she was married.

'If my honourable Luke had not stepped in, I cannot think what would have happened to Jeffrey or his mother. Alistair simply walked out and disappeared.'

'He returned.'

'Too late to be of any use. Oh, he promised Jeffrey would inherit, but the man is a rake. As debauched as they come. The title of dissolute Duke is well deserved. How can anyone trust such a man to do the right thing? And… You and he…' she waved a hand '…have not been celibate, I assume?'

'You can set your mind at rest.' Bitterness scoured her throat. 'There can be no children from me. The doctors have confirmed it.' Admitting being barren left her feeling raw. Useless. Empty inside. Tears welled. She blinked them away.

The Dowager's expression tightened. 'Your first husband was a man of declining years. He might have been at fault, not you.'

'The doctors say not. He has three daughters.'

The Dowager got up and prowled the room. The smile on her face when she turned to face Julia seemed less than sincere. 'I dread the *ton*'s reaction when they learn who and what you are. And they will. Alistair will not be able to face down the scandal this time. It is too bad the rest of us will be forced to suffer as well.'

'Suffer how?'

'None of us will be able to show our faces in town. This scandal will haunt us for years. We will be lucky if the King does not take an interest and make him forfeit the title.'

Julia's blood ran cold. 'He cannot do that, can he?'

'What the King giveth, surely the King can take away. Whatever the case, Alistair will be *persona non grata*. All of us will be ruined. Poor Luke. And Jeffrey.'

Poor Alistair, too. For all his faults, he had tried to help her. 'There is nothing I can do. We are married.'

The Dowager tapped her chin with her forefinger and looked thoughtful. Her face brightened. 'You could leave the country. Before anyone else has a chance to guess at your identity. I will pay Percy off. Besides, when I explain the damage that would result to his family, he will keep his mouth shut.'

'Where could I go?'

She shrugged. 'America. Ships leave from Portsmouth every day at this time of year. I will even give you the money for your fare if you need it.'

The thought of bringing shame and ridicule down on so many people made her feel ill. She'd known marrying Alistair was wrong. The last thing she wanted to do was cause him harm. She nodded. 'If I leave, you promise not to tell anyone what you know? You will stop Percy from speaking of it?'

'Why would I want to bring scandal down on my own head? Of course I promise. Much as I despise his morals, Alistair is the head of my family.' She touched Julia's arm. 'It really is the best for all concerned.'

It was. Alistair didn't want a proper marriage,

so why should she live a lie that could cause innocent people trouble and heartache?

'I'll leave right away.' But would Alistair let her go? Of course he would. Why would he not?

It would make things a great deal easier for them both.

Alistair opened the front door and somehow managed not to drag his wife over the threshold. When he got her inside, he shut the door with a rapidity that had her blinking.

'Where the devil were you?' The question came out more forcefully than he intended. 'Did you not recall I specifically told you to go nowhere without proper escort?'

'Why? Am I a prisoner?'

Her words made no sense. 'Don't be ridiculous.'

She stripped off her hat and gloves. 'I was accompanied. And besides, Grindle knew where I was. I received notice of a meeting of the committee.'

'Grindle,' he said, trying not to clench his jaw and to sound reasonable, 'is visiting his sister, as he does every Wednesday afternoon.'

She frowned. 'You know it really doesn't make sense to give all the servants the same half-day off. If you spread them out, you would not find yourself so shorthanded.'

He dragged his fingers through his hair. 'That is not the point. I asked you to leave the house with a minimum of two footmen.'

'I had John Coachman and Matthew. Two men. And here I am safe and sound.'

His temper subsiding, he noted an odd note in her voice, a sadness, and peered at her closely. 'Is something wrong?'

She lifted her chin. 'What could possibly be wrong? We have barely spoken for days. We might as well not be married.'

Those last few words she flung over her shoulder and marched into the drawing room.

It seemed another discussion about the state of their marriage was at hand. He followed her in and shut the door. 'We are married.' There was no getting around it.

'To your deep regret.'

'Julia, do not put words in my mouth.'

'I do not need to. I see them in your face. In what you do. Actions speak louder than words and right now they are shouting that you wish you had not married me.'

'I do wish it.' If he had made her his mistress they could have been perfectly happy. Perhaps for the rest of their lives, because at least then he'd be free to love her without this weight of guilt bearing down on his shoulders.

He froze. Did he love her? Heaven help him, he did. And by marrying her, he'd likely ruined her life by denying her the warmth and family she so obviously wanted, not to mention putting her very life at risk.

She was right, she would have been better off without him.

He clenched his fists.

Julia saw the movement and stilled.

Damn, didn't she know by now he would never raise a hand to her? Before he could speak she whipped off her bonnet and took a deep breath. 'Our marriage is a farce. I think it is best if I leave.' The pain in her eyes was hard to see.

'You cannot leave. You are my wife.'

'Then I *am* a prisoner.'

He raked his fingers through his hair. Wasn't this the conclusion he'd come to a couple of days ago? Then why would he not simply agree? 'I don't want you to leave.'

Sorrow filled her gaze. 'I—care for you, Alistair. I really do, but I want a proper marriage. Children, if at all possible.'

Wounded to the quick by her expressionless tone, he stared at her. 'I can't. You know that. You know why.'

'Then there is nothing in this marriage for either of us. Nothing. Will the dissolute Duke be happy to spend his life as a monk? Or will he be dashing off to find his pleasure and entertainment elsewhere? Or perhaps you will find a different way to be rid of an inconvenient wife.'

He flinched at the bitterness in her tone. 'What are you saying?'

'Someone was putting laudanum in my tea. Why not you? You were quick enough to spirit Mrs Robins to parts unknown when I discovered the plot.'

Fury coursed through his veins in a red-hot wave. He curled his lip. 'If I wanted rid of you, believe me you would be gone.'

'As your fiancée was gone?

Blankly, he stared at her.

'The woman your brother married on your behalf. You abandoned her.'

Ice filled his veins. 'So your meeting was with dear Stepmama.'

Her cheeks flushed. 'You know, you are really awful to your family. Your father—'

'My father let his second wife walk all over him along with the rest of my benighted family. I am not my father.'

'And you do not want or need a wife. I want you to let me go my own way. It won't make any difference to you.'

Not make a difference? His whole life had

changed since her arrival. He'd changed his whole way of life because she'd made him want to be worthy of her regard. But he wasn't. He never could be. And if she didn't want to stay, why would he force her?

He gazed at her. Took her lovely face in one last time as if he could imprint it on his mind. Saw the sweetness in her eyes. The courage in her determined chin. The passion. Things that had drawn him to her right from the first. Things he wanted, but had been doing perfectly fine without for years. He let a chill invade his soul and curled his lip. 'If you want to go, I won't stop you.'

Sorrow filled her face when he had expected satisfaction. She nodded. 'It is for the best.'

'Let my lawyers know your address. I'll have them set up whatever funds you need.' It was the best he could do.

She looked shocked. 'I don't want your money.'

Even his money wasn't good enough. A pang pierced his heart, ripping it open. He stuffed the tear with ice. Recalled the way his father had turned from him after his marriage to Isobel. How hurt he'd been.

He needed no one but himself, he'd proved that for years, but that didn't mean she had to go back to living in poverty.

He gave her his best ducal stare. The one designed to put mushrooms in their place. 'You wanted my money enough to marry me, I believe.'

She flushed as if he'd slapped her. 'I cannot deny I was desperate. But—'

'Exactly. You were desperate and we've both had a rollicking good time and now it is time to pay the piper. The carriage will be at the door to take you to London in an hour. I'll send along anything you cannot pack now. My lawyers will be in touch about the settlements.'

Unable to bear watching her go, he walked down to the stables, ordered the carriage, then saddled Thor and rode he knew not where.

Chapter Fifteen

It was late when Alistair, weary to the bone, rode into the courtyard and dismounted. No one came running to take his horse. He frowned. 'Halloo.'

No answer.

No doubt they were still down at the Wheatsheaf imbibing Prosser's best. And John Coachman and a groom were well on their way to London with Julia.

Surely, there should be one lad left on duty.

He removed Thor's saddle and began the task of grooming himself instead of seeking out the stable lad who must be around somewhere. It felt good to be busy. He knew it for what it was, of course. A way to put off returning to an empty house. For some stupid reason he'd hoped she might not have gone.

His gut roiled at the memory of what his stepmother had told her. Shame washed through him that Julia would believe he would have willingly abandoned a woman carrying his child. It seemed, even in her eyes, the dissolute Duke was sunk to the depths of depravity. Damn Isobel and damn Elise for not coming to him after their brief encounter. Instead she'd gone to his father, no doubt expecting him to force Alistair to the altar. Instead, he'd whisked his heir off to the Continent and required Luke to fill the breach.

Curse it all. What a mess his life had turned into.

A lonely mess, without Julia. He missed her already.

He glance up at a sound, expecting to see one of the lads coming to help, or take over.

Instead, he saw his stepmother, a lantern in one hand and a pistol in the other.

He frowned. 'What are you doing here?' And for once it wasn't a rude question. He couldn't recall a time when he had seen his father's wife in the stables.

'Waiting for you.'

He straightened and moved away from Thor, his gaze on the pistol in her hand.

Isobel glared at him. 'You weren't supposed to survive childhood, Alistair. And would not have if not for that interfering old governess. I could not believe you avoided my trap in Italy, either. But even you cannot survive a bullet to the heart.'

His gut lurched. Recollections of French soldiers chasing him away from the ship sent to bring him home surged through his mind. Memories of how they had seemed to know exactly when to arrive at the dock and the way they had singled him out. '*You* had me betrayed to the *gendarmes*?'

She glared at him. 'The clergyman your father hired to conduct you around Europe promised me you were dead. He said he saw your body.'

Pain shot through Alistair's chest. 'They shot the fellow I was with. A friend. I switched our papers, took his identity.'

She glared. 'It was supposed to be you. The Lords were hovering on the brink of declaring my son Duke and you came back.'

'Inconvenient, to be sure.' He edged away from the stall. He didn't want her shooting Thor by mistake. 'I suppose you had my girth cut, too.'

'A broken neck is a common enough occurrence.'

It could have been a broken back, leaving him paralysed. His blood ran cold. 'There were other accidents when I was a boy. The stone falling from a chimney. The leak in the boat on the lake. Was that you also?'

'You were such a hardy little beast.'

'And Julia? The poppy?'

'How *did* you figure that out? That stupid Robins woman, she could do nothing right.'

He shifted towards an empty stall. 'It was one of your servants I saw Robins with in Boxted. I knew I recognised him, but could not place him until now.'

'You always were too clever for your own good.' She waggled the pistol. 'Not clever enough. Don't make the mistake of thinking I cannot use this. Your father taught me well.'

His father always was a damned good shot. And a good teacher too. He held still.

'Why did you seek to harm my wife, when it is I who holds the title you want for Luke?'

'I won't risk having you leave behind an heir. Not after all my trouble to be rid of you.'

Cold fingers strolled down his spine. 'You will leave Julia out of this.'

'I wish I could. Actually, I didn't think she would go after our talk this morning. She actually likes you, more fool her. But I gather from my man she took me at my word and left. For some reason, she went to London instead of Portsmouth, but I will deal with her later.'

Not if Alistair could help it. He kept his gaze fixed on her face, tried to look harmless, confused. 'Your man? Another of your spies planted in my household?'

She shrugged.

He folded his arms over his chest, eyeing the distance, weighing the likelihood he could get to her before she pulled the trigger. 'How do you plan to get away with killing me in my own barn?'

'An unfortunate robbery, a duke cut off in his prime, a body to prove it, too, this time, and all but forgotten in a sennight when my son takes his rightful place.' Bending at the knees, the pistol held steady, she set down the lantern.

In the brief second she glanced down at the lantern, he risked another step closer. He needed something he could launch at her.

'You cannot kill my husband before a witness.' Julia stepped into the circle of lamplight.

Alistair wanted to shout at her to run, but feared that his stepmother might do something foolish like fire the damn pistol. Now he had Julia to worry about, too. Not that he was worried for himself. His father had been right. His younger brother would always have made the better Duke.

Pistol levelled at Julia, the Dowager backed against the wall of Thor's stall. 'Make one move, Alistair, and I will shoot her.' She shook her head.

'What are you doing here, girl? You should be well on your way to London. You are spoiling my plan.'

God help him, but the woman sounded irritated. 'Julia, you need to go.'

A look of hurt crossed Julia's face. 'I'm sorry, Alistair. I thought of something I wanted to tell you before I left.'

A thought that would get her killed, if he wasn't careful. 'You need to leave.'

Isobel's face turned sly. 'No. Stay. When the authorities find the Duke dead and the rubies in your wife's possession, they will know who to blame for your demise and everything will be as it should be.'

Alistair gazed at Julia. 'You took the rubies?'

'I did not,' Julia said, stiffening.

'You'd have been welcome to them,' he muttered, moving a step closer to his stepmama. 'They are said to be cursed.'

Isobel must have caught his movement from the corner of her eye because she shifted to keep him in view, but the pistol remained pointed at Julia. 'She has the rubies all right. Or rather an excellent version in paste. I had my man pack them in the bottom of her dressing case. With that and all the other evidence pointing at her, who will believe her protestation of innocence?'

The woman had run mad. 'You should have shot me when I first returned,' he said. He would have been glad of it. He hated the future of unmitigated loneliness he'd carved out by indulging in his lust with Elise. 'Or is this Luke's idea? He always did have a devious mind. I suppose he was worried he might be suspected, having the most to gain.'

'This is nonsense,' Julia said stepping between Isobel and Alistair. 'And you know it.'

The pistol wavered, then steadied. Mouth dry, he stepped out from behind Julia, causing the pistol to swing his way.

'Stand alongside your husband, Julia,' the Dowager said. 'Tell her, Alistair. Or so help me I will shoot her first.'

'And then what?' a male voice said.

'Good God,' Alistair said bitterly. 'Is everyone hiding in the dark in my barn? All it needed was you.' The odds had just got a whole lot worse.

'Luke, darling. Thank goodness,' the Dowager said. 'Tie her up, while I deal with him.'

Luke strode over to his mother and grabbed for the pistol. 'I'll take that, Mother.'

The gun went off. A searing pain crashed through Alistair's head. *Shot, by God—*

Everything went dark.

* * *

Julia screamed and went to her knees beside Alistair. Blood was pooling in the straw around his head.

'Fire!' someone yelled.

She looked up to see flames running along the floor catching straw on fire, little sparks and smoke dancing in the air.

'The lantern,' Luke shouted.

Isobel was backing away from the flames. 'You idiot,' she screamed. 'You have ruined everything.' She started reloading her pistol.

Luke rushed to Alistair's side and knelt down.

'Stay away from him,' Julia said, her heart pounding with fear.

He glared at her. 'We have to get him out of here.' He grasped Alistair under the arms and began dragging him. Smoke was all around them. Flames licking at her skirts. Heat. Thor squealed and kicked at the walls of his stall.

Luke glared at her over Alistair's inert body. 'Run. Trust me, I won't leave him.'

She saw truth in his eyes, the agony of loss, and ran for the faint patch of daylight already disappearing in a veil of black smoke.

Outside, she fell to her knees her eyes streaming, her throat burning. Gasping and coughing, she fixed her gaze on the open doors and the smoke billowing from within.

Where were they? Had she made a terrible mistake in trusting Luke? Moments seemed like hours and then Luke, carrying Alistair over his shoulders, staggered out. Behind him, Thor was screaming.

Luke turned to go back in. His mother came out of the smoke. 'Don't.'

He shook her off and, wrapping the cravat around his face, ran back inside.

'No,' his mother howled. 'No. My son. The Duke.' She plunged into the building.

Julia on the ground beside Alistair, pressing a handkerchief to his wound, could only stare in shock. A moment later, Luke bent double, his cravat now covering Thor's eyes, came running out of the barn. He led the horse into the paddock, removed the blindfold and the panicky horse galloped off. Luke was staring all around him.

'Luke,' Julia called out. 'Your mother. She followed you back inside.'

'What?' He strode towards the barn which was now a blazing inferno. Julia rushed to his side, held his arm when it looked as if he might try to dive in. 'There is nothing you can do. Think of your sons.'

He sank to his knees. 'Why did she do something so stupid? Blast it, she was safe.'

She put an arm around his shoulders. 'She was never going to be safe.'

Eyes glittering in a soot-covered face, he gazed at her, then buried his face in his hands.

The heat from the barn was dreadful, even at this distance. And they needed to help the living. Now.

'I'm sorry,' she said, patting his back. 'But, Luke, we need to get Alistair up to the house. He needs a doctor.'

Servants came running—some from the house, others on their way home from the village inn. Without a word they formed a bucket brigade.

Julia sent one of the younger lads to fetch a doctor. Luke, with one last despairing look at the blaze, hoisted his brother over his shoulders and carried him up to the house.

Two days later, Alistair reclined on the sofa in the drawing room with an interesting bandage around his head, wondering where his wife had gone off to.

Not that he was worried she would gallop off to far distant climes. She had promised she would not. Not yet, at least. But she remained unhappy. And she had been gone a long time, having promised him a tisane for his headache.

The sound of footsteps in the hallway had him

leaning back against the cushions. It seemed, from the heavy footfalls accompanying the lighter steps he recognised as Julia's, that they had company. Dash it all, and they still hadn't had a chance to talk. Now he was out of bed and dressed, he'd thought to have a discussion with her, lay all his cards on the table. And if she left him after that, he wouldn't blame her. Indeed, he'd do everything in his power to make her life easy.

A hesitant Luke appeared in the doorway. His face showed relief when Alistair beckoned him in.

'I won't stay long.' Luke turned his hat in his hands. 'I wasn't sure you'd see me despite what Julia said.'

His wife was a sensible woman. 'Sit down. Julia tells me you saved my life, little brother.'

Julia followed him in and sat down on the ottoman beside his sofa.

'Your wife saved your life.' Luke's voice was full of pain. 'I couldn't save Mother.' Luke perched on the edge of a chair. 'The inquest this morning declared her death an accident. The funeral is tomorrow.'

'We will be there. My condolences.' There was little more he could say. His sorrow for his brother's loss was genuine, though he could not grieve for his stepmother.

'She could not let it be,' Luke said, his voice harsh. 'She would not see that the last thing I wanted was the dukedom. You know that, do you not?'

'I wondered,' Alistair said. 'For a time. Especially after the cutting of my saddle at Beauworth.'

Luke bowed his head. 'That *was* my fault. I mentioned you were expected at Beauworth when I saw her. I had no idea what she planned.'

'She wanted to be sure Jeffrey inherited,' Julia put in. 'One can understand the motive if not the deed. He is the rightful heir.'

Luke groaned. 'That's what makes this all so impossible.'

Guilt rose in Alistair's throat in a solid lump, making it difficult to breath. Regret followed swiftly. One night of pleasure had ruined so many lives. He swallowed. 'I assured her he would inherit. I would never go back on my word.'

Luke made an odd face. His dark eyes were haunted. 'You don't understand. Elise had been having an affair with a married man for years before you and I ever met her. It was he who suggested she put the cuckoo in your nest, since you were one of the few unwed peers readily available. When Papa whisked you out of the country, she insisted on me instead. I hated you at the time, because I really did think you were Jeffrey's father. And later, after she told me the truth…' he shook his head '… I hated her.'

Alistair felt as if the air had been sucked from his lungs. As if he'd been struck a blow to the kidneys. 'He isn't mine? Are you sure? He looks more like me than you. Why the devil did you never say anything?'

'I didn't know Mother had told you he was yours until I heard what she said in the barn. By the time you returned from your cavorting in Europe, he was simply my son. Elise must have told her that Banbury tale years before, to account for Jeffrey's early arrival.'

Cavorting he had been. More guilt, but this time overwhelmed by relief. He didn't have a son. Something inside him shifted. Eased. He frowned. 'Then why did you want to have nothing to do with me?' He'd been more hurt by his brother's resentment than he had wanted to admit.

'Mother said you suspected me of appropriating more than my share of the estate's funds in your absence. After all I had done to keep things together, to hold them for you, I was furious.'

'Sadly, she always did try to divide and rule. I should have known better than to believe anything she said. How came you to show up in such timely fashion at the barn, may I ask?'

'Percy. He came to complain that Mother wasn't treating him right after all he had done for her and me. She'd paid him off, but he wanted more. Said Mother was on her way to seek you out. Not that I expected to arrive to see you held at pistol point.'

Alistair groaned. 'Families. I suppose I must do something about Percy right away.'

'No need. I told him that I would speak to his dear papa if he whispered one word about any of it. I hinted that it might not be in the Duchy's interest to help with the come out of his multitudinous sisters, should even a rumour escape. It was the idea of his mother's reaction to that little gem that had him sworn to silence. I'm afraid I committed you to a great deal of expense.'

'Worth every penny,' Alistair said, grinning at a brother who had always been good at complicated reasoning.

Alistair glanced over at Julia, who was looking terribly pale. He wanted to take her in his arms and ask her what was wrong. She had stayed with him because he was injured, because that was how she was. Kind. Generous. Far too good for him. And now he was improving, he feared she would take up his earlier offer and go.

A reason he had avoided talking about her decision to leave him. While he certainly didn't want to think about a future without her, he must, if that was what she wanted.

'I'm sorry, Luke,' he said, wanting to give his brother a hug, but not sure it would be welcome. 'Truly. Thank you for coming to the rescue. You always did try to stand between me and your mother. I am sorry things turned out the way they did. If there is anything I can do for you—'

His brother's expression darkened. He clenched his fists. 'You can tell me why you let me believe you were dead for nigh on two years.'

'The French soldiers in Rome made sending letters difficult.'

'You were imprisoned?'

'In a manner of speaking. If you could call the home of Rome's most famous courtesan a prison.'

His brother gave him a piercing look. Then cracked a laugh. 'Trust the dissolute Duke to end up somewhere like that.'

'It worked pretty well until I ran out of money.' He realised her betrayal no longer hurt. He didn't care. There was only one woman he cared about and she was planning to leave him. 'I don't suppose you would like to take on the job of land steward for the Duchy?' If so, he would go back to roaming Europe. If Julia didn't want him, there was nothing for him here.

'I cannot. I promised Beauworth.'

No escape then. 'His gain, my loss. But when your contract ends?'

'I will consider it.' Luke rose. Alistair remained where he was, knowing Julia would have his hide if he so much as raised an eyebrow. Luke leaned over him and kissed his forehead. 'Welcome home, Alistair.'

'Better late than never,' he growled, slapping his brother on the shoulder, but he could not help feeling pleased.

When he had gone, Alistair smiled tenderly at his wife. He knew it was a tender smile, because he felt exceptionally tender. And worried. 'We need to talk.'

She inclined her head, but her expression boded ill.

'I don't like to speak ill of the dead, Alistair,' Julia said, trying not to let her anxiety show, to continue to act the convenient practical wife as long as she remained under his roof, 'but I really think your stepmother had lost her reason. Yet she was clever, too. And ruthless.' Something the woman had accused Alistair of, but Julia knew it wasn't true. Had known it in her heart. She was babbling in the face of the far more important things that needed to be said. Things that would decide her fate.

She launched into the speech she'd been preparing in her mind all day. 'I should go. I cannot bear the thought of you being shamed because of me. Someone else may recognise me.'

'No. If you had not come back… I owe you my life.'

'As I owe you mine. There are no debts between us.'

Alistair pushed himself up and reached for her hand. 'Julia.'

She revelled in the warmth of his palm on her skin. She quelled the urge to rest her cheek against his thigh. 'The doctor said you were not to exert yourself.'

'I am well enough to exert myself with you, my love.'

She froze. 'I didn't think to hear you ever say that.'

'What, "exert"?'

She gave him a little shove with her shoulder. 'Not that.'

'Oh, you mean "my love".'

His voice was droll. Not possible. Her husband was never droll, though he was occasionally sweet.

The back of her eyes burned. She blinked hard and turned her face away. 'You shouldn't say things you do not mean.' Dash it, she sounded teary, when she had meant to sound teasing.

'And if I do?'

Perhaps teasing was not such a good idea after all. 'Your moods change like the weather.'

'You are a good woman, Julia,' he said softly.

'Tell that to the lace merchant in Cheapside. But for you I would have gone to prison or worse and now you are stuck with me as a wife and little chance of a true heir to your name. I should never have let you save me.'

He pressed his lips to the back of her hand. 'I would not give up one moment of these past few weeks with you in my life.'

The feel of his lips warm and dry against her skin made her eyes burn more. 'Nor I.'

He gazed at her steadily, but deep within his cool gaze, his shield against hurt, she sensed longing. 'Why did you come back?' he asked.

She hesitated, fearing his scorn. 'I was not speaking the truth when I said I cared for you.'

Hurt flashed in his eyes, a regretful smile formed on his thin lips. 'I deserve that.'

'Oh, no. I didn't mean it that way. I—'

He rubbed circles on her back and she wanted to arch like a cat. And possibly purr. How did he know exactly the right spot to caress? 'It is all right, Julia. I understand. I would like us to remain friends, if that is at all possible.'

Her heart nearly broke in two. 'Friends.'

'You did offer friendship a few weeks ago.'

The hope she had been clinging to so tightly began to wither. She shook her head. 'That isn't—'

'Very well. If it isn't possible, I quite understand.' His voice was soft and low and so full of pain, she wanted to weep.

'Alistair, let me finish.'

'Of course,' he said. 'It is your right.' He visibly braced himself.

Startled, she stared at him. What on earth…? 'Oh, Alistair, you mistake me.' She dropped her gaze to her hands in her lap, worried about how he would react to her baring her soul. 'When I said I cared for you, I should really have said I love you. I was halfway to the Bull and Bear when it occurred to me I had been lying to myself for weeks. I love you for your generosity. I love you for your honour and the way you protect your people. And the way you love your horse. I adored the way you counted me as one of yours from the moment we met. You are a good man. A kind one, despite all anyone says. Honestly, I think I fell in love with you at Mrs B.'s before I even knew any of those things. My heart knew. I love you with all my heart.' She swivelled to look into his dear face, to try to make him understand. 'Alistair, because of that I cannot allow my presence in your life to cause you harm. I promise, once I go, I will never trouble you again.' Her voice caught.

He sighed, a long soft expulsion of breath as if he had been holding it in for a very long time.

She glanced up at his face, but could not read his expression—the cool reserve had returned. A heavy lump settled on her chest. 'If you still want my friendship, then I will give it, gladly.'

'I cannot remember the last time I had a friend,' he murmured. 'Someone in whom I could confide all my secret hopes and not fear betrayal. I've been betrayed so many times, until I met you, I thought I could never trust again.'

He trusted her. Her heart lightened. 'I am sorry for what those women did to you: your stepmother, Elise, that woman in Italy. You did not deserve such treatment.'

'I thought I deserved nothing until you came along. But now you say you love me, yet you want to leave.'

'Hush. I don't want to leave. It is for the best. You need children. An heir.'

'I need you.' He pressed his lips to the top of her shoulder. The little hairs on her nape seemed to rise in welcome to his touch. 'The kindest, sweetest, dearest—'

'You are making me sound like a saint when you know perfectly well I am not.' Her voice sounded too full of emotion to go on, yet she finished what she had to say. 'You know what I did. My presence can only bring harm to your name.'

'Julia, darling,' he whispered softly in her ear. 'I love you so much, names mean nothing. When I thought you had left me for good, I was devastated, yet I did not want to keep you against your will. Your happiness is everything to me.'

He picked up her hand and pressed his mouth to her palm. Heat roared through her veins. She gasped.

'I love you, Julia. I want us to make memories together. Memories to drown out the past. I want the friendship you promised. And companionship. But most of all, I need your love.'

'You have it, my dearest sweetest man,' she whispered. Tears ran down her cheeks.

'You are crying.'

She choked down a sob. 'Happiness.'

'My life. My soulmate. Only with you do I feel like a whole man, instead of an empty shell. Love me. Please, darling.'

He curled a hand around her nape and brought her lips down to his.

'Alistair, your wound,' she squeaked.

He pulled off the bandage. 'My wound is fine, it is my heart that hurts with longing.' He kissed her deeply, until they both had no breath left.

She lay with her head on his shoulder and stroked his cheek. 'You really need to be careful of that head wound.'

He pressed a kiss to the tip of her nose. 'I have a gift for you. I wasn't sure I would ever have a chance to give it to you. Or if you'd accept it.'

'I told you, I do not need things to make me happy.'

'Please. I would like you to have this one.'

When he asked so nicely, how could she refuse? 'I don't want you getting up. Tell me where it is and I will get it.'

'In my writing table. Bottom drawer.'

She got up and found a small package wrapped in brown paper.

'Open it.'

He sounded excited, like a small boy at Christmas time.

Expecting jewels or something similar, she unwrapped the outer layer and discovered a red-velvet sleeve containing something cylindrical. When she opened the drawstring, a telescope... No... 'Alistair!' She gazed at him. 'A kaleidoscope. You remembered. How lovely.' She held it up to her eye.

'Point it towards the window, to get the best of the light,' he said. He started to rise.

She shot him a warning look. 'You have re-

ceived two blows to the head now and the doctor said—'

'Hang the doctor.' But he sagged back against
the cushions as if the effort had been too much.

She held the kaleidoscope to one eye and
closed the other. 'Oh, how pretty.'

'You turn it and the patterns change.'

In awe, she turned the tube, gasping at the
beauty created by the crystals inside. 'I love it.
I will treasure it always. A kaleidoscope of butterflies. Thank you.'

He looked so pleased with himself, she could
not resist. She bent over him and kissed him full
on the mouth.

He grasped her shoulders, pulling her down
until she once more lay beside him, changing
the brief brush of her lips into something much
more intense. On a groan, he broke the kiss and
rested his forehead on hers, his breathing ragged.

She snuggled against his shoulder. 'But,
Alistair, I cannot give you your heir.' Misery was
a painful ache in her heart.

'If children come along, I will be grateful, provided no harm comes to you. But truly, although
I did not realise it until recently, I already have
everything I want or need. Someone to love and
care for. Someone to call my own who cares for
me, not for my title or my wealth.'

'And you won't mind that some stranger's child will one day be the Duke?'

'You heard Luke. He considers Jeffrey to be his son in every way. And so will he be treated by us. I will teach him to be ducal and you can help him learn to be a gentleman around the ladies. We will be a family.'

'A family built on love instead of secrets.' It sounded perfect.

She pressed upward to seal their vow with a kiss and he groaned again. 'A bed, love. We need a bed.'

Epilogue

Banished to the garden with his uncle, while his papa remained in the drawing room cooing at the new addition to the Dunstan line, Jeffrey, small and blond and not in the least bit angelic, kicked at a rock. 'Babies are horrid. Girl babies are the worst.'

Alistair didn't think his baby was horrid. His was a perfectly beautiful little girl who already looked very much like her mother, even if she had come as a complete surprise to her parents. He was, however, quite in sympathy with Jeffrey in regard to the other two infants currently squalling in his drawing room.

There was the Beauworths' little boy, and strangely enough, his erstwhile amanuensis, Lewis, who turned out to have a title tucked away somewhere on his person, had arrived to wet the baby's head with his own infant progeny in tow. And a wife.

Or rather they'd come to attend the christening and enjoy a little libation afterwards.

Alistair, like Jeffrey, had found it all wonderfully overwhelming. 'You were a baby once. As was your brother Daniel.' The latter had remained firmly affixed to his father's side. 'Be assured, Jeffrey, a gentleman likes the ladies a whole lot more when he is older.'

'Yuck. Then I am never growing older.'

'But then you will never graduate from a pony to a horse and if I am not mistaken, your papa was talking about going to Tatts very soon.'

Young Jeffrey halted as if turned to stone. He gazed up at Alistair. 'You wouldn't jest about such a thing, would you, Uncle Alistair?'

A duke only jested with his duchess in private. 'It is too important a matter for jests.'

The lad clenched a fist and jabbed at a hapless red rose in the border of the walk. 'I'm getting a horse.'

'So shall we rejoin the party? I think Her Grace has ordered lemonade and cream cakes for tea.'

'A growing boy needs his sustenance,' Jeffrey said and tucked his hand around Alistair's arm.

Together they strolled back to the drawing room.

Sitting beside the Marchioness of Beauworth

on the sofa, Julia met his gaze with a beaming smile when he entered the room.

They had been very happy together these past two years, and a child, heaven help him, had added icing to the delicious cake of an extraordinarily sweet marriage.

With Jeffrey making straight for the desserts, Alistair felt perfectly comfortable taking his baby girl from her mother's arms. He was in love. With them both.

'Next time we will have a boy,' Julia whispered, getting to her feet.

'I'm not sure if I could survive a next time,' Alistair said. Not that his wife had been anything but healthy throughout, but the anxiety, knowing his mother had died in childbirth, had been hell on him.

Luke wandered over, cake plate in hand, to gaze down at Olivia. Smiling, his brother stroked the baby's petal-soft cheek. 'You are going to have your hands full with this one when she starts noticing there are two genders.'

'As you have your hands full now?' Alistair glanced over at Jeffrey and Daniel scrapping over the last bit of shortbread.

'Get your heir and a spare and we will all stop fretting.'

Alistair ignored the jibe. 'We'll take what we get.'

A baby set up a long drawn-out wail and Alistair barely managed not to cover his ears.

'What plot are you two hatching?' Beauworth asked, joining them. 'It wouldn't be a nice glass of brandy in the library, would it?'

Alistair glanced at Julia and she gave a small nod, interpreting his question with ease.

'Men,' Eleanor muttered. 'Julia, let me get you some of that delicious cake.'

Having rescued Lewis, or rather the Marquess of Dart, the men retired to the library, where Alistair poured them all a drink. 'To Isobel,' Luke toasted.

They stared at each other in contemplative silence.

Luke shrugged. 'If not for my mother, our family might never have been reunited.' He looked at Alistair. 'What? She loved me in her way. She was just a bit misguided. She would be thrilled to see you had a daughter.'

The other men chuckled and Alistair burst into laughter.

Families. Who needed 'em? He did. He had the most perfect family in the world and who was he to deny his brother his abiding love for his mother.

He raised his glass. 'To Olivia. The latest addition to the Crawford family.'

The men drank to this toast with a will.

'The new stables have turned out well,' Dart said, looking out of the window.

'It was a good thing all of your beasts were out to grass.' Beauworth said. 'I suppose you never did discover how she managed to set them on fire.'

'Knocked over a lantern,' Luke said.

'Since most of the lads were at the tavern in Boxted,' Alistair added, 'there was no one around to help her saddle a horse, the one man on duty being up at the house for his dinner.'

Beauworth frowned. 'Odd that she was there at all.' The man loved a mystery. Beauworth took his duties as peer very seriously and events in his past made him keen on seeing justice done.

'Let it lie, Beauworth,' Luke said. 'The family is satisfied it was an accident.'

'As you say.' Beauworth sipped at his drink and talk turned to other more important matters like crop yields and the best time for haying.

Later, when Julia and Alistair stood at the front door watching their guests depart, Olivia having been whisked off to the nursery by a doting Digger and an equally doting nanny some time before, Alistair could not resist a kiss on his wife's cheek. 'You need your rest.'

She smiled a naughty smile. 'That is just an excuse and you know it.'

'You know, it is a while since I have seen you wearing the Dunstan rubies.' It was their own private code for the naughty things they did in their bed.

'You are right. It has been too long,' she said, her lovely eyes smiling up at him. 'We have time with Olivia off having her nap.'

He put an arm around her waist and to the devil with the footman gazing at the ceiling and Grindle pretending to be invisible, he kissed her full on her delicious mouth.

Together they walked inside, there to beget the next Duke of Dunstan, who learned to love all of his myriad brothers and sisters very well indeed.

* * * * *

If you enjoyed this book, you won't want to miss the story of how Julia and Alistair met. Discover their past in:
ONE NIGHT AS A COURTESAN

This book also features characters who appear in:
WICKED RAKE, DEFIANT MISTRESS

And check out these other great reads by Ann Lethbridge:
MORE THAN A LOVER
MORE THAN A MISTRESS
THE DUKE'S DARING DEBUTANTE

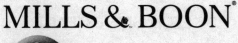

MILLS & BOON®

HISTORICAL

AWAKEN THE ROMANCE OF THE PAST

A sneak peek at next month's titles...

In stores from 26th January 2017:

- **The Harlot and the Sheikh** – Marguerite Kaye
- **The Duke's Secret Heir** – Sarah Mallory
- **Miss Bradshaw's Bought Betrothal** – Virginia Heath
- **Sold to the Viking Warrior** – Michelle Styles
- **A Marriage of Rogues** – Margaret Moore
- **The Cowboy's Cinderella** – Carol Arens

Just can't wait?
Buy our books online a month before they hit the shops!
www.millsandboon.co.uk

Also available as eBooks.

MILLS & BOON®

EXCLUSIVE EXTRACT

Prince Rafiq must save his desert kingdom's pride
in a prestigious horse race. But he's shocked
when his new equine expert is introduced…
as *Miss* Stephanie Darvill!

Read on for a sneak preview of
THE HARLOT AND THE SHEIKH
by Marguerite Kaye

Prince Rafiq could be wearing tattered rags, and still she
would have been in no doubt of his status. It was in his
eyes. Not arrogance but a sense of assurance, of entitle-
ment, a confidence that he was master of all he surveyed.
And it was there in his stance too, in the set of his
shoulders, the powerful lines of his physique. Belatedly
garnering the power to move, Stephanie dropped into a
deep curtsy.

'Arise.'

She did as he asked, acutely conscious of her dishev-
eled appearance, dusty clothes, and a face most likely
liberally speckled with sand. Those hooded eyes traveled
over her person, surveying her from head to foot with
a dispassionate, inscrutable expression.

'Who are you, and why are you here?' Prince Rafiq
asked, when the silence had begun to stretch her nerves
to breaking point. He spoke in English, softly accented
but perfectly pronounced.

Distracted by the unsettling effect he was having on her while at the same time acutely aware of the need to impress him, Stephanie clasped her hands behind her back and forced herself to meet his eyes, answering in his own language. 'I am here at your invitation, Your Highness.'

'I issued no invitation to you, madam.'

'Perhaps this will help clarify matters,' Stephanie said, handing him her papers.

The Prince glanced at the document briefly. 'This is a royal warrant, issued by myself to Richard Darvill, the renowned Veterinary Surgeon attached to the Seventh Hussars. How do you come to have it in your possession?'

Stephanie knitted her fingers more tightly together, as if doing so would stop her legs from trembling. 'I am Stephanie Darvill, his daughter and assistant. My father could not, in all conscience, abandon his regiment with Napoleon on the loose and our army expected to go into battle at any moment.'

'And so he saw fit to send his daughter in his place?'

The Prince sounded almost as incredulous as she had been, when Papa suggested this as the perfect solution to her predicament. The enormity of the trust her father had placed in her struck her afresh. She would not let him down. Not again.

MILLS & BOON®

Why shop at millsandboon.co.uk?

Each year, thousands of romance readers find their perfect read at millsandboon.co.uk. That's because we're passionate about bringing you the very best romantic fiction. Here are some of the advantages of shopping at www.millsandboon.co.uk:

* **Get new books first**—you'll be able to buy your favourite books one month before they hit the shops

* **Get exclusive discounts**—you'll also be able to buy our specially created monthly collections, with up to 50% off the RRP

* **Find your favourite authors**—latest news, interviews and new releases for all your favourite authors and series on our website, plus ideas for what to try next

* **Join in**—once you've bought your favourite books, don't forget to register with us to rate, review and join in the discussions

Visit **www.millsandboon.co.uk**
for all this and more today!